THE RESURRECTION OF JOHNNY ROE

A NOVEL

THE RESURRECTION OF JOHNNY ROE
Copyright © 2019 by Bruce Kirkpatrick

Cover Art by Julie Moore Design
Proofreading and Formatting by Maria Connor, My Author Concierge

This is a work of fiction. Names, characters, places, and incidents are either the product of the author's imagination or are used fictitiously.

Print ISBN: 978-1-7330410-0-3
Ebook ISBN: 978-1-7330410-1-0

DEDICATION

For Bob

ALSO BY
BRUCE KIRKPATRICK

Fiction

Hard Left
The Resurrection of Johnny Roe
The Carnival Chemist and Other Stories
Anyone But Me

Non-Fiction

Lumberjack Jesus
Raising God's Gen Z Teens

ACKNOWLEDGMENTS

Thanks to the men and women from my working days in Silicon Valley who helped explain software, robotics, and company operations, including Joe Lonsdale, Andy Housley, and Desire Smith. Any mistakes, assumptions, or omissions are all mine.

Thank you to my most enthusiastic, encouraging, and insightful editor, Virginia McCullough. I love working with you for all those reasons.

What a relief to find Maria Connor, whose eye for detail and imagination helped bring this book to completion.

And, as always, I thank God every day that he blessed my wife with an exorbitant amount of grace. She never runs out, and believe me, I test the limits.

ONE

JOHNNY Roe caught himself staring at Suzanne McLean, shapely and young enough to look awfully good in that short, black skirt. He had to admit, she sure had a knack for holding an audience. She'd been Johnny's best salesperson for the last three years. Today's presentation had him engaged and enthusiastic as she illustrated her ideas to win the business of one of San Francisco's most well-funded and anticipated start-up companies of the last decade.

She commanded the room, halfway through her pitch, a presentation to Johnny and the executive team illustrating how she would position their biggest prospect at the ad agency in what everybody knew was a competitive, crowded marketplace. The prospect, MarketSmart, aimed to offer online investors more research, more tutorials, more insights—and yes, more automation—at an even lower cost than Charles Schwab, E*TRADE, or TD Ameritrade.

Suzanne clicked through mocked up ideas rapid-fire from her laptop. Three examples of online ads. A Facebook business page. A press release and press kit with a special insert—a brand-new silver dollar. An idea for an extended financial library—virtual, of course. A series of old-school billboards. She was on a roll.

Johnny's thoughts wandered from Suzanne to a conversation he'd had with his wife that morning. It wasn't like she was mad at him or even annoyed. It felt like disinterest. How in the world could his wife be disinterested in his business and their life together? Was that what was really happening, or was he just imagining it all? He had tried to talk about the kids and what was on their schedules over the next several days, but all he got was a nod or a shrug. She even turned her head when he said an early goodbye that morning, and all he got was a peck on the cheek instead of how they'd started every day of their marriage—a passionate kiss on the lips.

"You know I can't hear you, Johnny, when I'm doing this," Samantha shouted over the roar of the blender. "Can't we talk about this later?"

"I'm just trying to understand what's on the agenda for the kids this week. Don't bite my head off."

Samantha just shook her head. "Whatever. I'm busy. We'll talk later."

She then turned to the two kids and with a motherly smile said, "Make sure you both finish those eggs. That's the protein that'll keep you going all morning."

Johnny blinked back to the conference room, trying to not look bored, even with the flare that Suzanne exuded with the presentation. Ten years into this advertising and public relations agency and he'd seen a lot of presentations. Most of the time when account managers like Suzanne presented ideas, ninety-five percent of them were decent but nothing special. Textbook gimmicks that had been done a hundred times before with limited success and even less imagination.

Johnny knew that true creative ideas came from the whole process. First, you did the research, then you did the competitive comparison, then you got down as many ideas as you could.

"Sorry to interrupt," Johnny said to Suzanne. "Do we have access to all the research these guys did? You know, the competitive landscape? That'd be interesting to see."

"Uh…not sure. I'll check," Suzanne said.

"Sorry, go on."

After the exhaustive download of creativity, you usually just had to set it to simmer for a while. It was rare that the one bright, shining moment of brilliance popped out and lay there on the table to be discovered. More times than not, it lay hidden beneath a layer or two or seven, and you had to peel away the accumulation, bit by bit, piece by piece. Everyone outside of advertising thought that creativity was simple, especially those who had a creative idea every once in a while. Just get it down, spice it up, and blast the heck out of it—easy peasy. But guys who ran ad agencies knew that the process—the long, long process to find the nugget—rarely came easy.

"Sorry, me again," Johnny said. "Just wanted to know, have you met the marketing guys at this company yet?"

"Uh…no. Not sure they have a big marketing team yet. I think they're depending on us to provide a lot of that."

"So, they're all financial guys?"

"Uh…I haven't met them all. We're still in the middle of the pitch. I'm really just trying to set the whole thing up…"

"Yeah, yeah, I'm sorry. I should let you continue. Go on."

As an excited Suzanne McLean peaked for her crescendo, Johnny doodled. Words or phrases, mostly. He would take an idea from a phrase he'd heard, maybe it came from Suzanne—at least he'd give her credit for it if the idea panned out—and just doodle with it.

MarketSmart.

MarketWise.

WiseMarket.

SmartMarket.

Reverse it, add to it, subtract from it, change one word, then the other. Use the built-in thesaurus in his brain. It was all part of the process. Johnny always used a pencil, never a pen. Always a notepad, never a computer. Who could doodle on a computer anyway? He liked the feel of graphite as it slid along the paper. About once a quarter, he bought a small box of Ticonderoga pencils. Yellow pencils with pink erasers. He loved their slogan—The World's Best Pencil—and thought that any company that had the gumption to call themselves the best in the whole world deserved his business.

He checked the presentation notes and found the tagline for this company he'd heard earlier. "Research. Training. Trades. For Every Investor."

Everything. For Every Investor.

From Research to Trades. For Every Investor.

Everything Any Investor Would Ever Need. Nope.

Educating Every Investor.

Research for Every Investor.

For Every Investor.

His agency, Troubadour (not Troubadour Communications or Troubadour Agency, just Troubadour), had won the business of a new company in the financial world that was going to make a killing on the web. Or so they said. Troubadour's job was to at least make them relative, so that some over-agitated biggy, like Google or Amazon—or heaven forbid, Schwab—saw enough of a threat to gobble them up, making instant zillionaires of the founders and putting the rest of the underlings back into the ranks of the unemployed. Plan B was to go public with a stock offering. The IPO market was gradually coming back from the brink of the recession and within a year or eighteen months should be overripe with money to heap boatloads onto a snazzy little social media gem.

As he was lost in doodle world, his iPhone buzzed. He had it on mute, but the text message from his administrative assistant, Laura, made the little machine shimmy slightly across the table like an excited puppy. It read: Need to talk to you NOW!!!

This could be important. We'll see.

If she stuck her head into the conference room in a couple of moments, he'd excuse himself and see what she wanted. If she waited until the meeting broke up, Johnny would tell her to tone down the exclamation points.

As soon as he began to put pencil again to paper, Laura opened the conference room door. She looked ashen, her eyes darted past him once, did a wild search of the room, then settled back and focused on him. She motioned abruptly with her hand to come outside. Johnny Roe immediately said a soft "Excuse me" to Suzanne and the other executives and hustled to the door.

Laura couldn't keep eye contact with him.

"There's someone here to see you," she said.

"You called me out for this," Johnny teased, trying to add a bit of levity to the moment.

Laura just stared at her desk and fidgeted with her hair. He'd never seen her rattled, but at the moment, he could see her hands shake as she straightened out the papers on her desk.

"A Mr. Worth is in the lobby."

There's something she isn't telling me.

"Okay, show him to my office."

Laura nodded. *Still no eye contact.*

"All righty then," Johnny said, almost under his breath as he slipped across the hall to his office.

He walked tentatively around his big desk. Johnny took a quick look out his eleventh-floor window at another gorgeous San Francisco morning, glancing at the blue of the bay and the splash of color from the adjoining buildings as he took a deep breath. American flags flew atop several buildings, flapping wildly with the onshore breeze. Tiny white caps in the bay signaled wind direction, and small sailing boats bobbed slowly about, in slow motion from this far away.

"Mr. Roe?" A short, bald man in a freshly starched police uniform stood just inside his office, his eyes looking at the carpet.

"Yes, sir."

"My name is Sargent Worth of the San Francisco police."

Johnny wanted to say, "Nice to meet you," but his mouth wasn't working. He felt his body temperature immediately rise. He felt the sweat break out on his brow.

"Mr. Roe, perhaps you should sit down. I have some terrible news."

TWO

THE funeral was a sick little affair. If it had been up to him, Johnny Roe would have skipped the whole thing. He would have let the funeral director pick out the caskets, arrange for the burial, and send him the bill. But his parents intervened. *You just have to have a funeral, John; it's the way things are done in the real world.*

The funeral convened in a little church Johnny and Samantha had attended on and off for the last five years. Mostly off, but it was the only church Johnny could think of to have a ceremony. The grandparents had spent thirty minutes the day before with the associate pastor who handled funerals, and they said he'd taken copious notes.

When the music finally stopped and tissues taken from purses and pockets, the pastor started his eulogy. He droned on and on about Samantha (just *Sam* to her close friends). What a good wife Samantha was, her background and life experiences before marriage, and what a great life Samantha and Johnny had shared together.

Then he talked about each child like he'd actually met them. Little Carson loved baseball and soccer and his dog, Buster. Cute little Cameron was a princess, an excellent dancer for her age, and now she was poised to spend the rest of eternity with Jesus. Why were they taken, the pastor lamented to the heavens? He didn't know, but he did know God worked in mysterious ways, and we didn't know what they were, and even though it made absolutely no sense that these precious people had been so savagely taken from our midst, it wasn't our job to question God because there was always a plan, God's plan.

Johnny thought, *Forget that.* Forget God's plans—he wanted his family back. Johnny hadn't had much use for God before the accident; now he had none at all.

He did his best to block out every sense of his that he could—his sense of hearing and feeling, his sense of sight and smell. He'd glimpsed the three caskets in front of the church—at least they weren't open. He'd had enough sorrowful looks from friends, relatives, and co-workers to last a lifetime, thank you very much. He even wanted to block out the smells, so he held his hand close to his nose, smelling only himself. He could swear he could smell the perfume Samantha preferred, or the wet furball of a dog, Buster, that was Carson's best bud, or the tangerine lotion that Cameron smoothed on after her bath every night. And if he had to hear much more of this morbid speech from this God-fearing man, he was sure he would run out of the church and blow his brains out.

The burial was even worse. The grandparents insisted on a short gravesite ceremony, and even though Johnny had initially refused to attend, he eventually relented. He never did think Samantha's parents liked him much so why push it. Both had been crying almost continually since they had arrived from Southern California. Not to mention Johnny's folks. When he said he wouldn't come to the burial, they were shaken up. They had lost grandchildren after all, so since this was what they wanted, he gave in.

They insisted he sit in the front row at the gravesite, within touching distance of the coffins. He first sat down, then stood and walked over to the edge of the plot, as far away as he could get without leaving the boundaries of the gathering, and stood by his wife's sister.

When the pastor finished his dust-to-dust, ashes to ashes speech, the small crowd stood and began to mingle in hushed tones.

"I'm so sorry for you, Johnny," Sam's sister, Julie Strausser, said, as she reached out to touch his arm.

"You're sorry that Samantha's dead," Johnny whispered back, almost inaudibly. He wanted to pull his arm away from her touch but resisted. She was so close he caught a whiff of her expensive perfume.

"Well, yes, and the kids, but mostly I'm sorry for you."

"Really? I didn't think you gave a hang about me one way or the other."

Julie's mouth fell open, but she didn't say a thing.

"Sorry," Johnny said, looking at his feet.

"I suppose, in some small way, I had that coming."

Now it was Johnny's turn to be shocked. He had never in his life heard Julie Strausser admit that anything was actually her fault. Their relationship had started out fine after Johnny and Sam were married, but in recent years had deteriorated dramatically. He had no idea why.

"You did," Johnny admitted, "but you didn't deserve it. Not today. Again, sorry."

Julie simply squeezed his arm.

"What are you going to do now?" she eventually asked.

"No clue."

"Are you okay financially?"

"Huh?"

Julie drew her arm away. She had been standing alongside Johnny, but not facing him. Now she turned her shoulder even farther away from him.

"Sorry, that's the lawyer in me. Not now. It can wait. I shouldn't have brought it up."

Johnny thought he saw just a tiny bit of sympathy in the eyes of his sister-in-law. He thought, *That's another first. That woman just might be human after all.*

Then the pastor approached, and Johnny Roe forgot all about the strange encounter with Julie Strausser.

THREE

JOHNNY craved a beer, but it was only nine o'clock in the morning. His alcohol intake had spiked dramatically since the funeral, and often he had slipped into the wet bar to sneak a large swig of his favorite bourbon, Buffalo Trace. It had the kick and spice of a good rye but was priced only slightly above Wild Turkey. His buddies had given him a bad time about drinking the cheap Turkey, so he graduated up to the Buffalo.

He decided to settle for a cigar. He grabbed one from the humidor and was about to head outside when he realized there wasn't anybody left to give him grief about smoking in the house, something Sam never let him do. She even made him close the windows and door to the back when he was on the patio lighting up. Of course, she had turned the kids against his smoking, but that was fine with him. He had to admit it wasn't his most attractive habit.

Johnny pulled one of the cedar sticks from the humidor, lit it, and used it to light the cigar. The kid at the upscale cigar store downtown told him it was all the rage to light your stogie with cedar. The mixture of cedar and cigar calmed Johnny. He slumped at the kitchen table and smoked.

It had been ten days since the funeral, but he still had no desire to check his business email or voicemail. Laura, his secretary, had called and texted him several times over the past week with questions, but surprisingly the workload from his office had almost disappeared. Either that or everyone was going above and beyond the call of duty not to disturb him. He didn't care what it was at this point.

Johnny wandered up to the master bedroom and plopped into one of the overstuffed chairs Sam had added to the huge room, which also featured a couch, coffee table, and 38-inch flat screen.

He remembered all those nights with Sam in this bedroom. They'd watch TV in the luxurious bed with all its fancy pillows, expensive sheets, and overstuffed down comforter. Sam mostly liked reality shows, but Johnny could talk her into an old movie, especially if it was a love story. Sam would get her popcorn—unsalted and unbuttered, the diet kind—and they'd settle in. She'd fall asleep way before the movie ended with popcorn scattered on her chest and the bowl on the bed. Johnny would always watch till the end. Then he'd carefully nibble the popcorn off her nightgown, letting his tongue linger, in hopes that she'd wake up.

He could see those times when she would stir, move a bit, her eyes fluttering open. After a beat or two, she'd smile that smile that said, *C'mon big fella*, and he'd turn off the light and make love to her.

Johnny sighed.

He was having a hard time sleeping in this bedroom, this bed. He tried the first several nights after the funeral but eventually had moved into the spare bedroom. It only had a single pillow, hand-me-down sheets they'd used when first married, and a thin chenille bedspread. It was a tiny separation, just a move down the hall, but he felt satisfied that he'd made even a small break from a life he would never know again.

He and Samantha Strausser had met in college at the University of California Santa Barbara—good ol' UCSB. Johnny ran into her at a frat party her freshman year. He was in charge of the Corona beer keg on the back porch, and she'd approached, needing a red cup refill. As he pumped the keg, only foam exploded out, and she got this pouty look on her face and said, "Now what?"

"Well, looks like my official work is done here. And I do have a private stash of something quite similar."

"Nice line. Like 'Do you want to see my etchings in my room'?" she said as her eyes twinkled. She followed him to his room.

Although he was two years older, she always seemed to be the more mature one. Johnny was the outside hitter on the university volleyball team, and for a school without football and a basketball team in the cellar of their conference, volleyball was big at UCSB. From the moment they'd met, they were inseparable. Sam had loved that Johnny was an athlete. She'd even nicknamed him Johnny. Said it had more flare than the name John Roe, the one always listed in the volleyball program. She said that sounded just like John Doe and how could his parents have done that to him. So he had become Johnny Roe.

As much as Sam loved that Johnny was an athlete in college, she loved even more that he knew how to make money. He always had a job, sometimes even during volleyball season. Mostly they were food service gigs at the frat house or the campus cafeteria. Sometimes both. How he kept his grades up, she never knew. Johnny confessed to her several years later that it was a combination of hard work, concentration, and the fact that he had what some people would call a photographic memory. She'd done a lot of research on the term, and she didn't think it technically was—but it was close enough for university work she supposed.

Still puffing on the cigar, Johnny slipped into the spare bedroom. Sam always called it his man cave. He had saved a few volleyball trophies, an MVP plaque from a tournament in Hawaii, his 2002 Most Inspirational Player award, and sports memorabilia. Sam had done a wonderful job decorating an old wall unit with the trophies, a few old uniform tops, team photos, and several framed photos of Johnny in action. He picked up a pair of Teva sandals that hung from a hook on the unit and reminisced about the summer between his junior and senior years in college.

He'd accepted an internship with the shoe company Decker Outdoor Corporation, headquartered in Santa Barbara. Somehow, he talked the marketing VP into letting him put together a road tour up and down the California coast in a van painted with the logo of the new water sandal line Decker had acquired, Teva. His volleyball coach had been furious that he was going to be gone for six weeks during the summer months and threatened to kick him off the team. And Sam wasn't too happy that she wasn't going along, but this was all business for Johnny.

Decker reluctantly agreed to stock the van with two hundred pair of sandals and told Johnny if he sold them all, they'd give him a commission. He'd sold them in the first week. During the tour that stretched almost eight weeks, he had ended up selling almost six thousand pair, many on consignment to surf shops and shoe stores along the coast. When he'd faxed in the last order, almost a thousand pair to a large outdoor sports chain store in Huntington Beach, the VP of marketing had offered him a full-time job on the spot. He wanted Johnny to forego his senior year and come to work immediately. Johnny said no.

In those eight weeks of traveling alone, Johnny Roe had discovered himself—and he liked what he found. First, he realized he was a risk-taker, but calculated risks, not crazy ones. It was risky to venture out on his own with the Decker plan; the only thing guaranteed was his gas and meal expenses. But he loved the sandals and knew they had big potential. If he could figure out a great way to showcase them to shoe stores and surf shops, he knew he could sell them. By parking the van as near to the beach as was legal, and in some cases not legal at all, blasting surf music, and being aggressive with the local beach girls, he was able to persuade them to try on the sandals and do an impromptu fashion show at local shops and stores. Bikinis sold sandals, he figured, just like sex sells anything. Boom!

He also discovered he could make his own way, figure things out when they didn't make much sense, and find the right way when he was lost, both literally and figuratively. He had the intuitive ability to not panic, to stop and think rationally, to not have so much pride that he couldn't retrace his steps or even ask directions. He'd read books about survival instincts and tried to put the ones that worked into practice in his business life. Most men who get lost, and eventually die in the wilderness, try to fit a mental map they have in their head about where they *think* they are to the surrounding terrain. But if that map doesn't match, they keep wandering, looking for a match. That almost always leads to nowhere. Rational thinkers continually look at their surroundings, and at the first sign of being lost, they stop right in their tracks. They don't push on. And if they have to retrace their steps to find terrain that is recognizable, they have the innate ability to concede they had better head back the way they came.

When Johnny Roe spent eight weeks driving the van, lost for the most part, and ended up not only with commission money in his pocket but also a job offer, he knew that when the path ahead was unclear, he'd be able to negotiate the terrain. To find his way. To make his own path. He knew he had the creative talent, the skills, and the innate abilities to succeed. For a twenty-one-year-old, that knowledge was more valuable than a college degree or an MBA.

After graduation, he and Sam took a month off and toured Europe, a rather old-school idea in the late 1990s when most of their friends headed off to grind out an MBA. Sam wanted immediately to go to

Rome, so they spent the first week in Italy. Their EuroRail train passes enabled them to go whenever and wherever they wanted. Sam got into the thrill of not knowing where they'd wake up in the morning. They took turns deciding the next stop on their itinerary. And they wouldn't tell the other. When it was Sam's turn to make the decision, they always ended up in well-known tourist towns like Barcelona and Madrid. When Johnny controlled the path, more obscure destinations became the town du jour. His idea of an ideal day was to rent bikes in Tuscany, find out-of-the-way wineries where they could compare dry Chiantis, and tiny restaurants to eat mounds of homemade pasta and try to guess the ingredients of the sauce.

Three weeks into the European tour, when Johnny checked in with his family, his dad relayed a message from the Decker VP he'd worked with the previous summer. They'd kept in touch. This message mentioned a connection the VP had with an outfitting and clothing company located in France who specialized in bicycle equipment.

They need help with the Tour de France. Right up your alley. You interested? They are. I pitched you! Call me ASAP.

The VP knew Johnny was an avid cyclist and thought the connection was ideal. The company was planning an event surrounding July's Tour de France and was looking for help. The *domestique* who ran the campaign took the bicycle training a little too hard and crushed his fibula descending one of the mountains on the racecourse. The VP pitched Johnny's skills hard, and the bike company was interested.

Johnny gave the company a call the next day, they detailed the plan, talked about logistics, asked how his French was, and then begged him to get to Paris as quickly as he could for formal interviews. He and Sam boarded the next train and arrived within eighteen hours.

When Johnny accepted the job, he quickly fell into twelve-hour days. For the first week, they only saw each other for a late dinner. During the second week, Johnny missed even those dinners because of the crushing workload.

One evening they were to meet at a small restaurant along the Seine at eight p.m. Sam arrived a little early in hopes that her enthusiasm for the evening would be equaled by Johnny's. At eight fifteen, she ordered her first glass of wine.

Twenty minutes later she ordered another glass of wine and got a little more depressed with each passing second.

At nine o'clock, she ordered dinner and a third glass of wine. Johnny finally got a phone message to her, delivered by the waiter, saying he'd meet her back at the hotel. Sam took a cab back at ten, and Johnny slipped into the room a little past midnight. Sam was asleep, and he didn't bother to wake her.

The next morning at breakfast, Sam was mostly silent.

"I feel horrible," Johnny began. "Horrible that you had to be alone all night and horrible how I treated you. I had no idea the job was going to be so demanding."

Sam sulked and nodded a faint acknowledgement of his apology.

"Maybe I should just go home," she finally said. "If this is how it's going to be."

"It's not how it's going to be forever. Just for now. I can't back out on them now. I have to at least see it through till August. But we've had a great time so far, haven't we?"

"Yeah, we have," she said with a smile.

"And we'll have a great time when I get back to the States, won't we?"

"We will."

"Okay. Let's look at some flights for you. And I'll get back to you just as soon as I can. I don't want to be away from you. Even for a little time. Okay?"

"Okay, mister."

They kissed a sad farewell two days later at Charles de Gaulle Airport. The night that Sam left, Johnny worked until five a.m., slept for two hours, jammed his body full of croissants and coffee, and was back on the job at eight. At night, he tended to work later than needed. He realized how much he missed Sam, and even the overload of deadlines couldn't keep his mind completely focused on work. He'd catch himself in a daydream of Sam and have to shake himself to get back to the task at hand.

He stayed with the company through July as the advance man for the caravan as it followed the Tour. He had a week's worth of work in August to finish up the financials, and they offered him a full-time job.

Almost demanded that he take it. He politely declined. He knew his future wasn't in Europe, and he missed Sam too dang much to be away from her anymore. Even though he had planned to spend the rest of the month exploring the fjords in Norway with a friend he'd met in Paris, he cut that adventure short after a week to get back to Sam.

One evening, after a few days in Norway, he and his buddy found themselves on a small boat heading up the west coast. As he shivered in his fleece jacket, he gazed at the steep rock walls on either side of the boat's bow and thought that if Sam were with him right now, she would no doubt be shivering even harder, since she was so thin and never wore appropriate clothes. She would not have a fleece jacket, maybe just a thin white cardigan. He rested his elbows on the boat's polished wood railing and imagined her leaning against him, trembling with the cold, his arm wrapping around her shoulders, around that thin cardigan, as their boat slowly churned past sheer rock walls that rose out of the freezing, dark-blue water.

The following day, he looked for a flight home. Flush with cash, confidence, and bravado, he headed back to Santa Barbara and Sam.

It took her two years to finally get him to propose. Johnny had wanted to wait until their careers took off and they had more money in the bank, but it wasn't like he finally just gave in to her wishes. He loved her deeply.

As Johnny finished his cigar in the man cave and stared at an advertisement he'd proposed (but never sold) for Guinness beer, he realized that their ten-year anniversary had been last week. *Man, I've been with that woman for almost a third of my life. Had been,* he corrected himself. Then he let the tears slide silently down his cheeks.

FOUR

"**Y**OU want to do what?" Jerry Ellis asked.

"You heard me," Johnny Roe said. "Do what you have to do to liquidate the 529 tuition savings account and then use that money to pay off the house mortgage. How soon can it be done?"

"Wait a minute, slow down, Sherlock. Let's talk about this."

"What's to talk about?"

"Well, for instance, all the tax ramifications you'll incur with the 529 plan and all the write-offs you'll lose if you pay off the mortgage early. For starters."

Ellis scrambled to find all of the account information for Johnny Roe. As his financial advisor, their twice-yearly meetings had always been well planned with all the paperwork in order in advance. But Johnny had appeared out of the blue with just a phone call, saying he'd be in the office in thirty minutes. Ellis' secretary was still searching for the latest reports.

"Yeah, I understand your concerns. I, on the other hand, don't give a flip about those concerns at the moment."

"I know, Johnny," Ellis said, his voice lowering. "But my job is to make sure we look at the long-range, the larger perspective."

"At the moment, I have no long-range."

"But, given time, you will."

"Jerry, good buddy, friend of mine, I'm not telling you to dissolve all my holdings and give my money to the Salvation Army, for crying out loud. I'm just saying, what the heck do I need a 529 college savings plan for anymore."

"You could save money on your taxes if you just designated those funds to somebody else in the family."

"Got nobody else."

"Nobody?"

"Nope."

"Don't you want to think about it for a few months? Maybe your viewpoint will change."

"The only thing that will change if you don't do what I ask is the address of my financial planner," Johnny said with only a slight smile.

Ellis had no idea if he was joking or not.

"I think the 529 funds won't quite cover the mortgage, so we'll need to figure out how to pay the rest of it off," Johnny said.

Ellis was taking notes with one of the slick, wooden Cross pens that were a permanent fixture on his antique conference room desk.

"It'll take me a few days to get the paperwork going and to figure out how much this is going to cost you. Then we can decide where to find the extra funds."

"Fine. When you get the figures, text me. But keep it moving. I want to get this handled ASAP."

"What's the rush?"

"I'm restless."

Ellis just nodded.

"One more request," Johnny asked.

"Sure, what?"

"You know Luke, the young man who makes the appointments, sends out the statements?"

"Yeah, what about him?"

"Good kid?"

"The best. Pepperdine grad, working on his Stanford MBA."

"Any qualms, any negatives, any skeletons in his closet?"

"Not that I know of. Why?"

"I'd like to hire him. For some part-time work. Something that he could handle off-hours. You okay with me talking to him?"

"For your agency? He's not the creative type. Just a real numbers guy."

"Exactly what I'm looking for."

FIVE

JOHNNY Roe gazed at a nervous Walt Mathews. Two weeks after the funeral, he'd set up the meeting in their downtown offices with Mathews, his partner for nine years, over the phone but didn't give him any inkling of what it was about. He knew Walt wanted a cigarette badly; he could always tell when Walt needed a smoke because he cracked his knuckles almost constantly.

Walt looked more like a well-dressed accountant than an advertising partner. Which was pretty much what he was. They'd met at one of the first accounts Johnny landed after starting the agency, and after working with Walt for a year on a major product launch, Johnny offered him a job. The product was ill-conceived, and David Ogilvy himself couldn't have made lemonade out of that lemon, so Walt jumped at the chance to join a young, hip ad agency in the heart of San Francisco's Financial District. He'd done well, made money, and added the operations functions to his financial duties.

"What's up, boss?" Walt asked, using the name he always called Johnny, a reference to one of their favorite movies, *Cool Hand Luke.*

"Shaking it here, boss," Johnny replied, keeping with the movie dialogue. "Well, maybe shaking it up is more like it."

"You know I never like it when you change everything up. It creates chaos for a while, and I hate chaos. I like order. Order," Walt said.

"You wanna buy my share of the agency?" Johnny asked.

"What the…wha…are you talking about?" Walt replied, barely audible.

"I gotta leave for a while, and I thought it just might be better if you ran the whole thing."

"I can't run shinola, you know that. We've talked about this before."

"You're a lot better than you give yourself credit for."

"Yeah, but I'm no you. I'm a pretty good number two, but I'd also be a pretty lousy number one."

"It still might work," Johnny offered.

"Well, well…how long are you going to be gone?'

"Don't know."

The two good friends looked at each other, then looked at the gray fog out the office window that covered the city. Walt continued to crack each individual knuckle, one by one. "Maybe…let's put an interim plan together," Walt suggested.

"Might work. What did you have in mind?"

"You take two weeks off, go to some far-off land, drink way more than your share of top-notch bourbon, and get your butt back to work and sell more advertising. But somehow, I don't think that's what you have in mind."

"You know me so well. You complete me," Johnny said, quoting from a movie they'd watched together a dozen times, *Jerry Maguire*.

"Screw you."

"Harsh."

"What are you doing, Johnny?" Walt said finally, holding eye contact with his longtime friend. "This is your baby. You created the whole thing. Why do you want to leave it all?"

"I don't know, Walter. I just don't have the heart for it. Not right now. Maybe I will again, sometime. Maybe not, who knows? I just don't think it's fair that I give a half-assed effort. You guys, all you guys here, deserve better than that."

Walt just nodded. He took a few deeps breaths and stared up at the ceiling.

"You heard my plan, now let me hear yours," Walt said.

"Right, a plan. We can put together a plan."

Walt began, "Let's call it an interim plan. Something that would work if you take the next month—or two months—off. Nothing permanent, just interim, right?"

They both stood up, walked around the office, in opposite directions. Johnny thought more creatively when he walked.

"Let's see. You can run the back end just fine, so we need somebody to head up creative and sales, right?" Johnny asked.

"Right. Pretty much the engine that runs the machine."

"First off, promote Suzanne. Head of sales."

"McLean? She's too green."

"Maybe, maybe not. She'll either sink or swim. I say swim. Besides, she's got the look for it."

"Fine, let's just say she can bring in some sales. Who runs creative during the next couple of months?" Walt asked.

"Are you writing this down?"

Walt grabbed his iPad and opened the Notes app. "Shaking it here, boss."

"Make it a team effort. The whole team participates on each project. Brainstorm like crazy. Make the conference room the war room. Tell everyone that it's imperative that the team come up with killer ideas. Find and nurture champions in creative. Rule by consensus for a while until somebody emerges. Somebody will; you'll recognize them."

"Can't we just conference you in on those meetings?"

"Let's assume not. For the sake of the plan."

Walt rubbed his eyes and tried to stretch the tension out of his neck by rotating it back and forth.

"And beef up the PR side of the business," Johnny added. "We've been getting bits and scraps of that for a year or two now. Go after the easy pickings. Find a good PR guy out there who wants to run his own show here with us. Offer him a job; tell him to sell the stink out of PR for six months and see where you are. Try Logan over at Hill Knowlton. I hear he's been looking around."

"We probably have enough backlog to sustain us for at least six months," mused Walt, as he caught some of the inspiration flowing from Johnny.

"Easy."

"But the ad side is cyclical. It comes, it goes," Walt said.

"Yeah, you still need to push sales there. But don't go after the big ones. Settle your sights down a bit, and go after lower hanging fruit. Check the prospect map we put together last year, the one where we ranked prospects."

Johnny suddenly stopped and closed his eyes. He took a deep breath.

"What am I doing?" he said. "You know how to do all this. We've been doing it forever. You'll figure it out. You're good at that stuff."

"I'm decent," Walt said, nodding his head.

"And stay away from hardware accounts. You don't know a computer chip from a buffalo chip. Stick with software, biotech, energy. Keep harvesting the venture guys for new companies; they typically have a huge need and cash. Stay away from consumer products—we've never had much success there. We're more nerds than we are Average Joe."

Johnny got a sudden twinge, deep inside. *What the heck am I doing? I'm giving this all up? Really? I guess so. Is that really what I want to do? No clue.*

"Back to Suzanne," Walt said. "What will we have to offer her for a raise? Twenty thou more?"

"Offer fifteen. But develop an incentive to increase business. Maybe increase the commission double for the first six months. That'll ignite her. If she closes a few big ones, she can make a killing. Then offer a bonus if she does well. Keep the bonus on sales, but if she brings in profitable business, shift it to a profit bonus. That'll be a good incentive for her to watch and learn the best business to tackle. Sink or swim."

"Six months? That long?" Walt asked, almost to himself.

"I love it when a plan comes together," Johnny said.

"I love the smell of napalm in the morning," Walt said, from the movie *Apocalypse Now.*

"Then," Johnny continued, "in a year or so, if it's going well, you and me talk, and we'll decide then if I should offer her my share of the company."

"A year?"

"Maybe."

"Then we're not partners anymore," Walt said, his eyes shifting back out to the gray fog.

Johnny felt that twinge again. It mingled somewhere inside, along with the despair and loneliness that was consuming him.

"Just don't sell your share to that eco-freak up in Marin," he said to Walt, getting back to business.

"What eco-freak? They're all eco-freaks in Marin."

"That eco-freak Jackson. If he offers you anything short of the Golden Gate for Troubadour, tell him to go jump off it. I'd rather be out of business than to see him destroy what we've built."

Walt Mathews looked at Johnny Roe, and Johnny knew what he was thinking. Walt never could hide his feelings well, his face showing the pain of what was happening.

Walt said, "Are you coming back? Ever?"

Johnny shrugged his shoulders. "Don't know." Then he thought for a moment and added, "Maybe…maybe not. Probably…who knows?"

That pained look expanded across Walt's face again.

"And I'm not destroying the company," Johnny said.

"What?" Walt asked.

"I can read you like a book, remember."

Walt looked away.

Johnny smiled. "You complete me."

"Oh, please," Walt said, trying not to grin.

SIX

JOHNNY set up the meeting with Luke Wacker at Pancho's Restaurant, a quiet little Mexican bistro near Jerry Ellis' office. He had located his financial planning office in quaint Lafayette, about thirty miles from San Francisco. He said clients liked to drive out to "the country"—a peaceful, quiet town, a great place to invest money. *You wouldn't want to invest money in some place that was crowded, noisy, hectic, and urban, would you?* Jerry always asked. Nope, people wanted their money to be peacefully invested. Like somehow it made a difference. Maybe Jerry just lived nearby.

For Tuesday's lunch crowd at Pancho's, only a handful of booths were occupied. The tortilla maker, a machine that was a major attraction in the restaurant, especially with kids, was either not working or had the day off for lack of business. They'd probably get leftover tortillas from the weekend.

"I'd like to offer you some part-time work," Johnny began, "but first I want you to answer one question as honestly as you can, okay?"

"No problem," Luke responded.

"How tough was it growing up with a name like Wacker?"

"Seriously?"

Johnny nodded.

Luke Wacker took several seconds to think about his answer. "Brutal."

"God, I can only imagine," Johnny said. "I read Tim Allen's book, you know the comedian? His real last name was Dick. Tim Dick. He said it almost killed him growing up with a name like that. He got the snot beat out of him almost every day, trying to defend that name."

"Starting in about sixth grade," Luke began, "I begged my father to change it to something else. Anything else. I even started to give him suggestions. Everything from Macker to Tracker to Backer, and all kinds of variations. Even suggested we pronounce it with a V, you know, like Vacker, the German company? He never went for it, said it was our legacy, that it would make both of us, my brother and me, stronger. I'm just glad I never had a sister, you know what I mean?"

"I didn't want to make a big deal out of it," Johnny said. "Just had to know that you'd be honest with me—on everything."

"Yeah, I figured it was a test."

"You passed." But Johnny hesitated. He didn't know Wacker well, and he was considering turning over part of his life to this…this kid.

What the heck am I doing?

"Good. What's the job?"

"I need a personal financial assistant."

"Sounds like a secretary."

"It'll start out that way, but you can make it much more."

Johnny had ordered extra-hot sauce and dipped a chip in, scooping what he knew would burn like the sun. Almost as a dare to Luke to do the same. He slowed the motion of eating the chip—right in front of his mouth—to emphasize how much sauce he was going to consume.

Johnny continued, "The salary will be fair to begin with, and there's a chance you can make some decent money. If you make me some money in the bargain." Johnny didn't want it to come out so much like a negotiation, but still, this was a kid.

"Okay, tell me more," Luke said, taking out his iPad.

"I want you to put all my expenses on a spreadsheet, to start with," Johnny began.

"Doesn't your CFO do that at Troubadour?"

"You can count Troubadour out. These are just my personal expenses…and my investments. Jerry's on board; he'll give you everything you need."

Luke started to take notes with a portable keyboard he'd attached to the tablet.

"Then set up as many of my bills for automated payment as you can. I won't be in the house for a while, maybe a long time. Cut as many expenses as you can, too. I'll be within email contact, but you can make decisions, to a point. Work with Jerry to put more money into dividend-yielding investments, so I have some cash flow."

"Maybe you should be talking to him about this," Luke said.

"Nope. I'm talking to you. How are you ever gonna run your own show if you don't take on projects like this? I'm giving you free rein, well, not quite free, but close. This'll train you on all aspects of handling a client—soup to nuts, as they say. Whatever soup to nuts means."

"Okay, keep going."

"As you get comfortable at that level, branch out. Look at my insurance. Car, life, property, medical, everything. I'll pay you hourly to start with, then once we figure out how many hours you're working in a month, we'll move you to monthly. But if you save me money and can prove it, I'll incorporate a bonus. If it works out and you like it, then we can talk about you taking a percentage of what you save me as your salary. What you really become is an efficiency expert. And when you're ready to set up your own shop—if that's what you want to do—you can incorporate that into your service. Clients will love it. You may not make much money doing the efficiency part, but it'll be a great way to keep clients and find new ones. You game?"

"Sounds interesting," Luke said as he nodded.

Johnny had to shake his head to get back into the conversation. He'd drifted away, remembering that Sam loved being in charge of the household money. She handed over the kids to Johnny a few times a month after dinner and headed into her little home office to balance the checkbook and pay bills. She always looked so proud when she emerged, like she'd balanced the national budget.

I'll never see that look again.

"One more thing, maybe not so interesting," Johnny said.

"Sure. What?"

"I need you to clean out the house."

"You mean like hire a service to clean it regularly?"

"Well, yes. And no. I'm talking about my wife and kids' things. I want you to clean out the master bedroom and give away anything of my wife's. Then move on to the kids' rooms. All of it, get it out of there."

"Don't you want to have some things, like pictures or toys, just to remind you of them?" Luke wondered.

"I'll pack up what I want and store it in the garage. Maybe a few pictures. But the rest of it, give it away, donate it. Then have the two kids' rooms repainted, new bedding, new pictures on the walls. A redesign."

"How do I do that?" Luke asked.

Johnny remembered the wall in the hallway leading back to the bedrooms. It was crammed, almost haphazardly, with framed photos of the kids. School pictures, vacation shots at the beach, their first time on snow skis. A very real depiction of their entire family life. Probably twenty-five photos, maybe more.

No more photos like that, ever.

"Did you hear me? I said, how do I do that?" Luke asked again.

"Find an interior designer. Give her a budget. Keep her to it. Figure it out."

"When will you be leaving?"

"Within the week, probably."

"Where you going?"

"Don't exactly know."

"How do I get in touch with you?"

"Email first, text if you need to talk with me. Either is fine."

"What about the mail?"

"Good question. I hadn't thought about that yet." Johnny shook his head.

"How about I handle that, too," Luke suggested. "We'll get a P.O. box. I'll handle the bills, trash the junk. If you trust me to do that. Do you?"

Johnny nodded as the impact of what he was going to do began to set in. It wasn't going to be so easy just to run away for six months or a year. The stakes here in Northern California were driven in pretty deep. But he was beginning to trust Luke Wacker; the kid was already getting into it, and even the purging part didn't seem to bother him.

"Listen, Luke, I don't…I just need to get away," Johnny confessed. "I can't live in that house right now, and I can't work at my company right now. I feel like everything…has just crumbled."

"Yeah." Luke averted his eyes.

"I just need somebody level-headed and career-oriented to take charge of this one aspect of my life."

"I can do that."

"Luke, I'm trusting you. A lot. With a big part of my life. Got it?"

"Yes, sir. I won't let you down."

"Good answer. Now let's work out the details over lunch. You want a beer?"

"No, sir."

"Another good answer."

As they ate lunch, Johnny couldn't shake the feeling that had been bubbling up inside him for days. Not one of sorrow or regret or loneliness—but one of revenge.

SEVEN

"**Y**ESSIR, how can I help you?" the burly man asked as Johnny walked into a small retail store called R&R Guns.

Several days after the meeting with Luke Wacker, Johnny had researched gun shops, finding this one about fifteen miles south of San Francisco.

"Need to buy a gun," Johnny answered.

"Well, name's Robbie. Any particular type you had in mind?"

"Something for self-defense."

"How big?"

"Big enough to hit something and to drop something."

"Something?"

"Yeah, something. Like a person. Or an animal. Or something…" Johnny said.

The gun shop, settled into a strip center just off the freeway, was set up like a jewelry store with counters surrounding all three sides of the store. Robbie—one of the R's in R&R, Johnny assumed—sat in a canvas director's chair. Heavy metal music came from a radio behind the counter, and Robbie reached behind him and turned down the volume. He was a fat man with thinning hair, a little too long to be fashionable, and the spider veins around his nose and cheeks told Johnny he liked his liquor.

"Well, we specialize in handguns. I figure people want to protect themselves, from something, from everything. Anyway, got any preferences?" Robbie asked.

"Nope. What're my options?"

"Well, let's see," Robbie said as he looked around the display cases, ambling over to the case to his right. "We got everything from this little Heinz Double Tap, a two-shooter…"

"What's a two-shooter?" Johnny asked.

"Holds two bullets."

Johnny shook his head.

"Something bigger then." Robbie searched the counter.

Johnny nodded.

"Well, over here," Robbie motioned back to his left. "We got a Smith and Wesson Shield, a Ruger Snubbie, that's a little snub nose, see that one there?"

Again, Johnny shook his head.

"Just holler if you see something you like. I'll let you hold it. That's really how you get the feel for something. Then we got a Springfield XD, a Beretta, a Walther…"

"Let's see the Smith and Wesson," Johnny said. At least he knew that name.

"An excellent firearm," Robbie said, as he reached into the case, grabbed the gun, and handed it to Johnny.

"Tell me a little about it."

Robbie puffed out his chest and began like he was describing one of his grandchildren. "The new Shield is the lightest and smallest 9mm personal-defense S&W has put on the market. It's only about six inches long, less than an inch thick, and weighs just nineteen ounces. Based on the full-size S&W design, it will undoubtedly be a big seller in the concealed carry world, know what I mean? The M&P9 Shield comes with one semi-staggered, flat-base, seven-round magazine and one extended-base, eight-round mag; the M&P40 model comes with one six-rounder and one seven-rounder. You're holding the 40. My personal favorite."

"Forget the sales pitch. What do you like about it?" Johnny asked.

"Well, when it comes to personal defense pistols in general, I'm pretty much like everybody else. As much as I appreciate big bore cartridge power and as familiar and good as I may be with a full-size revolver, those are probably not what I'm gonna strap on my belt or tuck in my waistband when I need to leave the house late at night for a quick trip to the local liquor store. In that situation, I'll be dropping something lightweight, compact, and inconspicuous into my pocket, something that's chambered for a cartridge with sufficient authority, if you know what I mean."

Johnny nodded his head. The gun felt heavy in his hand and a little foreign. The last time he handled a gun was…he couldn't remember. He gripped it tightly and noticed that it fit the shape of his hand—and almost gripped him back. Strange.

Robbie continued his description, but Johnny just held the gun, not listening.

"Feels good in your hand, doesn't it?"

"It does," Johnny concurred.

"In fact, the only problem I have at all with these tiny .380 pistols on the market is that I have to think very carefully about how I initially grab hold of them if I want to be secure in rapid-fire situations," Robbie said. "Oh, yeah. One more thing. It's got a uniform short, crisp trigger pull, which, again, is the same mechanism as found on full-size M&Ps."

"Is it powerful? I don't know much…about guns," Johnny said.

"Yeah, I figured. We're all looking to protect ourselves these days. It's only natural, and it's our God-given right. And yeah, that little sucker packs a whale of a punch, especially with the right ammunition. I'd recommend hollow points. Knockdown power and gets the job done right."

Johnny continued to look and feel the small gun in his hand. He finally remembered the last time he had held a gun. The shotgun when he took those reporters up to Boise to tour the Micron facility. They hired a guide to train them in a two-hour crash course in skeet sport shooting. Johnny remembered he could hit those flying clay pigeons pretty well if they were traveling from left to right, but not if they were going the other way. Something about his vision and his dominate eye.

"How much? With bullets," Johnny asked.

"Four-fifty for the gun, another thirty bucks, about, depending on how much you need, for the shells. You're out the door around five and a half."

"And how about if I need somebody to teach me how to use it?"

"We got a gun club just up the road. Lessons are pretty cheap. Fifty per hour, including shells."

"What's the waiting period?" Johnny asked.

"Ten days in California. Plus you gotta fill out the paperwork so they can do a background check. Then you gotta pass the safety exam, but that's a piece of cake. The gun club can do that for you."

Johnny nodded, weighing the gun in his hand.

"Cash or credit card, my friend?" Robbie grinned as he took the Smith and Wesson from Johnny's tightened grip.

EIGHT

TEN days later, dusk settled over Manteca, fading colors to gray. Johnny had all night to wait for Victor Gonzales.

Victor Gonzales. The man driving the truck that caused the accident. The one that killed his wife and children.

Johnny sat in his car, watching the sun set somewhere behind the East Bay hills. He always thought they called California the Golden State because that was the color the hills turned from about the first of May till the rainy season hit in October or November. The streetlights barely made a dent in the darkness as it overcame him. Must be cutbacks in the city of Manteca budget, he thought. It looked like half the streetlights didn't even come on with the first group of lights. Either that or they were burned out and not replaced. Johnny had read a lot about the Central Valley in California and how it had been sucker-punched by the recession.

Manteca was on the edge of the valley, not quite in the Bay Area, not quite in the Central Valley. Tons of inexpensive homes attracted the commuters who had the stamina to make the drive to the Bay Area, two hours each way. A commuter train came down from Sacramento, but like most rapid transit systems in California, it only got you close to your destination. All the dots were not connected, so you had to find another way, like a bus, to get the entire way from point A to point B. Most people just figured it was easier to drive. That's why the freeways were packed by five in the morning and never died down till eight at night. Even Johnny's trip east in mid-afternoon had lasted longer than most junior high school romances.

The Smith & Wesson rested in the cup holder, the nozzle pointing down as Johnny grabbed for it.

Johnny had never been to Manteca; its biggest claim to fame was that it was on the way to someplace else. Sacramento to the north,

Yosemite Valley to the east, and Fresno south down Highway 99 past the alliterative towns of Modesto, Merced, and Madera. The neighborhood where he was now parked had seen better days, if better days had ever visited Manteca. The apartment building directly in front of him was shaped like a U. Two-story, with a prominent red and white FOR RENT sign just below its name—Highland Gardens—that distinguished it from similar buildings up and down the road. Aluminum siding wrapped the complex in a faded shade of beige, and the iron gate that blocked the open end of the U had several vertical bars bent outward, almost like Superman had been trapped inside and needed to get out. The sign pointing to the office drooped to the right, tired from the thirty years or so it had been directing families who were looking for month-to-month stays.

He knew this was the right address; a call to Victor Gonzales' employer had easily revealed that. But Johnny didn't know what he'd do once he found Gonzales. He picked up the revolver and let it settle comfortably in his hand.

After meetings with the staff at Troubadour, Jerry Ellis, and Luke Wacker, Johnny yearned to slip silently away, to mourn the loss of his family on his own terms. It was a journey he knew he had to take, but he didn't know where it would lead, just that he hoped he came out the other end all in one piece. The two-week wait for the gun left Johnny alone, except for the ever-present Buster, his son's golden retriever. Johnny had been all set to give the dog away, but after long walks during the day, the dog began to grow on him. When Buster began sleeping on the bed next to Johnny at night, they became buds. And when each time Johnny returned home, no matter how long he'd been gone, Buster would jump up and greet Johnny with licks and the closest thing a dog can mimic to a hug, they became almost inseparable.

Even with Buster shadowing Johnny whenever he was home and tagging along in the car if possible, Johnny's depression had settled in. He drank too much Buffalo Trace, smoked too many cigars, and ate too little. He had managed to jump on his bicycle several times, and the endorphin rush of fifteen or twenty miles was always welcome. But his stamina was low, the rides only sporadic, and the joy of the ride fleeting.

Johnny had always been able to channel his anger constructively. On the volleyball courts at UC Santa Barbara, he could float on that edge between competitive and out of control. On his bike, he could hammer away at the pedals until he beat the anger down and let other emotions come to the surface. The bike had also been one of the ways Johnny had pushed through periods when his creativity was non-existent. Long, slow rides honed away the excess—whether body fat, bad emotions, depressed moods, or a lack of focus—and let the natural Johnny come to the surface. But he had trouble tapping into his natural, creative self since the accident. The anger kept growing, often sweeping over him, engulfing him. He grabbed the gun.

Buster wasn't with Johnny now. He sat alone in his car with his pistol.

The photo of Victor Gonzales in the local paper's online article was grainy, but as Johnny looked up, he recognized Gonzales getting out of the well-worn Chevy truck. After parking the truck by the curb, he leaned back in, searching in the cab for something, his back to the street. Johnny quietly slipped out of his car, pocketing the gun in his jacket, and took several steps towards the truck.

"Gonzales!" Johnny shouted.

Victor Gonzales jerked his head up suddenly, banging it on the top of the door jamb.

"Dammit! What!" Gonzales shouted back.

"Are you Victor Gonzales?" Johnny asked, immediately feeling a little stupid by asking a question he knew the answer to.

"*Si*, who want to know?" Gonzales asked, rubbing his head.

"You killed my family."

"What you talking about? I don't kill nobody."

"Two months ago, highway 580, the white Cadillac."

Victor Gonzales turned pale, and his face contorted up into a sorrowful frown. He dropped his hands from his head, and his shoulders slumped forward.

"*Trajico*…tragic," he managed to say, shaking his head slowly to look to the ground.

The anger in Johnny kept rising, suffocating any response to Gonzales.

"God, he no smile on nobody that day."

Johnny reached into his pocket and drew the gun out, hiding it securely in his right hand.

"You husband?" Gonzales asked.

"Not anymore."

"I so sorry, *señor.* I don't know else to say."

"You…you killed my family."

Johnny raised the gun, pointing it straight at Victor Gonzales. His arm shook, the gun unsteady in his hand. He felt his neck and shoulder muscles clench.

Gonzales' eyes opened wide when he saw the gun, and he slowly began to raise his hands.

The two men stared at each other, standing fifteen feet apart. Neither moved.

"Goddamn you!" Johnny said through clenched teeth. He could barely breathe, the anger choking him.

"Yes," Gonzales said, nodding his head in agreement. "Goddamn me. God will damn me, *señor.*"

"You killed my family," Johnny managed to mumble.

Johnny put his left hand on his right wrist, trying to steady the gun, the anger uncontrollable now, rising on a wave, sweeping over Johnny's head like a swell in the ocean. He imagined Gonzales accelerating away from the accident, not caring about what he'd left behind. Laughing.

Gonzales put his hands together in prayer and slowly sank to his knees.

"Please, my family," he pleaded as his eyes darted quickly between the apartment building and Johnny Roe.

"You ruined my life," Johnny said, his voice trembling. "It's gone, all gone."

Gonzales lowered his head to the pavement. He sharply exhaled, a moan.

Just then, Johnny glanced to his right and saw a short, pudgy woman holding a small child in her arms. She perched on the top step to the apartments and looked from Johnny to Gonzales. She hugged the child closer and tried to turn his head away from the scene unfolding before them. Gonzales noticed them, too, and motioned with his hand for them to go away. The child's outstretched arm reached out, and his fingers fluttered like he was beckoning to the man.

"My family," Gonzales said, barely audible.

Johnny lowered the gun as emotion caught in his throat. The swell of anger subsided. He took a deep breath. Then another. A deep headache emerged across his forehead. He slipped the gun back in his jacket and walked slowly to his car. Victor Gonzales now had his head close to the ground, his hands still in prayer outstretched in front of him, his head nodding up and down, as a gesture of gratitude.

Johnny started the engine and pulled away from the curb. The darkness had completely engulfed Manteca.

NINE

EVEN though the decision to leave had been made weeks before, as Johnny and Buster pulled out of the garage, Johnny was gripped with emotion. He couldn't seem to take a deep breath, and his head and shoulders ached, the muscles frozen in place. Memories flashed repeatedly, like a Facebook collage gone wild. Pain from the loss of his family traveled from his midsection to head and back and bounced around the rest of his body without a place to settle. He leaned down to let Buster lick his face and somehow found the resolve— he could always tap into the resolve—to direct the car to the freeway. *Just go, just go,* he thought.

The Jeep had lost that new car smell after only a few weeks. It now had an old Buster smell, but that was fine with Johnny. He'd outfitted Buster with a San Francisco Giants kerchief made for dogs. Seemed only fitting since he'd been named for Buster Posey, the Giants' catcher. His bed was on the floor in the front seat, and his favorite blanket covered the shotgun seat.

Johnny jumped on Interstate 80, heading east early in the morning. The California morning was clear and mild. He lowered the passenger-side window a few inches so Buster could search for new smells.

They drove for four hours before Buster made them stop just east of Lake Tahoe. After a twenty-minute walk around a city park, they found a little deli with an outside table and shared a turkey sandwich. The deli had a bowl of water for their canine customers, and Buster indulged. Johnny settled for a caffeine jolt.

Since they were under no time pressures, really didn't have a destination in mind—basically, nowhere to go or nobody to see—they returned to the park and took another walk.

Johnny said hello to a few people, mostly older men or younger women, walking their dogs. One particular woman who looked to be in her late twenties smiled at Johnny and said he had a beautiful dog. He wondered if that was a pick-up line. She did have a nice figure with long legs.

Whoa! He hadn't had a thought about another woman since the accident. It was only a brief thought, and it left quickly, but at least he had smiled back at the pretty woman and said thanks. It was a good thing he hadn't seen any kids playing with dogs. He didn't want to see that; he wasn't ready to see that.

The Lake Tahoe morning was cool and crisp, most of the snow gone, with spring beginning to poke its head out after a winter slumber. But Johnny wasn't into gorgeous, so they kept driving east, away from the sunset and into Nevada.

Johnny drove, barely noticing the landscape or the road signs. He wasn't looking for a particular exit, didn't have a final destination to keep him alert.

He'd always been a man who focused on goals. Ever since high school, he'd kept track of everything he was aiming for.

Finish college by age 22
Get a good job with an innovative company
Obtain a nice salary (Range: 50-75K)
Start a company by the age of 30 (35 at the latest)
Fall in love and start a family (2 kids? 3?)

First, he had a notebook, then he transferred his goals to the computer. He would update them yearly, refocus, rearrange, delete, and add on. When one goal was complete, he'd check it off and add another. Whenever he felt he was teetering in life, off-balance, his goals centered him. He felt safe around them, like the goals themselves provided peace, instead of the life they'd actually produced for him.

But now, he had no goals. No targets, no compass. He was spinning—maybe not out of control—but certainly not under control either. At least not his control.

Around midnight, with Buster asleep in the shotgun seat and Jason Aldean's *Relentless* CD wailing with a nasal twang, a song struck a chord with Johnny. Aldean lamented about losing a woman and how trying to get her back was going to be as easy as putting smoke back in a cigarette. A line in the chorus Aldean sang with such pathos that Johnny began to cry.

He spotted a turnoff—a narrow country road, not paved after the first several hundred feet from the highway. He exited the two-lane they'd traveled since Tahoe and drove a quarter-mile or so down the road. He couldn't breathe, needing more air than the car allowed.

He stopped the car just off the road and got out, leaving his door open. As his eyes adjusted to the darkness, the night sky sparkled with more stars than he'd ever seen. The Milky Way, visible in a luminous swatch of sparkling light sprinkled from one horizon to the other, looked like it had been painted by a star-happy wizard with a heavenly paintbrush. Stars illuminated the surrounding high desert landscape, even with the moon not yet out. Shrub bushes resembled solitary sentinels, keeping guard of the road. Johnny again looked to the sky. Then he sank to his knees.

His tears came, first as a trickle, then a stream. He mourned the loss of his wife and children. He mourned the things he'd miss. Carson's baseball games and the way he mimicked big league pitchers on the mound, adjusting his hat and spitting often. Dance recitals where Cameron would try not to look at the other girls to remember the steps, her eyes darting quickly right and left. The funny way Sam had of scratching his face with one of her long fingernails, making that screech-screech sound, as an indication he could probably use a shave.

He sobbed uncontrollably, but he didn't try to rein it in. He'd been keeping this darkness of mourning inside for two months, and now it had to come out. He pounded the dirt with his fist.

Buster tentatively poked his head out of the door and stared at Johnny. The dog looked like he wanted to jump out of the car and rush to his owner, but he hesitated, waiting for the command. Johnny simply patted his thigh, and Buster cautiously stepped out and walked to him. Then he put his muzzle in the crook between Johnny's neck and shoulder. The dog seemed to understand Johnny's sorrow.

Buster moved closer. It felt to Johnny that the dog was trying to absorb the grief from him. Buster licked Johnny's chin as Johnny hugged him. Aldean's singing was a lamenting background chorus as the two sat by the side of the road in the Nevada desert. They eventually ended up lying on the ground, side by side, hugging.

Johnny decided it wasn't a waste of his breath to call their names, so in a voice he'd never heard before, he groaned out *Samantha, Carson, Cameron* over and over and over again. He kept repeating their names. Buster began to wail, not like a wolf and not too loud, but in a soft doggy voice.

Johnny called and called; Buster wailed. Aldean's music faded below the surface.

When he could no longer find a voice to cry out, the tears subsided. Johnny took several long, deep breaths. He had no idea how long he'd been on the ground, but his back hurt and stiffness spread through his legs.

They both slowly rose to their feet, Johnny stretching out his legs and Buster doing his stretch and shake routine, his collar jingling in the head-to-tail choreography. Johnny felt like he needed to do a similar shake but figured God gave that particular skill to dogs only, so he settled for more stretching and deep breaths. Buster began to sniff the air and look around.

Johnny wiped his nose on his sleeve and tilted back his head to look at the Milky Way again. His chest felt more open like he could finally breathe.

Buster barked, ready for a treat. And Jason Aldean had shifted into a country rocker with a strong guitar riff.

TEN

FOR the next month, Johnny and Buster headed in an easterly direction with no particular place to go.

They stayed away from interstate highways and kept to back roads. When Johnny got tired of the car, they found a nice, clean motel and set up camp for a day or two or three. They rose at dawn, mostly Buster's idea, and went to bed whenever they felt like it. Johnny took long afternoon bike rides while Buster napped in the car or the motel. Then they grabbed long walks in the afternoon so Buster could explore and mark new territories.

They meandered their way east through Nevada all the way to Salt Lake City. Johnny had been there only once, so they spent a week. Then they detoured almost directly north to Pocatello, Idaho, and continued north to Butte, Montana. Johnny had spent some time in Montana with a client at a dude ranch, and he was eager to explore the Big Sky country. They traveled east, in the direction of Lewis and Clark's journey back home, keeping close to the original route of the 19th century explorers. Out of Butte, Johnny drove past the B towns of Montana—Bozeman, Big Timber, and Billings—and sliced down into Wyoming's Bighorn Mountains. He rode horses outside of Sheridan at a dude ranch, drank Moose Drool beer (best name ever, he voted) on tap at the Mint Bar in Sheridan. He thought of how both Cameron and Carson would have giggled at the name—Moose Drool!—and how Sam always teased him that he must have been a real rootin', tootin' cowboy in a past life. And how the word *tootin'* would have sent Carson off to Giggleland again. Johnny smiled at the memories.

His taste for bourbon subsided, and his frequent bike rides cleansed not only the alcohol from his body but his moodiness. Buster enjoyed being tied up outside The Mint to a lamppost in the late spring air. The bartender (Johnny really wanted to call him a barkeep, but resisted) opened the door, so Johnny had a clear view of his pooch. In doggy heaven, Buster accepted back scratches and ear rubs from all the locals. His new outfit consisted of a new collar that looked like a gun belt and a leash made from a lariat.

Although Johnny loved hanging out at The Mint—the animal taxidermies on the walls were hellacious conversation starters—he wasn't drinking much. He had finally lost the craving for the buzz. His alcoholic friends had always explained that the buzz was the holy grail of why people drank. Alkies loved the buzz, more than life without the buzz. It just plain made life different, and for most, different in a good, happy way. For others, darkness emerged when the buzz presided. Johnny had developed a craving for the buzz after what was now known in his mind as *The Accident*. But with this trip, the long bike rides, and the long hours of introspection, the craving subsided. Somehow, he'd gotten over the hump. He loved a Moose Drool or two, and even a good sip of bourbon now and then, but the buzz craving had left the building.

Johnny had purchased a Stetson cowboy hat in Bozeman, and although he was a little self-conscious that it looked brand new, he wore it proudly and fit right in with the local crowd. He wore his Tony Lama roper boots, purchased a few years ago during the dude ranch outing. He hadn't worn anything but blue jeans for the past couple of months. He felt comfortable.

The first month after The Accident, Johnny stayed in touch with the office daily. That pattern was changing. They called and texted less now, and Johnny only checked in occasionally, mostly to let Walt Mathews know that he was still alive and doing fine. Business was usually a secondary conversation whenever they talked. The agency suffered a bit right after Johnny left, and a few accounts cut ties with them entirely. But the staff had bonded together and won new clients. Even though most companies were hoarding cash like Imelda Marcos hoarded shoes, some segments went gangbusters. The agency tapped into the stronger segments and made money.

He checked in with Luke more often. The boy wonder of personal service and accounting had moved all of Johnny's transactions online and shown Johnny how to access everything from electrical bills paid to investment dividends received.

One day in late May, Luke sent a text to Johnny, wanting to talk.

"Luke, my man, what's up?" Johnny asked when Luke answered the ensuing phone call.

"Johnny, good to hear from you. Where are you?"

"God's country. Sheridan, Wyoming."

"Never been there. Not even close."

For the next twenty minutes, they reviewed what had happened the last month or so, how the investments were doing, and how life in Northern California was treating the young bachelor.

"One thing that stumps me, though," Luke said as the conversation wound down.

"Fire away."

"Do you guys…er, did you guys, sorry, give away a lot of gift cards?"

"A few, I suppose, during the holidays mostly, some to employees. Why?"

"Well, I've been investigating all of these automatic withdrawals for the past six months from the main checking account, and they're all for gift cards."

"Gift cards for what?" Johnny asked.

"That's the part that has me stumped. They're from everywhere. Gas, shopping, coffee…."

"Huh, what the heck are you talking about?"

"Every month there were huge charges for Arco, Texaco, Chevron, Nordstrom, Starbucks, Macy's, American Express, and a few others. Some are twenty-five dollars, some are fifty. They stopped right after…the accident."

"How much we talking about?"

"About two thousand a month."

"A month?!"

"Yep, like clockwork."

"Can you do some digging? Find out who authorized these and when. Then cancel them all and see if we can get them credited back to the account."

"Sure. If I need any authorization, I'll just say I'm you. What passcode do you typically give credit card companies?"

"Town I was born in, Huntington Beach, California."

"I'll get on it right away and let you know what I find out."

"Thanks, man. Take care."

Johnny hung up and wondered why Samantha would buy so many gift cards without his knowledge.

He and Buster stayed in Sheridan, Wyoming, the better part of May as the weather cleared and the sun warmed the northern prairie. But a man could only drink so much Moose Drool, and Johnny's bike wasn't meant for dirt roads, so as the calendar flipped to June, they ventured back on the road again. Buster seemed to cherish his shotgun spot and the crack in the window. Johnny had thrown away the Jason Aldean CD and invested in more upbeat music.

They made quick work of South Dakota, stopping only to see Mount Rushmore and the Badlands. Once they found the Missouri River halfway across the state, they followed it straight into Iowa. The landscape turned decidedly flat, but the sun was warm, the cornfields were thriving, and the early summer days were getting longer.

They stopped at the outskirts where smaller signs, such as the Farmer's Guild and the Chamber of Commerce, surrounded the big Welcome to Booneville sign. After stretching their legs and after reading the mishmash of signs, they decided to look around.

They almost never left.

ELEVEN

JOHNNY sat in the Jeep as Buster sniffed close by the town sign. He'd pulled up Wikipedia on his phone and quickly found a page about Booneville, Iowa.

He discovered that Booneville was the county seat of Boone County, Iowa. Smack dab in the center of the county, just west of Ames. The county was named after Nathan Boone, son of Daniel. The website told him it was a small town, not much more than twenty thousand people, and that figure included the half dozen smaller towns that surrounded it.

"Well, pup, let's do some exploring, what'd you say?"

As Johnny powered up the Jeep, Buster jumped back in, and they headed toward the town. The homes were a mixture of two-story brick, rectangle ranches and farmhouses. Gardens visible in the back or along the side sidled up alongside the homes, green lawns in the front edged by white picket fences. Gravel driveways outside of Booneville introduced each house. Large, deep ditches paralleled the roads that took the water from storms off property, Johnny surmised. Paved driveways appeared closer to town, not with blacktop but real concrete. As Johnny rode down Main Street, he knew Norman Rockwell had depicted a few of these homes in his paintings. Johnny didn't think Frank Lloyd Wright had designed many homes in Booneville, Iowa. As Johnny and Buster drove the Jeep slowly down Main Street, puffy white clouds filled the sky. The air smelled clean and fresh.

Johnny pulled off Main Street at a small diner called Buddy's for breakfast. It was mid-morning, and the place was crowded, which Johnny figured was a good sign. He didn't frequent restaurants that were empty; it usually meant the food was not a big draw. He parked the Jeep in a parking space across the street from the diner, cracked all the windows for Buster, and gave him a few biscuits from the bag in the back seat.

The diner looked like it hadn't changed much from the 1950s—a counter with red vinyl stools in front of the kitchen, booths surrounding the rest of the interior, and a meeting room to the left, with a sliding plastic curtain drawn closed. Johnny heard voices, some raised to near shouts, coming from the room. The smells of syrup, coffee, and bacon hovered in the air. He settled down at the counter and grabbed a menu, glancing at the small mini-jukeboxes with the flip pages in front of him. He wondered if they had any Jason Aldean. Twenty-five cents for a single play.

The waitress behind the counter waved politely to him and mouthed that she'd be right with him. She wore a faded red uniform with puffy sleeves and a white apron that included a bib, tied with a big bow in the back. Her hair was raised in a tight bun, a pencil sticking out above her left ear. A few strands of hair flopped on her forehead, and she nonchalantly tried without success to tuck them back behind her ear. It looked like she'd had a long, busy morning.

Johnny flipped through the pages on the jukebox and saw a lot of country songs, a few tunes from the '60s, mostly Motown, a page of Frank Sinatra, one of Elvis, one of Merle Haggard, but nothing for Jason Aldean. *Just as good,* he thought. He fished around his pocket for a coin but came up empty.

"I think they got it turned off," said an elderly man sitting two seats to Johnny's right. "Big meeting going on, and they don't want to be disturbed."

Johnny nodded and said, "Thanks for the tip."

"Don't mention it," the man said, extending his right hand out. "Doc Enbright."

"Johnny Roe."

They shook hands, and Johnny noticed that the old man had soft, warm hands and smelled of antiseptic.

"New in town? I haven't seen you around."

"Just passing through, really," Johnny replied. "Got hungry, and this place looked pretty good."

"Been here seventy years or more," Doc said. "Actually was run by Buddy Parcel, but he passed in 1995. Now Floyd and his wife Wendy run it. Floyd's in the back on the grill this morning. Been busy in here."

"You seem to have a pretty good take on the pulse around here. What's good for breakfast?"

"Pancakes are the specialty of the house. And you don't look like you'd mind the calories. Actually, you look a little peaked. You feeling okay?"

"Fine, thanks," Johnny said. He turned to look at the menu again, trying to ignore the friendly inquiry.

"Sorry, didn't mean to stick my nose in your business. But once a doctor, always a doctor. Retired now, though. No offense?"

"None taken," Johnny said, smiling at the old fellow.

Johnny ordered the pancakes and looked around the diner as Doc Enbright settled into the crossword puzzle in his newspaper. Framed photos with "Best Wishes" and autographs on each blanketed the diner walls. Many of the photos were old and yellowing; some looked as old as the diner itself. Johnny didn't recognize anyone in any of the photos. Locals, he thought. On one wall, a series of stacked plaques verified that Buddy's was a long-standing member of the Rotary, Chamber of Commerce, Kiwanis, Knights of Columbus, and a couple other clubs Johnny didn't know. The walls looked like they'd just had a fresh coat of white paint, and the white-and-black-checked linoleum, except for a stray straw wrapper or napkin, almost sparkled. Floyd and Wendy did a good job of keeping the place clean and tidy, and yet they kept the old-time flavor of the original Buddy's intact. Johnny liked the friendly atmosphere, the friendly people, and the buttermilk pancakes.

"Good, huh?" Doc asked as he slid to the stool next to Johnny.

"Um huh!" Johnny said as he shoved another mouthful in, smiling and trying not to lose any of the pancake.

"You mentioned you were just passing through. Where you headed?" Doc asked.

"No place special. Just kind of winding our way east," Johnny replied.

"Our? Means you're not traveling solo?"

"My dog and me."

Doc nodded and smiled.

Suddenly, the plastic curtain to the private room to Johnny's left burst open and a tall gentleman dressed all in denim and an old baseball hat yelled, "You idiots have no idea what the Sam Hill you're talkin' about!"

He then pushed the curtain aside even farther, forcing it off its tracks, and walked hurriedly toward the door. He slammed it as he left.

"I take it that's not a Chamber of Commerce meeting," Johnny said.

"Keen observation," Doc joked.

The denim guy's departure had the room in an uproar. Somebody tried to get the curtain back on track, barely succeeded, and closed it again. But the curtain didn't snap shut with the latch at the end, and it drooped open again.

"Those guys have been in there every Saturday morning for a month or two," Doc offered. "It always seems to end the same way—lots of arguing. Probably isn't too healthy for those boys to be carrying on so."

"Lot of things ain't healthy in this world, Doc, including pancakes," Johnny said.

"Where'd you hear that malarkey? Pancakes never killed anybody!" Doc replied, smiling broadly.

"Hey, I kinda like this old town. Maybe I'll get a room and look around," Johnny said. "Got a recommendation on a nice hotel?"

"Well, most travelers stay at that Courtyard out by the freeway. You get a free breakfast, but I'm told it tastes like cardboard. If you want a real taste of Booneville, I recommend the Best Western just out that-a-way on Main," Doc replied, gesturing with his arm. "Tell Irv and Donna that Doc Enbright sent ya. They might even give you a good rate!"

"Thanks, will do. Nice meeting you," Johnny said as he shook the doctor's hand again.

Doc Enbright looked deeply into Johnny's eyes and held the grip for longer than normal. He peered in at Johnny to the point that Johnny began to pull his hand away. But the doctor's grip was strong, and he didn't let go.

"Son, I don't know what's bothering you, but you got a pallor about you. It kind of surrounds you, engulfs you."

Johnny didn't say a word, just stared back at Enbright.

"I can see it in your eyes. Sad...or something. Can't quite pin it down."

"Just tired, that's all," Johnny said as he flipped a ten-dollar bill on top of the check. "Been a long trip."

"You cannot pull the wool over the doctor's eyes, son."

"I'll remember that. See ya around."

"I'm here every mornin'. No appointment necessary."

Johnny quietly closed the door as he left the restaurant. He turned around to see Doc waving goodbye to him. Old coot, Johnny thought, as a big smile spread across his face.

TWELVE

AFTER checking into the Booneville Best Western and making friends with Donna at the front desk, Johnny leashed Buster and headed out to survey their newest town. They spent the rest of the morning walking the streets of downtown and the outlying areas, getting in a good five miles. When they returned to the motel, Buster crashed on the bed, and Johnny took a leisurely bike ride. A ten-miler took him in a counter-clockwise circle around Booneville and the farms that nestled close to it. He passed several small businesses—an upholstery shop attached to a used car lot, a dog food manufacturer, several veterinarians, a food packager—and a large farm equipment rental lot. One particular business called U.S. Johnson Controls had several people picketing out front, something about keeping America manufacturing in America, but Johnny didn't pay too much attention.

The next morning, Johnny returned to the counter at Buddy's for more pancakes. He tried the buckwheat cakes and liked them even more than the buttermilk.

Doc Enbright slid onto the stool next to him.

"I see that the slow-paced life of Booneville has kept you around for at least another day. Or maybe it was the pancakes."

Johnny chuckled, "Definitely the pancakes, but the bike ride through the country roads was nice yesterday, too."

"Motorbike or bicycle?" Doc asked.

"Bicycle. Just can't get enough of the outdoors these days."

"Settles the mind, doesn't it?"

"Indeed."

As the old man sipped his coffee, he said, "I've always looked for activities that settle the mind. I used to go for long walks. I could walk for hours, it seemed. Whenever I had a problem or situation I was facing, I'd just start out walking. Sometimes I'd be five miles away from the house before I knew where I was. Like a trance, working on that problem. Lately, my knees and back have been a little cranky, so I don't walk much anymore. I miss it. Therapeutic."

The two men ate in silence with only the clatter of silverware and murmured conversations.

"Are you a fisherman, Mr. Roe?" Doc asked.

"Johnny, please. And no, never been."

"Never?"

"Maybe once, but deep sea fishing, and I don't think that's what you mean."

"Nope. I'm talking lake fishing. Catfish. Interested?"

"I'm game."

"Splendid. I'm always looking for company when I go fishing. I'll pick you up at Irv and Donna's in one hour."

"What do I need to bring?"

"Hat, sunscreen. And your pooch is welcome, too."

"Good. He was getting lonely in the motel."

"See you then. Gotta go get some nightcrawlers."

Within two hours, Johnny, Doc, and Buster had nestled into a small boat with an outboard motor on Great Flat Lake, poles in the water, sun shining.

"Are you allowed to talk when you fish?" Johnny asked.

"Talking is usually the purpose of fishing unless you're alone. Then thinking takes precedent."

"It doesn't bother the fish?"

"Not unless you're talking politics."

Johnny smiled. Buster had been skeptical of the water at first, but he seemed to be settling in now. He still sniffed the air, but his movements in the boat didn't seem to bother Doc.

"I'm surprised you let Buster come along," Johnny said.

"Didn't think you'd join me if I excluded him."

"Appreciate it."

"He seems to be enjoying it. We'll see what happens if we snag any catfish."

"Is that what we're fishing for?"

"Yep. Anything else we throw back. Catfish are pretty big this summer. And tasty."

"What's the strategy?" Johnny asked.

"For fishing? Not much other than throw the line in and see what bites."

"Seems a little more complicated than that."

"Doesn't have to be."

"But it is?"

"Well, bait is important," Doc continued. "The bigger the lake, the bigger the fish, and that dictates bait. For instance, this lake isn't real big, and most fellows would recommend using live minnows or frogs, but lately, I've found that nightcrawlers seem to be getting some play. Plus, they're a little more available, not to mention easier to put on the hook."

"And these fish stick close to shore?"

"Good observation. I'll make a fisherman out of you yet. Most catfish hover around eight to ten feet below the surface, so we don't want to get too far out in deep water. Plus they like vegetation like these reeds. Again, close to shore."

"I thought maybe you were sticking close to shore in case Buster took a header into the water."

"That happens and the boat tips over, every man and dog for himself."

"Let's try and not let that happen."

"Good plan."

"What's the limit on catfish?"

"Eight. Or sunburn, whichever comes first."

The two men fished in silence for several minutes. Buster fell asleep in the bottom of the boat on a blanket. The early summer air warmed them all, but a slight breeze made the late morning temperature comfortable.

Finally, Johnny asked, "What's all the hoopla going on in the private room at Buddy's? Those boys were at it again this morning."

"Everyone's agitated about what's happening out at the plant."

"What plant?"

"Johnson Controls. Excuse me, U.S. Johnson Controls."

"U.S. as in United States?" Johnny asked.

"U.S. as in Ulysses Samuel Johnson, the owner of the plant."

"What's the agitation about?"

"U.S. wants to close the plant. Seems the Chinese have just about near run him out of business."

"That's not uncommon."

"Around here it is. Couple hundred folks stand to lose their jobs. And there aren't many other jobs like that nearby."

"What do they make?"

"A kind of motion controls, powered mostly by pneumatics, and then they go into robotics. Automaton-type stuff."

"You seem to know a lot about them."

"Was on the board for a few years before they kicked me off."

"Why? What happened?"

"Didn't like my suggestions."

"Which were?"

"Well, I told 'em they shouldn't be letting the Chinese make their products in the first place. Told 'em they'd steal their ideas. Which they did."

"That's not uncommon either."

"Yeah, well, crap happens, I suppose. Excuse my French. But then I told them to find something else to manufacture. That's when they voted me off the board. Didn't like that idea."

"Sounds like a good one to me."

"Ulysses didn't much like it, and he runs the board, which in my humble opinion, are a bunch of brown nosers."

"Suck-ups, heh?"

"Worst kind. Ulysses pays 'em nice and takes 'em on a trip up to Canada once a year, hunting and fishing as a perk, and they all just get off on that stuff."

"Well, in case you haven't heard, plants have been shutting down all over America lately. A lot move to China, but Korea, Taiwan, Singapore, even Vietnam and India are luring companies away. It's hard to compete with the wages those countries pay."

"Heck, son, I know that. We aren't completely in the sticks out here, you know," Doc said as he smiled at Johnny. "Trouble is, the employees own part of that company. Ulysses had to offer them stock a number of years ago when times were tight. They're going to lose it all if he just shuts it down and takes off for good."

"Who are the boys in that backroom at Buddy's?" Johnny asked.

"Mostly managers, guys with most of the stock."

"What're they planning?"

"Some of them want to take over the plant. Kick Ulysses out. That isn't ever going to happen. Others want to install some pretty drastic measures to keep the doors open. Like cuts in pay, reduced benefits, forced time off, anything to try and win business back. Some are one hundred percent behind Ulysses. His cronies, I suspect."

"Again, you seem to know a lot about what's happening."

"Small town. Still got friends in that room."

"How come you're not in that room?"

"Good question. Probably should be. If they'd let me."

"In my experience, the best way to win business is to make a better product. Cutting expenses only works for a time. The quality slips or people quit because they can't afford to work there. Just kind of goes downhill."

"You a manufacturing guy?" Doc asked.

"Nope, but I've worked for a ton of them. Not much different if you're making computers or motion controls."

"Sure would hate to see that old plant close down."

"Might be the best thing."

"How so?"

"Seems like they're trying real hard to hang on to the past instead of reaching for the future." When Johnny said that, he paused, feeling almost like he was talking about himself.

"Yeah?"

"Well, when you're hanging on, you're typically not looking at how you can change. You're looking at how to stay the same, just better. And if they've been doing that for a long time, there isn't much fat left to trim."

"I see what you mean."

Johnny thought he got a bite on his pole, and Buster raised his head from his nap, but the bite was gone as quickly as it had appeared.

"Let me ask you a question," Johnny said, after a few minutes.

"Fire away."

"What did this town produce two hundred years ago?"

"Cows, corn."

"How about a hundred years ago?"

"Corn, cows, maybe some apples."

"I'm sensing a pattern. Fifty years ago?"

"I think that's about the time the plant started, although they weren't making automation. It was mostly gearing for the auto industry. Ulysses' daddy ran it back then. What're you getting at?"

"Times change, people need to change with them."

"Uh, huh. Go on."

"Plants making buggy whips and typewriters and slide rules don't make that kind of stuff anymore. They change the products when the time comes—or they're out of business."

Doc nodded.

"I don't know much about motion controls," Johnny continued, "but if the Chinese have the technology and now make it cheaper and better, it's not like you can sue them. That won't work—it ain't a fair world out there. So you either compete against them, you change the playing field some way, or you adapt and start manufacturing a new product. Or you quit and go back to raising cows."

"Hard work, and smelly, too. Not much glamour in going back there," Doc replied.

"Then chart a new path."

"These boys are hardworking and smart, but I'm not sure they're real worldly. Suppose they don't know which path to choose?"

"There are companies out there that could help if you found the right one. Sort of guide them along the path. But…"

"What?" Doc asked.

"They gotta go forward. They can't go backward. And the first thing they gotta do is make up their mind, cut the ties, say the heck with the Chinese, let them have it. We're going to do something bigger and better."

"Hard choice to make."

"Yep. But if they don't, they're toast."

"Maybe not so hard after all, you put it that way. God's will be done, huh?"

Wow, a God reference, Johnny thought. *Haven't paid much attention to him in a long time. Haven't missed him much either.*

"What's the plan for the rest of the day?" Johnny asked.

"Lunch, then maybe we talk a bit."

THIRTEEN

EARLY the following morning, Doc Enbright slowly slid open the plastic curtain to Buddy's backroom and stuck his head into the daily meeting. The group had expanded their meetings to weekdays. A few disgruntled looks didn't dissuade him from entering and finding an empty chair. For a few minutes, he just listened.

The discussion between the thirteen men in the room hovered around the point, made by two men who worked directly for Ulysses Johnson that it made no financial sense for him to keep the doors to the plant open. Terms like *they're eating our lunch, we're getting killed out there, we just can't complete, they stole our technology,* and Doc's favorite, *those Chinese* dominated their argument. The team of plant managers had little to say, offering only weak arguments centered on their need to work and take care of their families.

Finally, Doc spoke up. "Mind if I ask a question?"

"Is this any concern of yours, Enbright?" said Joe Dunham, who was representing Johnson and did most of the talking for shutting down the plant.

"Dunham, isn't it?" Doc asked.

"Yeah, that's me."

"What is it again you do out there? I don't remember you working at the plant."

"I work for Johnson."

"Doing what?"

"Doing none of your business, that's what."

"Okay, Joe, settle down," Norm Boswell, quality control manager at the plant, said. "Doc's an old friend of the company, and most of us have known him all our lives, so there's no need to get nasty."

"And there's no need for him to be here, far as I can tell," Dunham replied. "He's got no interest in this business."

"You're right," Doc answered, "but I have an interest in this town."

"Yeah, whatever," Dunham said, the last word coming out as two. He poured himself another cup of coffee.

"It seems to me that there are only two options on the table," Doc continued. "Either shut down or not."

"Brilliant," Dunham said, half under his breath.

"Go on, Doc," Boswell said without looking at Dunham.

"Times change, people need to change with them," Doc said.

Most people in the room nodded, Dunham shook his head, and several literally threw up their hands.

"Now, now, listen a bit further," Doc said.

"We're listening, but we aren't hearing much," Dunham replied.

Doc Enbright was used to listening to patients, asking them questions, then working out a solution with them for a return to health. He always liked to think of himself as one who listened for a minute or two, prescribed medicine, but never shooed you out of the office so he could see his next patient. He prided himself on his bedside manner. But he felt out of his league with tough guys and intimidators like Joe Dunham. So he ignored the comment and plunged ahead with the conversation the way Johnny and he had discussed it the day before over roast beef sandwiches and Miller Lites.

"Seems like the Chinese have been pretty much eating our lunch for a long time now. They do that in the world," Doc continued. "And it seems like you're trying real hard to hang on to the past instead of reaching for the future."

Joe Dunham raised his hands in front of him and said, "Get to the point, old man."

"When you're hanging on, you're typically not looking at how to change. You're looking at how to stay the same, just getting better. Seems like you've been doing that a long time. There may not be any fat left to trim. Maybe you should start looking at changing the product you make."

"What're we going to make, Doc?" Norm Boswell asked. "We've been making controls forever."

"No, not forever," Doc said. "Fifty years ago that plant made automotive controls."

"Gearboxes, actually," a voice chimed in from the crowd. Doc noticed it was Josh Brown, an old-timer at the plant.

"Right," Doc said. "So if we made buggy whips or typewriters or…" Doc couldn't remember the third product Johnny had mentioned. "…or something else nobody wants to buy anymore, we'd be out of business, right?"

"You ain't included in the 'we', Enbright," Dunham said. "I still don't know what the Sam Hill you're talking about."

Doc ignored him and pushed on. "So cut the ties with controls. Move on. Say screw the Chinese. We're going to make something bigger and better."

Most of the men in the room nodded in agreement. Doc Enbright wasn't a polished public speaker, but his age, his stature in the town, and his likeability tended to be persuasive.

"All that takes capital. We…got…no…capital," Dunham said.

"I didn't know you spoke for the whole company, Joe Dunham," Doc countered.

"I speak for U. S. Johnson."

"Well, it sounds like we need to hear that from Ulysses, Joe," Norm Boswell said.

"He's been telling you that for months now, Boswell, hasn't he?"

"No, *you've* been mostly telling us that. Besides, we haven't really taken a hard, calculated look to see if we could migrate this production line to another product," Boswell said.

"That takes money. That's what I've been trying to tell you," Dunham said, his voice rising. "There's no money to do the research, buy new equipment, find new customers, all that stuff. Time's run out."

"Easy for you to say," Doc continued. "But except for old Josh Brown there and a few others, most of you aren't ready to retire or pack it in. You still have kids to put through college or to save for your own retirement. But what you do have is time. Time to do the research and find a new product line. There may even be companies out there that could help you do that. What've you got to lose? You fellows want to go back to raising cows or crops?"

That silenced the crowd. Doc let it sink in. Dunham just kept shaking his head. Everyone else looked lost in thought.

"It may not be easy, and it may not work," Doc said, "but this isn't working either. You boys are hard charging and smart. I've known most of you since you were tadpoles. You've never backed down from a challenge. It's a hard choice to make, but if you don't make it, you're deader 'n catfish in the bottom of the boat."

Dunham had picked up his cell phone and was texting a message, probably to U. S. Johnson. Doc had won the day's argument—and the crowd was thinking in a new direction.

"Where do we start?" Norm Boswell asked.

"I got an idea. You boys pick a small committee, maybe three of you. Then let's get together at my place tomorrow evening after supper."

Arrangements were made, and the group sipped more coffee. Some left to return to the plant and start their shifts.

As the men headed out of the restaurant, Joe Dunham grabbed Doc Enbright's arm and rudely steered him out the door, away from the entrance, and down the block.

"What in the world?!" Doc said.

Dunham kept pushing him halfway down the short block.

"We don't much like what you had to say in there, old man," Dunham said in a hushed tone.

"Who's 'we'? Most liked what I said."

"Just don't be sticking your nose into something that ain't none of your business. You might get hurt."

"You're threatening me?"

"Advising you, old man."

"Let go of my arm," Doc demanded.

Dunham squeezed it harder, digging his powerful fingers deep into the triceps muscle on Doc's right arm. He moved closer to Doc, his face only inches away. Doc could smell the powerful odor of coffee on Dunham's breath.

"Take the advice. Stay out of it!"

Johnny had arranged to pick Doc up and was pulling into a parking space in front of Buddy's as Dunham was manhandling Doc. Johnny quickly jumped out of the Jeep and shouted toward the two men.

"Doc, you ready to go?"

Doc looked to Johnny, and his eyes pleaded for help. Dunham turned around slowly, relinquishing his grip and forcing a smile onto his face.

"We just finished up, right, Doc? And we just got everything settled, right?"

Doc rubbed his arm and slowly walked toward the Jeep. When he reached Johnny, his face was white, and he was shaking noticeably.

"You okay?" Johnny asked.

"Jerk," Doc said, looking back toward Dunham, who was writing down the license plate of Johnny Roe's Jeep in a small notebook.

FOURTEEN

"**Y**EAH, whatcha got?" Joe Dunham said as he cradled his cell phone between his ear and his shoulder while grabbing at a pen on the desk.

"The Jeep belongs to a John Roe, R...O...E, no W," the raspy voice replied. "Address is in the Frisco area. Owns an advertising company called Troubadour. Want me to spell it?"

"Nah. I got it. He have any business you know of in Iowa?"

"Nothing shows up."

"Wife, kids, family?"

"Mostly deceased. And recently."

"What do you mean, recently?" Dunham asked.

"March, this year. Wife and two kids killed in a car accident."

"No family in Iowa, huh?"

"No connection to Iowa shows up."

"Keep looking," Dunham instructed as he clicked off his phone.

"What did he say?" U. S. Johnson asked as Dunham paced in front of his office desk. The soundproof office was hidden away in a remote corner of U.S. Johnson Controls manufacturing facility. The office was traditional and showed only glimpses of the man behind the company. On the oversized desk sat only a phone, a computer, and a giant Rolodex. Several filing cabinets, a bar built into the wall, and a huge Winchester Big Daddy floor safe filled the rest of the room.

"Nothing much. We got a name, an address in San Francisco, a business, and absolutely no idea what he's doing in Booneville," Dunham answered.

"Keep an eye on him, 24/7. He wipes his butt, I wanna know how many times."

"I got the Bettcher boys tag teaming him."

"Great, dumb and dumber."

"They ain't the brightest dogs in the litter, but they're loyal. Inconspicuous, too. They look like every other farmer around here."

"Dunham, listen. We cannot—I repeat—we cannot screw this up," Johnson said as Dunham saw him twirling the tiger's eye ring on the third finger of his right hand. "Our job is to close this plant and do it by September first. If the Chinese see even a hint of something going wrong with that plan—and believe you me, just as sure as God delivers rainfall, them guys are watching every move we make—they walk. And we get doodily squat. I repeat, doodily!"

"We won't let Enbright interfere."

"I'm not worried about that old man. He's been around forever, preaching the same old mumbo jumbo."

"Well, he's preaching new jumbo now. And people are listening."

"Then it ain't coming outta his mouth. Find the source."

"Don't worry. I think we found the source. R, O, E, no W."

"Well, if this no-W is stirring the pot and he's got no business here in Iowa, then get rid of him. Send him packing back to Californ-i-ay. Or beyond. Get my drift?"

Dunham nodded.

"And remember, doodily!"

FIFTEEN

JOHNNY wondered how long Luke Wacker would take to return his text message when the phone rang.

"Hey, Luke, that was quick," Johnny said.

"Yeah, I was just working on your account."

I'm an account now? Impressive.

They exchanged pleasantries, and Johnny got the update on all the aspects of selling the 529 plan and paying off the home mortgage early. Then he asked about the elephant in the room.

"What did you find out about those gift cards?"

"Well, I was able to trace each one back to when the first one was purchased," Luke began. "It all started in May four years ago with a series of Starbucks cards, twenty-five dollars a month. Then it branched out to gas cards, Texaco and Chevron, national brands. As a matter of fact, all of the cards have that in common."

"What in common?" Johnny asked.

"They're all cards of national brands. Nothing regional or local. No Piggly Wiggly, for instance. No Peet's Coffee."

"What in the world is a Piggly Wiggly?"

"Grocery store. We used to crack up when we saw them down south when I visited my cousins. Love that name."

"Yeah, okay. Go on."

"I made a spreadsheet of all the gift card purchases, including the start date of each card, end date, and total charged. I'll email it to you."

"Samantha made all the purchases?"

"As far as I can tell. The cards were charged to several…actually, quite a few come to think of it…credit cards. Did you guys change your credit cards a lot?"

"Sure. Sam always said if a good deal with free mileage came along, we should switch. Grab the miles, use the card, then cancel it."

"Probably not a good idea if you're trying to build up your credit score," Luke offered.

"Yeah, well, maybe you're right. We were never too worried about that. We always paid our bills, never paid an interest charge."

"The credit score companies frown on lots and lots of credit cards. It's always better to use two or three, keep them a long time, and pay them off each and every month."

"Got it, professor, thanks for the lesson," Johnny said with a chuckle. "Let's get back to the gift cards. Were you able to stop them?"

"Yessir, every one of them. Not a problem."

"What's the bad news?"

"Sir?"

"What's the total spent in gift cards since 2009?"

"Just over $40,000."

"Holy Mother…!" Johnny almost shouted. "What happened to them all? Did you find any in the house?"

"Well, I was a bit hesitant to go looking in every drawer, but if you'd like me to, I can spend some time at your home."

"Every nook and cranny, Luke. Do you mind?"

"Oh, no. I love a treasure hunt."

"Thanks. If you find them, I'll let you keep two Starbucks and one Texaco card for yourself."

"Even better, an incentive! What if I find all $40,000 worth?"

"Three Starbucks, one Texaco, and a partridge in a pear tree."

"That's what I'm talking about! Hey, Mr. Roe, one more thing."

"Yeah, what's up?"

"How're you doing? You sound pretty good. Better than last time we talked."

"Right. I am better. I'm actually kind of, sort of, working on a new project."

"In Iowa?" Luke asked.

"Yep, Booneville, Iowa."

"Cool. You know, Iowa has been tagged the 'Silicon Prairie' by some of the pundits."

"You mean like Silicon Valley? They're making semiconductors in Iowa?"

"Well, not necessarily products on silicon. Just high-tech stuff. Probably the Chamber of Commerce just latched onto that name. You know, like Silicon Forest in Oregon, Silicon Glen in Ireland."

"Really, where in Iowa?"

"A lot in Des Moines. Some in Omaha, some in KC."

"Luke, you do know that Omaha is not in Iowa, right?"

"Duh. I just meant that whole stretch out there on the prairie. Turning barns into bandwidth, they say. A real renaissance."

"No kidding? Whodda thunk it?"

"Probably all those guys who can't afford to buy a home in the Bay Area. Like me."

"Or pay all those taxes. Hey, Luke, one more favor?"

"Yeah."

"Do some research for me. Send as many links as you can about the Silicon Prairie."

"Sure, no problem. Is this for your new, sort of, kind of project?"

"Kind of. Sort of. Maybe. See ya."

"Later."

As Johnny hung up the phone, Buster snuggled close.

"You're feeling better, too, huh, pup. Yeah, both of us, a little better."

SIXTEEN

DOC Enbright and Johnny Roe slid the small outboard boat off the trailer as Buster snooped in the nearby bushes for animals unknown. Once the boat was properly situated, Doc pulled the car and trailer up the ramp and parked. On a Tuesday morning, the lake was empty of boats, people, and noise. A peaceful serenity encamped the lake, and only the lapping of water at the shoreline broke the silence.

Buster jumped in, and they pushed off, again staying close to the shore. Doc had brought a thermos of coffee, several doughnuts, and a few dog biscuits for Buster.

"Grab a doughnut," Doc said.

"I thought those things will kill you," Johnny replied.

"Well, if you eat them every day, I suppose the fat would mount up. But once in a while, it's a treat."

"What's the occasion?"

"Nothing too special. We just seem to be making progress at the plant."

"How so?" Johnny asked as he reached down and scratched Buster's ears.

"Well, the guys liked my idea…your idea, really…of looking for another product to build. The meeting at my house last night went well."

"Good to hear."

"I think you should start coming to the meetings."

"I'm not really a manufacturing guy, you know that, right?"

"You're a thinker. That's what we need."

Johnny baited a hook from the new batch of nightcrawlers Doc had brought and let his line out about six feet. He stared at the water, willing a fish to latch on to the hook. He let the last request from Doc simmer a bit in his brain. He hadn't decided whether he wanted to stay in Booneville much longer. On the one hand, he was getting anxious to keep moving. On the other, he was intrigued by the dilemma facing the plant. It had been a while since he'd been a part of a team, and he missed that. Only so much could rattle back and forth in your own brain until you needed to bounce ideas off of somebody else. Buster provided great companionship, but he had limited communication skills.

"You thinking about it?" Doc asked after several minutes.

"I am."

The two continued fishing as Buster snapped at a fly. Morning humidity hung in the air while the sun played peekaboo behind a thin layer of clouds.

"I fashion you as a modern-day Cyrano de Bergerac, you know," Doc said, breaking the silence.

"How so?"

"You as Cyrano, me as Christian, putting words into my mouth to woo the lovely Roxanne."

"The lovely Roxanne, pray tell?"

"Well, it's not a perfect analogy, but Roxanne could be the plant or even the town. We are trying to save the town after all," Doc said as he laid the fishing pole across his lap and leaned closer to Johnny

"Ooo-kay then."

"I really have remembered most of what we've talked about over the past few days. My memory is still pretty sharp."

"Never doubted it for a second."

"I just couldn't keep up with the malpractice insurance. That's why I closed my practice. It wasn't that I didn't still love it or that I'd lost my touch."

"Too bad. I thought maybe you just wanted to retire."

"Doctors never retire. They always want to practice. Well, most of us. Too many sick people out there. And it seems lately that good men and women just aren't getting into the profession," Doc continued as he straightened up and looked directly into Johnny's eyes. "Too costly to get started. Too costly to keep a practice running. With socialized medicine bearing down on us, it's not going to get any easier."

"That bad, huh?"

"Worse, probably."

It wasn't that Johnny didn't want to talk more about medicine, but it seemed to depress Doc, so he switched back to the conversation about the plant.

"Let me ask you about the guys at the plant," Johnny began.

"Sure, what do you want to know?"

"Are they resilient, determined? This process could take a while, you know. I may have overstated how easy it would be to make a transition."

"Are you asking if they will stick to it? Not give up? Even if it gets tough?"

"No, not really like 'when the going gets tough, the tough get going.' More like if the payroll stops, will they keep working."

"For how long?" Doc asked.

"It depends. It might be easier to find a new manufacturer who wants to buy the plant rather than trying to convert to a new product. If that happens, they may have some of their own people, and for sure, they'd have to retrofit the old plant. That could take a while."

"What have we got to lose?"

"For one thing, they could lose their jobs," Johnny said, the last few words coming out barely above a whisper.

"That's happening now. It's not like these guys can just go work someplace else. A lot of them were born here, and they don't want to leave."

"I'm just saying, it could get tough."

"They'll be tough."

"And you?"

"Me? How tough do I have to be?"

"Tough enough not to get roughed up by Johnson's goons. Somebody doesn't want you interfering."

"I noticed that. Wonder why?"

"Good question," Johnny said as he reached down again for Buster.

SEVENTEEN

"**T**HOSE two are thick as trees," Jim Bettcher said. "I seen them everywhere together."

Joe Dunham just shook his head. Talk about how hard it was to find good help these days. It was all he could do not to strangle the moron. He was going to correct Bettcher on the saying but thought better of getting into a discussion with the guy he considered the village idiot.

"Everywhere, like where?" Dunham asked.

"Everywhere. Buddy's, out at Doc's house, fishin'. I 'spect if ol' Doc could ride a bike, they'd be doing that together, too."

Dunham just got a quizzical look on his face like he didn't know what Bettcher was talking about.

"That guy, he rides that bike of his dang near every day," Bettcher said.

"You able to tell what they're talking about?"

"Lots of stuff, but mostly they're talking about the plant. That feller from California got some different ideas, and old Doc's just taking it all in. Sometimes he even takes notes."

"He still staying out at the Best Western?"

"Yep, paid up through the end of the week. I could probably get that credit card number if you really wanted it," Bettcher said, almost beaming.

"What would I want that for?"

"I dunno. I was just tellin' ya I could get it, that's all," Bettcher replied, looking somewhat hurt that Dunham didn't want the number.

"Just be careful. I've told you a hundred thousand times, you're not a private detective. I pay you to do what I say. This time, all I said was follow him. Don't let him see you, don't stick your nose into his business. Just follow him and report back to me who he sees and what he does.

You got that?"

"That's what I been doin'."

"Make sure your brother knows it, too. Got it?"

"Got it. You don't need to worry about Earl. He follows my lead. I'm the leader in this family. Earl ain't quite as smart as me, you know," Jim Bettcher said as he stood up tall and puffed out his chest.

That was a mighty scary thought, Joe Dunham said to himself as he picked up his cell phone to call Ulysses.

EIGHTEEN

"**T**HOSE two," Ulysses said, "they're gonna muck everything up. Now all these ideas are floating around the plant. People are getting their hopes up. We had that hope thing squashed. That Doc's killing me."

"I think it's the Roe guy that really is the brains behind all those ideas," Joe Dunham replied. "Doc was content to sit on his stool at Buddy's and spout off now and then, throwing his two cents in. But he doesn't have the business brains to pull this off. Roe's the problem."

"Man, that No-W guy," Johnson said as he took a long swig of whiskey. He and Dunham sat in his office after the plant had closed for the day. "You think it's possible that they could actually pull this off? I hear they think they can convert this factory into making something else? How easy would that be to do anyway?"

"It's hard enough making what we make," Dunham said. "Don't know how they can just switch it over to something else. They gotta find a buyer, then they gotta find customers, they gotta be competitive. You just don't start off building something, then take over the market."

"Maybe the Chinese are double-crossing us?" Johnson speculated as he fondled his tiger's eye ring.

"Nah, they pretty much got us where they want us. Why'd they want to try and get the plant to make something else? They're paying us to get out of the business. They don't have to do anything but let the plant die its own death."

"Well, maybe you're right, but I don't trust those guys. It wouldn't surprise me if they're covering both sides."

"Doesn't make sense. I think," Dunham said as he paced around the large office, "that Roe guy just happened to be in the wrong place at the wrong time. We can't find any connection between him and Doc Enbright. Or him and Booneville. Or him and anybody around here. He just seems to have fallen right outta the sky into Doc's lap."

"Maybe we should just burn down the plant. Arson," Johnson said with a squinting gleam in his eye. "We could find somebody to do that, easy."

"Man, that's awful risky," Dunham countered. "Even if we could find a pro, and I'm not sure we could. This is Booneville, Iowa, you know. Say we bring in somebody from Chicago. Any trace they leave behind, the cops start investigating, then your debts are found. All things point back to you."

"And you. Don't forget, they point to you, too. You're up to your ass in this, too."

Dunham stared back at Johnson but didn't hold the stare more than a blink of an eye.

"Maybe we can scare Doc out of this idea?" Johnson finally said.

"What good would that do? The seed has already been planted. The hope, as you say, is already on the rise. Besides, Doc won't scare. He's too old and cantankerous. What's he got to lose, he's dang near dead already."

"Okay, genius, I don't hear you coming up with any ideas!" Johnson said, pushing back his shoulders and stretching his neck from side to side. "You don't like any of mine, what've you got? We just can't sit around here and take it in the shorts, you know. If we don't close that plant by September first, we are up the proverbial creek. So you better start coming up with something. You're killing me here now!"

"Calm down. Jeez, you'll have a heart attack."

The two sat there and sipped whiskey. The sun was setting over a warm Iowa evening, and the air conditioning had clanked off several minutes ago. The air became stale, and the humidity rose as Johnson lit a cigarette and the pungent odor waffled around the office.

"Let's attack this from the other side," Dunham finally said. "We know Doc won't scare, but we don't know about No-W. If I'm right and he just showed up outta the blue, then he doesn't have a horse in this race. He's just doing it out of the goodness of his heart or something. If that's true, then maybe he scares."

"Fine. Bring him in here, and we'll talk to him," Johnson said, nodding his head.

"Nah, that just implicates us. I think we gotta let him know somebody's on to him, somebody really doesn't want him around, scare the crap out of him."

"How, genius?"

"I got an idea."

"Well, whatever your idea, you better do it soon. Real soon," U.S. Johnson said, finishing off his whiskey and reaching for the bottle.

NINETEEN

ULYSSES Johnson pulled his Ford F-350 into his garage later that night. He teetered, almost falling down as he stepped out of the truck. After he and Dunham left the plant, U.S. had stopped at the Elks Club and had a few more pops. He never much liked going back to his farmhouse since his wife left him five years ago. In fact, he hadn't much liked going to it when she was there. That's probably why she left, he thought. They married young, fueled by passion and pregnancy and had a few kids quickly, but U.S. never adapted well to family life. He liked his freedom too much and didn't appreciate his wife telling him how he should spend his money. To spite her, he often spent it recklessly and frivolously. Trips to Vegas with a buddy or two. A new shotgun. A new truck every eighteen months.

His wife had kept the place looking nice at least, spending his hard-earned money on new drapes and couches and other assorted furniture that was in the French Colonial style or whatever it was she liked. He had to admit, it looked pretty good five years ago. But he had done nothing to keep the house up except have it cleaned every once in a while. He barely used more than the TV room, the bathroom, and the bedroom. The rest of the four thousand-square-foot home just gathered dust.

But regret regularly appeared when he was alone in the home. He never admitted to his friends, but he missed his wife. At least the companionship. Somebody in the house. He remembered how she looked when they were young. Her figure, the hair, the smile in her eyes. Whenever he thought of her, she was still twenty years old. Young, vibrant, full of life and hope. He remembered the attraction, sexual mostly, but not entirely. His thoughts wandered in the past, trapped there by a wall of stubbornness, unable to escape.

He took a long swig of OJ right out of the bottle in the fridge, dropped into his favorite chair, and was about to turn on SportsCenter when he heard the distinctive ring of the special cell phone. He knew who was on the other end. Dunham had purchased a cheap phone and put minutes on it so that when Mr. Cheng wanted to talk with him, the call couldn't be traced. Mr. Cheng now wanted to talk.

"Hello?" Johnson said.

"Mr. Johnson, this is Mr. Cheng."

"Hello, Mr. Cheng, how are you?"

"No time for pleasantries, Mr. Johnson. September first is approaching very quickly. I call to make sure everything is going to plan. Can you assure me it is?" Mr. Cheng said in his slow, deliberate English.

"Well, we are doing our best to close the plant by that date, but you know that the employees own a portion of the plant, and they would like to see the plant stay open. But I don't foresee any problems. Do you think we could get an extension, say maybe till October or November, even the first of the year."

"That not our deal, Mr. Johnson."

"Oh, I know, I know, and I'm not saying there are any problems. As a matter of fact, we were just brainstorming tonight how we are planning to solve these…er…this situation. So I think we got it all planned out. But maybe it takes us a few extra weeks, you know?"

"Mr. Johnson, we have paid you very much money for this technology. And you have promised for this payment that the plant shut down. That is our deal, is that not correct, Mr. Johnson?"

"Well, yeah, sure, but…"

"And incremental payments have been advanced to you for your gambling problem, is that not correct, Mr. Johnson."

"Well, I don't really have a gambling problem…where'd you hear that?…and I appreciate those advancements very much, but…"

"Then if the plant is not shut down by September first, then no more payments. Is that not correct, Mr. Johnson?"

"But you see, the plant does not want to make those motion controls. They want to make something else. Something altogether different than motion controls. Hell, I don't even know what they want to make. So it wouldn't be like we were competition anymore for what you guys are doing, you see what I mean?"

"I do not understand," Mr. Cheng said.

"All I'm saying is that even if the plant was to remain open after September first, that should not interfere with our arrangement, that's all," U.S. Johnson replied.

"No, Mr. Johnson. Arrangement was if plant open after September first, deal off, no more payments. Is that not correct Mr. Johnson?"

"Well, yes, that is what we agreed on, but all I'm saying is—"

"Do not try to renegotiate, Mr. Johnson. I do not like to renegotiate."

"But I need those payments to continue. You haven't paid me everything you owe me!" Johnson raised his voice. The liquor had worn off, and he had a splitting headache, and he'd had just about enough of Mr. Cheng. But he still needed the money.

Cheng was silent. Johnson wondered if he'd pissed off the Chinaman.

"Okay, okay, listen. We will get the plant shut down by September first, okay?" Johnson said, his voice under control now. *Don't piss off the Chinaman.*

"Mr. Cheng, are you there?"

"Yes, I here," Cheng said.

"I know, I know, it's not your problem. We'll get it done, don't worry."

"I not worried, Mr. Johnson. You worried."

Then Mr. Cheng hung up.

Shoot, Johnson thought, he'd pissed off the Chinaman.

TWENTY

ENJOYING a mid-morning bike ride along a two-lane highway west of Booneville, Johnny Roe heard a vehicle approaching from behind. He never listened to music while riding, instead enjoying the sounds of nature and the thoughts that randomly came to him. Music tended to drown out where his mind wanted to wander. He also enjoyed the quiet because it let him be aware of the sounds of the road.

He could tell the vehicle approached fast and much too close. He'd ridden enough to know when drivers were moving off to the opposite lane as a courtesy when they passed or whether they only moved over in their lane a few inches—or not at all. Johnny pulled his bike closer to the side of the road, but there was no bike lane or paved shoulder. Any farther and he'd end up in the gravel roadbed, and that was never a good thing on a bike with skinny tires.

"C'mon!" Johnny yelled as the truck missed him by less than a foot. It wasn't a prayer, but Johnny had a strange sense that maybe it should be. He looked up to see the driver and passenger both crank their necks back to look at him as the vehicle swerved to the left. The older brown Ford truck continued on. Johnny noticed the letters F-O-R-D in white against the brown background of the tailgate. He shook his head violently to let the driver know he didn't appreciate the close call, but he knew from past experiences it wouldn't make much difference.

Johnny had forgotten about the close call and was deep in thought about the last conversation with Doc about the plant when he looked up and saw the Ford bearing down toward him. The truck straddled the centerline.

As it got closer, it seemed to pick up speed. Johnny looked into the truck's cab, but the sun was behind the truck, and all he saw were shadows. But it sure looked like the truck was aiming right at him. The gravel to his right sloped off to a ditch about five feet deep, then sharply came back up. Trying to take that ditch on his bike, if he made it through the loose gravel, was impossible. It was too steep on the other side. The Ford made a sudden turn right into his path, and Johnny made a split-second decision.

Jerking his body and the bike drastically to his right, Johnny laid the bike down, taking the brunt of the fall on his right shoulder. The loose gravel absorbed most of the impact as he slid onto the grass. The left front fender of the Ford missed the front wheel of Johnny's bike by a few feet. The truck spun into the gravel and kicked up the stones, showering Johnny like a hailstorm from a rock quarry. The driver struggled to gain control of the fishtailing truck, swerving the steering wheel back and forth, sending more gravel toward Johnny. The truck finally escaped the gravel and accelerated away.

After his heart rate subsided and he got his breathing under control, Johnny took stock of the situation. A queasiness settled in his stomach, replacing the adrenaline rush he'd just experienced. Johnny had broken his collarbone once before after taking a fall on his shoulder, and although it was sore, he knew the bone wasn't cracked. He had purposely tucked his right hand into his body so his wrist wouldn't be broken trying to break his fall. His arm was bruised and cut up a bit from the gravel but definitely not broken, although it had begun to bleed, pooling in several places near the elbow. His right leg looked like it would develop some nasty road rash, but his foot had clipped out of his pedal and avoided too much damage. As he stood up and took a few deep breaths, he noticed some pain in his hip. His bike shorts had been ripped up, and he caught a glimpse of the reddening, dirty skin beneath. Then he surveyed his bike. The chain hung loosely, and the seat was skewed and torn from the gravel, but the bike had no structural damage that he could see. The derailleur would need some adjustment, and the whole bike needed a bath, but it seemed to Johnny that the bike made it through better than he did.

Johnny looked back toward the truck, but it had disappeared over a small rise in the road.

He stood by the side of the road and continued to check his bike and make adjustments. Then he walked around on the road surface a bit to test his body. He brushed himself off and swabbed his arm and leg with an antiseptic towelette he carried in his seat bag. He got on the bike and did a few circles, checking the gears and the chain and how well his legs were working.

Then the truck reappeared.

It advanced slowly toward him, going no more than ten miles an hour. Johnny looked right and left for an escape route. He saw nothing but a flat road ahead of him and large ditches on either side that led to overgrown fields. Even if he could make it to a field, he saw no escape, the brush too thick to get through. The truck would eat him up.

He thought about trying to outrun it—but not for long. He wasn't about to let the truck have another shot at him. Then his anger kicked in. That darkness. He hadn't felt this way since the encounter with Victor Gonzales. It slowly engulfed him and took away his rationality. His mind clouded with thoughts of revenge and snowballed until his vision narrowed and the surroundings faded away.

If the truck could play chicken, so could he. Besides, maybe he could get a look at the license plate number, he thought, as logic surfaced and quickly subsided.

So Johnny pointed the bike toward the truck and started to pedal slowly. The two advanced toward each other, about two hundred yards apart. The truck began to pick up speed. Johnny rose from the saddle and pedaled harder. Then he darted quickly to his right. The truck swerved to its left, and now both of them were in the same lane, fifty yards apart. And closing fast.

Johnny swerved all the way across the road and hugged the far left, close to the gravel. He peered at the license plate, but it looked blurred. He couldn't make out any letters or numbers. Johnny accelerated and pushed to his top speed. Sprint speed. The truck gunned it. Johnny stayed far left and hugged the brim of the road, being careful to not hit gravel. He glanced at his speedometer—twenty-eight miles an hour. He forgot about the license plate and tried to figure out his next move. If he stayed left, the truck could merely run him into the ditch.

His only escape was to the right. But if he moved too soon, the truck had him dead on. At this speed, he could maneuver the bike quickly and precisely. He pedaled harder—and waited.

One more glance at the speedometer—twenty-nine miles an hour. The truck was only about twenty yards away. *Wait for it, wait for it,* Johnny kept repeating.

Suddenly, Johnny turned hard right and, standing on the pedals, tried to get around the onrushing Ford.

He saw the truck veer toward him, and he concentrated all his energy on the narrow passageway between the front fender and the gravel to his right.

Johnny thought he'd make it. He stared at the fender of the truck as his bike barreled down the highway, inches from the gravel. He pulled his head away as the rearview mirror swiped at him.

He didn't make it.

The truck's rear fender caught Johnny's rear tire. The truck spun Johnny around so violently that his front tire veered left and struck the tailgate of the truck. Then, nothing.

TWENTY-ONE

A sharp pain in his left wrist brought Johnny awake. He tried to open his eyes. Then he noticed they were already open as he focused on the ceiling. He turned his head away from the bright florescent light. He remembered only the brown truck. Lying flat on his back, a thin sheet covered his body.

"Hello, there," a soft voice said, coming from his right. He glanced that way, but his eyes wouldn't focus. He closed them again.

"Don't go away," the soothing voice said. Again, he opened his eyes.

"Hi, Mr. Roe. Are you back?" the voice asked.

Where did I go, Johnny thought. He couldn't remember.

"You're going to be fine, Mr. Roe. You are in Parkside General Hospital. We're taking good care of you."

Johnny could only nod his head.

"My name is Emily Brownell. Can you see me?" the soothing voice asked.

Again, Johnny tried to focus. A brown-haired young woman stood next to him.

"Can you do me a favor, Mr. Roe? Can you wiggle your toes?"

Johnny tried to look at his toes, but his head wouldn't move. It felt like an anvil was sitting on his forehead.

"No, don't try to get up or look at them. Just wiggle them, okay?" the voice said.

Johnny had to think about where his toes were. He finally found them and first wiggled the toes on his right foot, then his left.

"Perfect! Good job. Now, can you wiggle your fingers?"

First the search for his fingers, then wiggling. The right hand first, wiggle, wiggle, ouch, then the left, wiggle, wiggle, big ouch. He winced.

"Great, that's good. A little painful though, huh? We might have something going on there," the voice said, almost to itself.

Johnny drifted back to sleep. A gentle hand touched his right arm.

"No you don't, big fella. I want you to stay awake now."

Johnny opened his eyes and stared directly at Miss Brownell. He blinked several times and tried hard to focus. Beautiful eyes, he thought to himself.

"Can you tell me your first name?" she asked.

"Johnny," he said after several seconds, clearing his dry, raspy throat.

"Do you know where you are?"

Johnny thought hard and tried to remember.

"Iowa?" he guessed.

"Good. What town in Iowa?"

Des Moines? Omaha? KC? Johnny remembered bits of a conversation.

"Here's a hint. Rhymes with…Swoonville?"

"Omaha?" Johnny answered.

"Close enough for hospital work," Miss Brownell said, smiling to nobody in particular. "You can go back to sleep now. I need to clean up some cuts and bruises."

Johnny wanted to know where the cuts and bruises were, but he wanted to sleep more.

"Wait. One more question. Can I call somebody for you? The number on your ankle bracelet was in San Francisco."

Johnny shook his head no.

"Wife? Brother? A relative?" she asked.

"Buster," Johnny managed to say.

"Who's that? Your brother?"

"Dog."

Miss Brownell smiled and said, "He might be hard to contact."

"Motel," Johnny said.

"Which one?"

"Irv and Donna."

"Got it," she said as Johnny drifted away.

TWENTY-TWO

S EVERAL hours later, Johnny woke up. He glanced at his right arm and saw a tube leading to a large drip bag on a stand. His left arm was outside the covers of his hospital bed. A large splint covered the arm from wrist to elbow. He tried to shift his weight, but a sharp pain stabbed him in his lower right hip. He shifted the other way and noticed the pain ran up and down his spine. The anvil still squeezed his head. He wiggled his toes and fingers again and noticed that every toe and finger hurt when it moved.

"What did you run into, a truck?" the soothing voice of Miss…Miss…he couldn't remember the name of the dark-haired lady with the pretty eyes.

He nodded yes.

"Really, a truck?" she asked.

"You're Miss…?" Johnny wondered aloud.

"Brownell. Nurse Brownell. Emily. But most people call me Emmy."

Johnny smiled at her and winced.

"We haven't given you any pain relief yet. We wanted to know if you're allergic to anything, but we couldn't get that information out of Buster," she said, smiling.

"He okay?" Johnny asked.

"I called Donna out at the Best Western. She said she'd go get him, feed him, and let him stay in the hotel office for a while."

"I'd like to see him."

"Visiting hours for dogs are frowned upon here at Parkside. But we'll see what we can do."

"How long am I going to be here?"

"It depends. You'll be a little limited. Do you have someone who can care for you? Cook for you? How's Buster's cooking?"

"It stinks, just like Buster most of the time."

She giggled. Johnny enjoyed watching her work, and he enjoyed making her giggle. Emmy Brownell checked the bandage on his right leg.

"Are you allergic to anything?" she asked.

"Nope."

"Good, I'll get you something to ease the pain."

She quickly returned with a needle, raised the hospital gown at his left hip, swabbed his cheek, and immediately he felt the cold liquid squirting through his body.

"That should take effect pretty quickly. Then you'll get sleepy," she said. "Want a quick review of the damages before you drift off?"

"Sure."

"Okay, here we go. Broken left wrist, but not bad, just a hairline fracture. Chip fracture in the right elbow, but we won't even splint that. Very small fracture in one of your vertebrae, but we almost missed it the first time. But every time we touched up and down your back, you winced, even when you were a little bit out of it, so we checked the x-rays again. It's tiny; should heal fine on its own. Mild to moderate concussion, but your helmet, may it rest in peace, saved the day. And quite a few scrapes and bruises on your legs and arms."

"Terrific."

"Oh, and a few stitches. Eighteen, I think, in your forehead. We had the resident on-duty do the work. We usually ask if you want a plastic surgeon to do the stitching, but you were not very responsive, and the only plastic surgeon for miles around is on vacation for two weeks."

"Again, super terrific."

"Actually, he did a great job. Some of the sutures are right above the eyebrow line, almost hidden. I'm sure you won't even notice them in a few months. And what man doesn't look just a little more manly with stitches on his face, huh?"

"Is it bad?" Johnny asked.

"No, they weren't deep, and if you take really good care of them over the next couple of weeks, they'll heal fine. In a few years, they'll blend right in with all the other wrinkles."

Johnny smiled and tried to touch his forehead with his left hand, but the pain in his wrist stopped him.

"You know, we don't put plaster casts on anymore," Emmy said, pointing to his wrist. "That's just a splint. The doctor will want you moving those fingers just as soon as he sees you. Which should be any minute now. He's on rounds. Same with the elbow. It's going to be stiff, but if you don't start moving it, it'll stay stiff."

"Duly noted. Uh, I have a request," Johnny said.

"Sure, what?"

"I need to use the bathroom."

"Well, how about a bedpan. We don't want to get you up until the doctor okay's it."

Johnny looked at his injured wrist, which throbbed, and the opposite elbow, which was immobilized at the moment with the drip bag. How was he going to manage that, he thought? It showed on his face.

"I could help. I'm a nurse."

"That's okay. I'll hold it. Until the doc comes."

"Or I could hold it…it being, you know…and you'd feel a lot better," Emmy said, smiling at him.

"How long have you been a nurse?"

"How long have you had to go to the bathroom?"

"Long time now."

"Me, too. I mean, being a nurse." She giggled, trying not to smile too broadly.

"Okay…let's do it," Johnny said, looking away.

"Hey, we were talking about number one, weren't we?" Emmy said, her eyes smiling and her face scrunching up like she smelled something bad. "I mean, I haven't been a nurse that long!"

"Just get the bedpan."

She reached under the bed and grabbed a metal bedpan about the size of a large frying pan.

"Dainty, aren't they?" she said, folding back the sheet and reaching for his gown as she slid the pan under him.

"Cold, too," Johnny commented.

"The pan? Or my hands?" Emmy asked.

"No, your hands are just fine, thanks."

"I bet you say that to all the girls." And they both laughed.

"Are you always this cheerful when you're helping somebody go to the bathroom?" Johnny said.

"Yep. Most of the time. Are you feeling better?" she answered, pointing with her head toward the bedpan.

He took a deep breath in. "Yeah, thanks. I needed that."

Emmy Brownell smiled at Johnny Roe, and he smiled back.

"By the way, I am getting kind of sleepy," Johnny said.

"That almost never happens to me when I've got a hold of…you know," she said, motioning again with her head. "Almost never."

He smiled at her again as he drifted away.

"You go to sleep now. I'll take good care of you."

TWENTY-THREE

AFTER the doctor visit and a long nap, Johnny was watching TV when Emmy Brownell stuck her head into his room.

"There is an Officer Bowen from the State Patrol here to see you. Feel up to it?" she asked.

"Sure, show him in."

A tall officer in the Iowa state trooper uniform of chocolate brown and tan ambled toward the bed while taking out a notebook from his back pocket.

"Hello, Mr. Roe. My name is Trooper Bowen, from the Iowa State Highway Patrol. I'd ask you how you're doing, but from the looks of you, you've had better days."

"Yeah."

"Could I ask you about the accident? We always follow up with an incident like this."

"Sure," Johnny said as he thought about the brown Ford truck.

"Was this a solo accident or was there another vehicle involved?"

"Well, I'm having a little trouble remembering exactly what happened."

"Yes, the nurse mentioned you have a pretty significant concussion. What do you remember?"

Johnny searched his brain for details as the trooper stood beside his bed. He remembered almost everything that happened out on the road except the details of when the truck won the chicken battle. He knew the brown truck was out to hurt him but probably not kill him. Since he'd been lying in the hospital, Johnny had thought a lot about why he'd been the target. The only answer that he could come up with was something to do with his involvement with the plant. Johnny wanted to talk with Doc before he gave away all the details about the accident to the State Police. He felt safe for the time being in the hospital, and he didn't want to miss his chance to find the two guys in the truck by having the State Police scare them off. He needed more time.

"Well, I remember fighting for space on the road with another vehicle, a small truck, I think, not much else."

"When you say a small truck, do you mean a pick-up truck or more like a maintenance truck or a rental truck?"

"Like a pick-up, I think," Johnny said, blinking his eyes several times, then closing them like he was trying to envision what happened.

"What color?"

"Brown."

"Brown like my shirt or brown like my pants?" the officer asked, pointing to the dark chocolate brown of his uniform top and his tan pants.

"Sort of in between."

"Was the vehicle coming toward you or coming up behind you?"

"Behind me."

"So, you didn't get a good look at it?"

"Not really."

"But you knew it was a small pick-up truck, in an in-between brown color, huh?"

"I looked behind me because I heard it coming and it seemed really close. I can tell how close a car is and almost how fast it's moving just by the sound, I've been riding so long. But I just got a glimpse."

"Did the vehicle strike you?"

"I don't think so. I think I just lost control because I thought it was too close and ran off the road."

"So, you're not sure if it hit you or not?" The trooper focused his eyes on Johnny, skepticism etched in his eyes and brow.

"Not really. But I don't think it did."

Just then the phone on the table beside Johnny's bed rang. The trooper waited for Johnny to answer it. Finally, the trooper reached over, picked up the receiver, and put it carefully into Johnny's left hand.

"Hello?" Johnny said.

"Johnny, it's Julie. Are you okay?"

"Julie?"

"Julie Strausser, your sister-in-law? Remember me?"

"Oh, hi, Julie, I just didn't expect to hear your voice, like way out of context. What're you…? Why are you…?"

"The guys in your office called me when they got a call from the hospital. What happened?"

"Uh, hang on. I'll be with you in a second," Johnny said. Maybe he could use this interruption to end the conversation with Trooper Bowen.

"I really need to take this. Are we done for now?" Johnny asked the trooper

"Sure, for now. Maybe you'll remember more details in a day or so. You're not planning to leave town, are you?"

"No, sir. I don't really feel much like getting out of this bed, to tell you the truth."

"I understand. Here's my card. Feel free to call me if something comes to mind that you think I should know," the trooper said as he placed the card on the bedside table.

"Sure, will do, thanks."

The trooper put his flat-brimmed hat back on but didn't immediately leave the room. He stared at the notebook for a few seconds as Johnny held the receiver close to his chest. Then the trooper looked at Johnny for another few seconds, squinted his eyes at Johnny, nodded his head, turned, and walked out of the room.

"Julie, I'm back. Tell me again how you got this number."

"I guess when they found you…where are you, in Iowa?…the hospital called your San Francisco office. That's the number they found on you. Since the office couldn't reach your parents, they called me."

"Oh. Got it. Well, thanks for calling, I guess."

"What happened? Are you alright?"

"Bicycle accident, a few broken bones, but I'll live."

"Oh, that bike of yours. Sam never liked you riding it in the first place. How long will you be in the hospital?"

"They say I can probably leave later today, maybe tomorrow."

"Where are you staying?"

"A local motel, with Buster."

"He'll be a big help. Why are you in Iowa?"

"Just passing through."

"On your way to where?"

"No place special."

"Fine. What bones are broken?"

"Wrist and elbow, but I'm functional. I can walk around. A little sore. I can even go to the bathroom by myself now. Regretfully," Johnny said with a mock frown.

"What?"

"Never mind, inside joke. Julie, why are you calling? I haven't heard from you since Sam …."

"Well, I was concerned."

"Bull."

"You're my brother-in-law. Of course, I'm concerned."

"I repeat, bull."

"Listen, Johnny, I like you. I always have. There are just things you don't know about that have made our relationship … well, difficult."

"What things?"

"Just things between me and Sam."

"Julie, what are you talking about?"

The telephone line was silent. Johnny could almost hear Julie's mind humming in thought.

"Maybe we should do this in person," she finally said.

"Do what?"

"Talk."

"Julie, just tell me."

"Johnny, Sam wasn't the perfect wife like you think she was."

"What do you mean?"

"She wasn't always nice."

"Nice? To who?"

"You."

"Sure, she was."

"Even in the last year?"

Johnny thought about all the times the year before Sam's death and how often she just seemed out of touch with their marriage.

"Most of the time, she was fine. Nobody's perfect," he answered.

"Oh, Johnny…."

"Dammit, Julie, just tell me!"

"No, not on the phone. I can't do that to you. Where in Iowa are you? You can't be too far from me."

"Booneville. Parkside General Hospital. But I'm staying at the Best Western."

"I'll be there Saturday. I'm sorry, Johnny."

"Sorry for what?"

"Just sorry. See you Saturday." Then she hung up.

"I'll count the minutes," Johnny said to the empty line.

TWENTY-FOUR

"**O**KAY, now that you can walk on your own," Emmy Brownell said later that day by Johnny's bedside, "and you've taken all the joy out of nursing by going to the bathroom by yourself, they're kicking you out."

"I'm getting out of this place?" Johnny said, his eyebrows rising.

"You can leave this afternoon."

"Oh…good…I think."

"I've arranged for a little help for you. Actually, I didn't have much to do with it. Doc Enbright will pick you up at three o'clock."

"Doc?"

"Yep, what better nursemaid than a retired doctor? He'd really enjoy it if you stayed with him. Seriously. Ever since his wife passed away, he's been kind of like a lost little puppy dog. It would do him good."

"Buster, too?"

"Who do you think has been watching the pooch since you've been in here?"

"I thought you said Donna was taking care of him?"

"She started to. Then yesterday, Doc picked him up for a walk and just kept him the whole day."

"You seem to know a lot about my dog."

"Just part of our full-service hospital care. Donna took it upon herself to pack up your room and load it into your car. She drove it over to Doc's place so it all should be there when you get there."

"Geez, that's really nice."

"We're a full-service town."

"How long have you lived here?" Johnny asked.

"All my life. Except for five years in Iowa City at the university."

"You must like it."

"I do. The people are nice, honest. I've known most of them since I was a kid. It gives you a sense of belonging like everyone is a part of your extended family in a way. That's one of the big advantages of a small town. I like the seasons. I like the Midwest. Of course, I've never lived anywhere else for any length of time."

"You never had the desire to explore the world?"

"Not really. Oh, I vacation in different places, all around the States mostly. I've been to Europe twice. But I'm really a down home girl, I guess. How about you?"

"I like exploring. Been doing it all my life. Kind of on an exploration now."

"What are you looking for?"

"I'm not quite sure. I guess I'll know when I find it."

"But if you don't know what you're looking for, how will you know when you find it?"

Johnny thought for a few moments about the question, but he wasn't sure how to answer. He hadn't really thought about what he'd been hoping to find.

"I just needed to leave what I had, to get away. Maybe I'm looking to find myself again."

"So, that implies that you found yourself once, but now you're lost again. That about right?"

"You ask a lot of questions."

"You started it!" Emmy said in mock disbelief, her eyes wide. Changing tone, "So, are you lost?"

"A little." Johnny stared at Emmy and noticed that her eyes were brown with little orange specks.

"Were you getting away from a woman?"

"A woman?"

"Men tend to run away from women. Especially when it gets messy."

"Voice of experience talking?"

"I've been hurt, sure. A couple of times. Haven't we all?"

"That's for sure."

"You didn't answer my question about running away."

"Hand me my wallet, top drawer there," Johnny said, pointing to the small table next to his bed.

Emmy Brownell retrieved the wallet and handed it to him.

"My wife and kids," he said, showing her the photo.

"Oh, I didn't know … you weren't wearing a ring … they're beautiful."

"They were. They died in a car accident several months ago."

"Oh, my…" she said as her eyes began to water. "I'm so sorry."

"That's why I'm a little lost."

"I can't even imagine…"

"Yeah, I couldn't imagine I'd end up in a hospital in Booneville, Iowa, either. Some things just don't turn out like you planned."

"We all need time to heal. And most of us don't understand what God has planned for us either."

God, Johnny thought, *who's he? And where's he been lately?*

"I'm finding that out, the hard way I suppose."

"You're quite a mess at the moment, aren't you?" she said, putting her hand on his.

"Just a little lost."

"It looks like you lost your razor, too," Emmy said to break the tension.

"Yeah."

"Maybe you'll look good in a beard," she said, rubbing the stubble on his face. He liked the touch of her hand.

"Thanks," Johnny said.

"For what?"

"For taking care of me."

"I'm a full-service nurse," Emmy said. "You can get dressed now. Doc's always early. He'll be here any minute, I bet. Need any help?"

"Nah. I'm good."

"You'll be even better when you find yourself again."

Johnny smiled.

TWENTY-FIVE

"**L**ET'S go for a walk," Johnny said to Doc Enbright as they sat on chairs on his front porch. "Or maybe just a stroll. I've been cooped up in that hospital room forever."

"It's a mighty fine day for a stroll around the block. Buster need a leash?"

"Nah, he'll be fine."

The early August day was warm and humid, so the two men stayed on the sidewalk, under the shade of the maple trees that lined the block.

"What's been happening at the plant?" Johnny asked as Buster sniffed the new territory.

"Lots of the same. Ulysses is threatening. Dunham is being vocal. The boys are searching out new ways to make it work. Not much has changed since your accident."

"I don't think it was an accident."

"What do you mean?" Doc asked as he stopped walking.

"That truck made three runs at me. Finally got a piece of me on the third one."

"Nothing like that in the police report."

"How did you see the police report?"

"I've been doctoring the Bowen family for thirty years. Heck, I brought Dan Bowen into this life. Delivered him myself. We go way back. He gave me a peek."

"I wasn't sure how much to trust him."

"All the way. You want me to call him, get him over here?"

"Not yet. I'd like to try and figure out why they went after me. If Bowen finds whoever did this, they'd just deny it. Their word against mine, and there were two of them."

"But you got a hunch, I reckon."

"I do. I think it must have something to do with what's going on at the plant. Maybe somebody was pissed that I was sticking my nose where it doesn't belong."

"Johnny, we appreciate what you've been doing for us, but it isn't worth getting killed over."

"They weren't trying to kill me, I don't think. If they were, they were pretty bad at it."

"Well, I hope you don't take offense at what I'm about to say, but the way you look, they came pretty close."

"Not even. I think they were just trying to run me off the road. Except I don't like to be run off any road. Then I got pissed, they got pissed, and I lost the pissing match."

Buster chased a squirrel, his front paws four feet up the trunk of the tree where the squirrel had disappeared.

"Buster, come," Johnny shouted. The dog stopped barking but kept looking at the tree as he trotted back.

"So what's our next step?" Doc asked as they continued to walk.

"I'm going to stay low for a while. May even head down to Des Moines for a few days. I've been doing some research, and there are a few people down there I'd like to talk to if I can get some meetings with them."

"And me? Got something for me to do while you're gone?"

"You might want to stay low for a while yourself. You're in the middle of this whole thing, and if somebody came after me, they could come after you, too."

"Oh, heck, son, I got nothing to lose. They don't scare me."

"Just the same, I'd take it easy. Don't get caught out on a country road all by yourself."

"Gotcha. Hey, you don't look like it's going to be real comfortable driving. Maybe I could drive you down."

"Sure, that might work. Let me ask you something," Johnny continued. "Who has the most to lose if the plant closes down?"

"Everybody loses if that plant closes. Everybody owns a piece of it. The whole town's going to suffer."

"Maybe I'm asking the wrong question. Maybe the question is, who has the most to gain if the plant closes down?"

"That may be easier to answer, but I'm not sure," Doc replied. "You do have a unique way of thinking outside the box, don't you?"

"Advertising guys don't make much money if they keep thinking inside the box."

"Is that what you do? I thought for sure you were a professional bicycle rider just having a bad week," Doc said, making them both laugh.

"Maybe I can get some appointments for Monday. What are you doing Monday?"

"Road trip."

"Oh, I forgot to mention. I'm having a visitor on Saturday."

"Let me guess. Emmy Brownell?"

"Nurse Brownell? No, why did you guess her?"

"Oh, no reason."

"It's my former sister-in-law. Ah, shoot, I told her I'd be at the motel."

"Donna will send her our way. Big pow-wow?"

"Big mystery."

"Sometimes mysteries are better than pow-wows."

"Let's hope. I wouldn't want to get into a pow-wow with that woman, that's for sure."

TWENTY-SIX

THE doorbell rang Friday evening just after Doc and Johnny were enjoying hamburgers and corn on the cob on the grill and a few Goose Island Bourbon County stout beers. Doc and Buster answered it.

"Hey, Johnny, a friend is here to see you," Doc yelled to Johnny, who was still sitting on the back patio.

"Don't have any of those around here."

A forlorn-looking Emmy Brownell stuck her head out the patio door.

"I'm a friend, aren't I," she asked, looking sad.

"Oh, yeah, sure you are," Johnny managed to stammer. "What brings you around?"

"Nice to see you, too."

"Well, yeah, it's nice to see you, I just meant…"

"I'm making a house call."

"I didn't know nurses made house calls."

"This one does."

"Full service, right?"

"Exactly. How are you feeling?"

"Better. Yeah, better. Doc and I have been walking a bit and eating well."

"And drinking well, I can see," Emmy said, pointing to the pint glasses on the patio table.

"For medicinal purposes only. Doctor's prescription."

"One of Doc's favorite prescriptions, as I remember."

"Would you like one?"

"No, thanks. I'm on duty."

"Really?"

"Kind of."

Just then Doc emerged with Buster on his leash. The dog nuzzled up to Emmy, rubbing his head on her thigh. She scratched both ears.

"Me and Buster are heading out for a walk. A stroll, really. Probably a slow stroll. See you later," Doc said as the front screen door slammed.

"Have you been doing your exercises?" Emmy asked.

"Not really, it's pretty sore."

"Uh huh. You been using that squeeze ball they gave you in rehab?"

"A little. Some. Not so much."

"Uh huh. Have you been keeping the road rash clean, at least?"

"Doc's looked at it a couple of times, changed the bandage."

"Well, that's something."

"And I'll have you know, I've been doing my best to consume most all of those pain killers they gave me whether I need them or not. Yes, indeed."

"Just don't overdo it."

"Yes, Nurse Brownell."

"You know, that road rash doesn't prevent you from bathing?"

"What are you implying?"

"That Buster smells better than you."

"It's too hard to take a shower. I'm not supposed to get these stitches wet, and when I take off the brace, well, that wrist is still pretty useless."

"And that beard, I was wrong. Doesn't make you look more distinguished."

"Yeah, I never could grow much facial hair. And it itches like crazy," Johnny said, scratching vigorously at his chin and cheek.

"Then that settles it."

"Settles what?"

"You're taking a bath. It won't hurt the rash, and will probably help your back. I'll get it ready," Emmy said as she headed up the stairs.

Johnny waited a few minutes, then followed her up the stairs at a much slower pace. He stuck his head into the bathroom and saw Emmy bending over the tub, swirling her hand in the erupting bubbles.

"A bubble bath?" Johnny asked.

"Well, not really. I couldn't find any bubble bath, so it's a combination of Epsom salts and dishwashing soap. I guess Doc's not a bubble bath kind of guy. But it'll feel good and get you clean! You jump in, and I'll check back with you in a second or two," she said as she left the room.

Johnny gingerly slid off his shorts, unbuttoned his shirt, and stepped into the water. It was hot at first, but as he settled in, it felt just about perfect. After a minute or two, Emmy opened the door and stuck her head in.

"I was thinking you might like some help washing your hair. Yes?" she asked.

"Sure, I was wondering how I was going to do that."

"Once you finish soaking, come on downstairs, and we can use the kitchen sink, okay?"

"Sure, thanks."

"I'll see you in about half an hour."

"A half hour? That long?" Johnny said as he made little waves in the tub with his fingers.

"It'll do you good. Just relax and enjoy it."

As Johnny slid down farther into the tub, his knees emerged like a double periscope. He splashed water over them to keep them warm. And his thoughts drifted to Sam. There was a period just after Cameron was born when she became almost obsessed with bubble baths, at least in Johnny's opinion. She would feed her baby girl and make sure Carson was plopped in front of his favorite video and tell Johnny that she absolutely needed an hour alone. She cocooned herself in the bathroom, took a long, leisurely tub and shaved her legs. If both kids fell asleep, Johnny would try and invade her privacy, but most times she'd shoo him away.

Now Johnny tried to let the water sooth his body ache—and wash away his heartache.

When he entered the kitchen later, he saw Emmy sipping a cup of tea and reading a magazine. He noticed she had a chair in front of the sink and several bath towels on the counter. She didn't notice him right away and was tapping her foot to an imaginary beat.

He coughed, and she raised her head, a smile quickly spreading across her face.

"Feel better?" she said.

"Yeah. You were right. I needed that."

"Good, now let's get that hair washed. Have a seat," she said, motioning to the chair that was facing away from the sink.

She grabbed a towel and placed it over the top of the chair.

"Lean back," she said to him. "That comfy?"

"Sure."

She ran warm water over his head and began to massage his scalp. She dug her fingers into the muscles at the bottom of his skull, rubbed behind his ears, and began to methodically use her fingernails over his entire head. She could feel the muscles in his neck begin to relax as she used a little more warm water from a cup to keep his head warm.

"Wow, that feels great. Where'd you learn to do that?"

"I volunteer out at the assisted living facility once a month. Mostly I just visit with a few folks I know, nothing professional or anything. Then I noticed," she continued, never stopping his massage, "that the ladies got their hair done once a week. Standing appointment in the little beauty shop right there on the premises. They always looked forward to that weekly shampoo. But the gentlemen never got that chance. They'd get a haircut but nothing as luxurious as a shampoo and head massage. So I started to do that."

Johnny smiled. "Nice."

"Most were pretty hesitant at first. They didn't really like another woman touching them like that. But eventually, word got around. Now they enjoy it. It's fun. I get to talk with them, they're lonely because many have lost their…" She stopped.

"Their wives?" Johnny said.

"Sorry."

Johnny only nodded.

"Anyway, they just seem so lonely, and I hate that, and when I show up, well, I can at least get a smile out of them…and we talk, about anything…and they don't seem so lonely."

Emmy finished the shampoo, rinsed his head, and toweled it dry, running her fingers through his short-cropped hair. She sat back down in the chair as Johnny said, "Those men out there are awfully lucky to have you do that."

"It's just a way to keep connected and give back a little. Most times I wish I could do more to help," she said, looking away.

"So let me ask you something. Why'd you come here today?"

"Uh…it's my day off. No plans. Just thought I'd check up on you. And…."

"And what?"

"I felt so bad, after your accident…I thought…I could help, in some way."

Johnny nodded, rose from the chair, and began to walk slowly around the kitchen, stretching his back as he walked.

"Well, I do smell better, that's for sure."

"That's a start. Sometimes you just have to start somewhere. Small baby steps."

"Ah, you're a philosopher, too, huh?"

"As a matter of fact, I'll have you know," she said with just a bit of mock indignation and a poorly concealed smile, "I minored in philosophy in college. A nursing major but a philosophy minor."

"We all need to figure out life in college. And other times."

She sat in the chair and smiled up at him, but looked away.

"Like now?" she said as he circled behind her.

He looked at the back of her head, but she didn't turn around.

"Well, thanks again, for the bath and shampoo. I appreciate it."

"I should go," she said as she headed toward the front door. She looked back and waved goodbye as the screen door closed behind her.

Johnny stood in the kitchen, hand raised but not waving, as she stepped down the stairs and walked away.

"Hey, wanna beer?" he called to her.

She turned around and walked back toward him. "Thought you'd never ask."

TWENTY-SEVEN

ON Saturday, Johnny woke early, jumped in the shower to rinse off, and got the coffee brewing. He hadn't been able to shake the conversation with Julie Strausser that day in the hospital. *Sam wasn't always nice.* What in the world did she mean by that? Johnny let his mind wander over the last year of his marriage and tried to find clues to what she might be talking about, but he kept thinking of Emmy Brownell.

After the tub incident, they'd shared a beer before Doc returned. The three of them had talked into the evening about Iowa, corn, medicine—just about everything except what was going on at the plant. The conversation was spirited and lively, and they all laughed at every opportunity. Johnny had noticed that Emmy had no pretensions, shared about herself easily, and had an endearing quality of humility.

"I've been reading a lot about robots lately," she'd said. "How they're going to replace almost half of the jobs around today. Even nurses. Of course, I suppose that's not too farfetched. Empty bedpans, give shots, take blood pressure…"

"Robots can't shave people, can they?" Johnny asked with a smile.

Doc perked his ears and leaned closer.

"Maybe. Who knows? I'm sure I don't. I'm not the sharpest blade in the pack."

"Way sharper than you think, huh, Johnny?" Doc said.

Johnny smiled but couldn't keep eye contact with either of them.

As Johnny sat at the kitchen table sipping his coffee, he watched the dawn. He was attracted to Emmy. But something about the feeling wasn't quite right. The day his wife and children died seemed like yesterday. He could still feel the emptiness in his heart. It was a physical feeling, like a migraine headache, a torn muscle. No less painful than a broken bone— this feeling centered in his chest—and it almost never left him.

Johnny didn't know whether he wanted to remember everything about his family or try to forget. He rubbed his newly shaven chin and thought about Emmy. Then images of Samantha crowded into his brain. His wife had a hurt look on her face that he would even entertain ideas about being with another woman. Then he saw images of his kids, and he grimaced. His breath seemed to be sucked right out of him.

But he forced himself to look for happy times. He remembered a time his son was playing Little League baseball and how he ended a game with an unassisted double play. He envisioned that image being stored in a cardboard box, like the shoebox he used to keep his baseball cards in when he was a kid. He imagined the box labeled "Carson" and covered the box with a lid.

He remembered the dollhouse that his daughter used to play with almost every day. He looked into each room and saw her there, in miniature. In one room she was dancing with her preschool friends, each looking to the other to find the right step. In another, he saw her reading a book aloud to one of her dolls, making up the words as she went along, acting out the story with her hands. He managed to close each door to every room of the dollhouse as he struggled not to cry. How he missed them. Good God, how he missed them. *Are you even there, God? Can you even hear me? Where have you been through all of this?*

Would he ever heal? Could his heart heal like his wrist or his elbow? Would he ever have full use of it again? Maybe Emmy was right—it would take some time, and then he might be able to find himself. Somehow. Somewhere.

A little after two o'clock, Julie Strausser pulled up in front of Doc's house. Johnny had been reading one of Doc's fishing magazines on the porch. Julie drove a new 529 BMW, a perk of her financial services business in Chicago. But she wasn't dressed in her typical women's power outfit—blue or black two-piece business suit with a white blouse. Today, she sported khakis and an over-sized, long-sleeved blouse, sleeves rolled up. Quite the preppy, Johnny thought.

"You could have told me you weren't at the Best Western," she said as she got out of the car. "It took me another half hour to try and find this house."

"Nice to see you, too, Julie," Johnny countered.

"Sorry, it was a long drive. I'm not used to being in the car for six hours."

"Well, I appreciate you coming. How was the traffic?"

"Not bad. I just pointed the car west. Seems Booneville is almost directly west of Chicago. You've looked better. How are you feeling?"

"They've been taking good care of me, thanks."

"Your face is bruised pretty badly."

"You should have seen me a couple of days ago. Would you like to use the bathroom or can I get you something to drink?"

Julie had been pacing in front of the porch but hadn't come up to sit in a chair next to Johnny. She hadn't given him a hug or shook his hand. She'd kept her distance, constantly running her hands through her short-cropped hair.

"Sure, maybe a Coke or something."

"Coming right up. Come on in," Johnny said as he opened the screen door.

"Whose home is this? A doctor, the lady at the motel said. Is that right?"

"Doc Enbright. But he's more like a friend than my doctor. He just offered me a place to stay until I got better."

"Friendly town, I suppose."

"Very."

They finally settled at the kitchen table, Johnny making small talk about his journey East and Julie pacing around the kitchen. Finally, Johnny broke the ice.

"Okay, let's hear it. What was so important that you had to drive six hours to tell me?"

Julie took a deep breath and sat down across the table from him.

"I don't know how to break this to you gently, so I'm going to just have to tell it to you bluntly. I'm sorry if I hurt you. It doesn't seem like a good time to lay this on you right now."

"Fire away."

"Samantha was my sister, and I loved her very much. I didn't always agree with everything she did in her life, but she was my sister."

"Yeah, I think all that's been established. Just spit it out, Julie."

"She was making plans to leave you," she said as she walked away from the table, over to the door to the backyard.

"What?" Johnny said, his eyebrows shooting upward.

"She'd been making plans for a couple of years to leave you when the time was right. Like I said on the phone, she wasn't always nice. She was using me to help her. And I wasn't proud of it."

"What do you mean 'making plans'? What plans? Are you sure about this or is this just another of your games, Julie?" Johnny asked, trying to get her to look him in the eye. He clenched his jaw and balled his right fist.

"She wasn't happy, Johnny. She would call me at all hours of the night and tell me how she didn't like her life, how it hadn't turned out how she wanted, and how she needed to change it."

"She never mentioned anything to me."

"You were always working. You weren't available to her," Julie said, her voice barely audible.

"That's a bunch of bull! I was providing for my family. She seemed to like all the perks that my business gave her." Johnny stood up and threw back his shoulders, his right fist lightly punching his right thigh.

"I'm sorry. I didn't mean to blame you. That's just what she told me."

Julie backed away from him as he began pacing the kitchen, too. The two of them were like boxers in a ring, each circling the other, waiting to deliver—or receive—the next blow.

"How were you involved?" Johnny asked.

"More like her confidant. Although…she did ask my advice about hiding some money."

"Hiding money? What are you talking about?" Now his hands were raised outstretched in front of him, pleading for answers.

"She'd send me money, and I'd invest it in her name."

"How much money? Where did she get money? She wasn't working, she was taking care of the kids."

"I didn't ask where the money came from, I just did the investing."

"Right! You didn't want to know where she was getting it?"

"I figured she was getting it from you. One way or the other."

"Like stealing it?"

"Dammit, Johnny, listen to me. She was taking $500 here and there, I guess out of her checking or savings account and sending it to me. I'd invest it in a special account, in her name only. Get it?" she said, now looking him in the eye.

"Why, what did she need it for?" Shaking his head, he moved closer to her.

"For when she left."

"Was she having an affair? I want to know. Tell me, was she?"

"Johnny, I have no idea. She never mentioned anything like that. It didn't have anything to do with some other man. She just wanted out of the marriage." She looked away and backed up a few steps.

Johnny had opened the refrigerator and taken out a beer. He opened it and took a long swallow, then another. He continued to pace, breathing deeply, refusing to believe what Julie was telling him.

"Why tell me now?" he demanded, looking out the kitchen window.

"Because it's your money. And it was...deceptive. And...you deserve to know."

"How do I know you're telling the truth?"

"Why would I lie about a thing like this?"

"I don't know. Is that all of it?"

"No."

"What else?"

"She was, I don't know what you'd call it...hoarding, I guess...gift cards."

Johnny stopped pacing, stopped breathing for a few seconds.

"Gift cards," he said but not as a question, as a confirmation. "Like gas cards and American Express cards and cards from ... everywhere."

Julie nodded, unable to look at him.

"You knew?" Julie said.

Johnny didn't answer.

"It was all part of the plan," she said.

"Milk me dry," he said, his head in his hands, palms over his ears like he was trying to block the words.

"I'm sorry, Johnny."

"Sure."

The anger rose in Johnny, that darkness again. He let it rise, not wanting to control it. The anger generated heat, from his midsection up through his head. He didn't know what to say or what to ask. He felt sick to his stomach, then lightheaded, then empty, then devastated. He wanted to smash something.

"As the only heir, I can have the money sent to you," Julie said. "I think the gift cards are in a safe deposit box. A bank in San Francisco. They shouldn't be too hard to find."

"How much?"

"The cards? I don't know."

"Forty thousand. I meant the money. My guy found a record of the cards. We were trying to figure it out. But I had no idea…it was something like this. How much more in money?"

"Approximately fifty-five thousand."

"Oh, my…," Johnny said, wondering how long she had been taking money from their savings. "A hundred thousand dollars." *How did he miss a hundred thousand dollars?*

"I have a copy of the death certificate. I'll submit that and have them send you the money directly. Where do you want me to send it? Here?"

He had to take a few breaths before he could answer. "No, send it to my bank in San Francisco. My guy Luke will take care of it. We'll send you wiring instructions."

"I'm sorry, Johnny."

"You keep saying that! But you weren't sorry when it was happening, were you? It was like a little conspiracy! The two of you. You were in it together!"

"Like I said, she wasn't always nice. And I'm not proud of what I've done. I can only offer my apology."

"Is that all? Anything else? Any other stashed money I should know about? More safe deposit boxes? Accounts in the Caribbean? Swiss bank accounts? Anything like that?" He began to pound his fist into his thigh again, this time with more power.

"Don't get carried away, Johnny. She wasn't that smart. Just devious."

"But you are, aren't you?"

They both stopped pacing, the question focusing Johnny. He stared at her, anger in his eyes.

"It was all I could do just to help her out. I didn't want to be a part of it. She was my sister. But I didn't like it."

"You didn't like it, but you did it."

Julie nodded, her eyes downcast.

"Have a nice trip back to Chicago," Johnny said with absolutely no sincerity in his voice.

TWENTY-EIGHT

O N Monday morning, Johnny and Doc started for Des Moines. Johnny had arranged a meeting with a professor in the business department at Drake University. They'd talked on the phone about Johnny's idea. The professor said he didn't know how much he could help, but Johnny got the sense that the guy had his hand on the pulse of start-ups and venture funding coming into Iowa and the surrounding region. At least it was a place to start.

Doc drove his ten-year-old Volvo, Johnny in the passenger seat, doodling in a notebook.

"You've been kind of quiet the past few days, ever since your sister-in-law left," Doc said.

"Ex-sister-in-law."

"Okay, ex. Something she said get you down?"

"Oh, no, nothing. Just that my whole life has been a lie, that's all."

"Well, we only got a little over an hour down to Des Moines, but if you can do the short version, I'm a pretty good listener."

"Yeah, okay. I gotta tell somebody."

For the next half hour, Johnny told Doc the whole story, starting with his college days, his marriage, his business, the accident, and the last several months. Doc deliberately slowed the car down to 60 m.p.h. He wanted to hear the story—and knew Johnny needed to tell it—more than they needed to be on time for their appointment. Johnny expressed anger and bewilderment at the same time. He couldn't understand how a woman could keep such secrets. He continued to vent, sometimes vehemently, as Doc just listened.

Finally, Johnny sat back in his seat, spent. He'd gotten most of it out and was breathing deeply, trying to exhale the anger and resentment. Trying to stay under control.

"Did your wife ever keep secrets from you?" he asked Doc as they exited I35 on the outskirts of Des Moines.

"In the fifty-five years of our marriage, only once, that I know of," he replied. "Oh, I'm sure there were times when she thought it best that I didn't know something, but I wouldn't call that keeping secrets. Just keeping bad news away I didn't need to hear. Wouldn't have done me any good. It was more like she was taking care of me. She was always good at that."

"What was the one time, if you don't mind me asking?"

"It was on her deathbed. A couple of days before she passed. She told me that for the past five or six years of our marriage, she'd faked her orgasms," he said, a smile spreading across her face.

"Seriously?"

"It was the only time in all those years when she wasn't truthful with me, but I didn't consider that too deceitful. Like I said, she was always looking out for me."

"Did you ever lie to her?" Johnny asked.

"I never had to. I never had to fake it, know what I mean?"

"I wasn't talking about orgasms."

"Except that one time. I got into the peach brandy pretty good during a Christmas party and the old sucker just kind of didn't want to finish up his business, if you get my drift."

"Yeah, got it, happens to all of us."

"Really? That's darn comforting. Thought it might have only been me."

"You pulling my chain? Uh, no pun intended."

"No sir, I'm still a passionate man. Gracious, son, if that Emmy Brownell wasn't making googly eyes at you, I'd take a run at her myself. That is, if I were forty years younger."

"Googly eyes?"

"Okay, then what do you call it these days?"

"I don't know. I'm not sure. Been too long."

"You'll figure it out."

As they checked the GPS on Johnny's phone, they turned into the campus of Drake University. The professor was teaching a summer school class and agreed to meet them for coffee.

"Hey, all this talk about orgasms and googly eyes isn't going to throw you off your game in there, is it?" Doc said, smiling.

"Hold on, I'm googling googly eyes. Seeing if the two are related somehow."

"Get your head in the game, son, head in the game."

The small coffee shop on the ground level of the business building exhibited few signs of activity this time of the morning. Johnny texted the professor that they were there and in five minutes, he entered the shop. Jason Sonderling had the look of a professor—short-cropped hair, a well-trimmed graying beard, button-down shirt, and loosened tie, with khakis and penny loafers. Johnny couldn't remember a single professor when he was in college at Santa Barbara wearing a tie, and that was almost fifteen years ago.

After they had introduced themselves, grabbed some coffee, and exchanged introductions, Johnny asked, "Dressed pretty formal for summer school, aren't you?"

"Yes, maybe, but I try to teach the kids in my class that presentation matters. They watch movies like *The Social Network* and think that everyone becomes a billionaire like Zuckerberg wearing sweatshirts and blue jeans," Sonderling said. "They show up in my class wearing hoodies and flip-flops. I try to tell them that most times, it doesn't work that way. But times are changing. Every once in a while, I get through to them; sometimes they get through to me. That's why I like teaching. It's usually a two-way street."

They exchanged ideas about kids these days, and Doc chimed in about kids in the old days. All three chuckled that even though the way kids dressed had changed, kids in college were pretty much the same, no matter what the era.

"Tell us a little about the venture capital situation in this neck of the woods," Johnny said. "I know the VC scene in California, so I have a pretty good idea of how it works. We'd just like to know what's available around here."

"You've read those articles, I take it, that proclaim us the Silicon Prairie, right?" Sonderling responded.

"We did, yeah."

"From what I can tell, anywhere from fifteen to twenty start-ups are established in eastern Nebraska each year. And that figure is at least triple what it was a few years ago. Most all are tech related in some way. The state has over $300 million venture money available to attract start-ups. It's not California, but they saw what Texas and most recently New York has done to get businesses to move in, like tax credits, and they're getting aggressive. Five years ago, there wasn't anything. Zilch."

Johnny was jotting notes in his notebook.

"Last month," Sonderling continued, "Google Fiber installed an ultra-fast internet connection in a Kansas City business park, and within a week, twelve start-ups had moved in. And over the past six months, over sixty start-ups have presented their ideas in Kansas City at weekly forums organized by a few guys who manage a lot of money for several big name foundations. So the lure of getting funded is bringing them out of the woodwork."

"How about closer to home?" Johnny asked.

"I was getting to that," Sonderling said. "Des Moines has an incubator funded with both private and public money, close to a million dollars, and they've heard over a hundred and fifty pitches over the past two years. I can find nine that they've funded."

"Not much money, so each is only getting a hundred grand or so," Johnny said.

"Like I said, not California, but it's on a pretty aggressive track. If the money is still available, they're supposed to do at least another nine this coming year."

"What kind of start-ups? Tech like in KC?" Doc asked.

"Not necessarily. There's a website called Local Ag, a marketplace to sell meat. I know, it doesn't sound fancy, but it's attracting money. Got another one that verifies your identity with eye scans, and there is another that sells tickets to concerts so bands can manage their own sales. It's really all over the board. We have start-ups in Des Moines that cover everything—biotechnology, medical devices, advanced manufacturing."

"Now we're talking," Johnny said.

"There's an online newspaper. I can give you the URL. They follow the activity," Sonderling added. "After you called, I checked, and they can track over eight start-up companies in the whole region just in the last four years. And that doesn't count another fifty or so that have produced mobile or web apps. It's really quite amazing, especially for a guy like me.

I've been teaching here for almost twenty-five years. Back when I started, it was mostly agricultural business the kids wanted to know. Now it's completely changed."

"What's the shortage?" Johnny asked.

"What do you mean?" Sonderling replied.

"Talent wise. There never is a shortage of new ideas, but most companies fail because they can't execute the idea."

"Around here, far as I know, it's mechanical engineers. Hardware guys."

Johnny smiled directly at Doc. "Hardware engineers aren't a problem, I wouldn't suspect, are they?"

"We got 'em coming out our ears," Doc said, exaggerating only slightly.

After another thirty minutes of the details of what Sonderling knew about specific start-ups and entrepreneurs looking for money, they jumped back into the Volvo for the return trip to Booneville.

"So let me see if I got this straight," Doc said, obviously excited about the hour they'd spent with Jason Sonderling. "Iowa is like this mini hotbed of new businesses. The state has incentives to start the business around here, mostly tax incentives, right?"

"Yep."

"And there seems to be one heck of a lot of them, right? I mean companies looking for money."

"Never has been a shortage of ideas in this country. That's what we're famous for. Japan, China, all those Asian countries, they can manufacture anything. But America, we come up with the idea, for the most part."

"So why would one of those companies want to locate in Booneville?"

"Because you have manufacturing capacity and the talent. Like Sonderling said, most of these ideas fail because they don't have hardware engineers that can make the product work. Somebody has a great idea, in theory, and they think they know how it *could* work. Those creative types just have those kinds of minds; they're always thinking of what doesn't work in the world and coming up with ideas how to make it work. But they need engineers to figure out how to put the idea down on paper and then manufacture it. An idea without a means to reproduce it on a large scale is like…well, like…weaving straw into gold. What was that story?"

"Rumpelstiltskin."

"Yeah, right. Great idea, but really hard to make it happen."

"So now what?" Doc asked.

"We have to do some matchmaking," Johnny said. "We find an idea, then we find some money. And we lure them to Booneville."

"Sounds easy."

"Famous last words."

TWENTY-NINE

"**W**HY in the world would they go to Drake University?" Ulysses wanted to know, and he wanted to know right now.

"All we know," Joe Dunham said, "is that they were talking to a professor."

"A professor of what?"

"Business."

"And what did this professor of business say when we asked him what they wanted?"

"They didn't ask."

"Dumb and dumber."

"You haven't really given me the money to hire respectable investigators," Dunham replied. "Those two boys are doing the best they can with what God gave 'em."

"Which was nothing. It doesn't matter what they were talking about, now does it? What we know is that California No-W did not understand the subtle hint that was delivered out on the highway. He's still poking his nose into our business."

"That seems like a fair assessment."

"And Cheng is ready to pull the plug on the payments unless the plant closes on September first."

"Seems so."

"So I say we torch it!" Ulysses said, both arms rising in the air, like the explosion he envisioned.

"We've been through this before. Let's take another run at No-W. Let's not be so subtle this time. Maybe he'll get the hint and get out of Dodge."

"And if he don't?"

"We gotta keep the pressure on the guys at the plant. Make it tough on them to come to work. Criticize them, humiliate them, make them hate their job. Tell them it's all over, doomsday, the final lap, whatever we got to say to convince them to quit."

"That's what we've been doing, genius, for the last three months. Those suckers seem slow on the uptake."

"Then let's do a forced shutdown, two weeks," said Dunham. "No pay. We'll tell them there isn't enough work. Pinch 'em, stretch them a little. Make it hard for them to put food on the table, buy their beer."

"They know we got backorders."

"Tell them they're full of crap. Tell them we don't have enough to pay them even if we made the orders. Tell them anything, just don't tell them the truth."

"Brilliant."

"And I'm gonna take another run at No-W. Get up close and personal. Make it real messy. He ain't no hero, he's just an advertising guy."

Ulysses just shook his head and headed to his office bar for a drink.

THIRTY

"WE are patient men, don't you agree, Mr. U.S. Johnson," Eddie Walnuts said as he applied the nutcracker to the pinky finger of Ulysses. He squeezed enough pressure to cause extreme pain to shoot up the arm, and Ulysses wondered exactly when the knuckle might crack.

Eddie Walnuts was not his real name, of course, he'd boasted several times in front of Ulysses. His friends in Chicago slapped that moniker on him. In fact, he'd been in this line of work, persuasion he liked to call it, so long that not many people remembered his real name. Those that did weren't talking, he'd said.

Joe Dunham slumped in a chair in the corner of the office, a big man dressed in an ill-fitting suit hovering over him. Dunham didn't move; he stayed quiet.

"I did not hear an answer from you, Mr. U.S. Johnson. The question was, are we not very patient men?" Walnuts repeated.

Johnson stared at his pinky finger and the nutcracker but managed to say, "Yeah, yeah, sure, you've been very patient."

"And do you not agree, Mr. U.S. Johnson, that missing a payment to us is very disrespectful?"

"I'm sorry. I can explain that."

"Explanation at this point would be good. But you know that my employer does not like explanations. He prefers cash payments. On time."

"Would it be possible to not crush my finger?" Johnson asked. "That way I can think better during my explanation."

"Your explanation, Mr. U.S. Johnson, should not take thinking. Just tell me," Eddie Walnuts replied as he torqued more pressure to the nutcracker. "I usually know exactly how much pressure it takes to crack a knuckle. But I'm not a perfect man, I can miscalculate. And of course, not every knuckle is built the same.

"You don't have to call me Mr. Johnson," Ulysses said through clenched teeth. "All my friends call me Ulysses."

"We are business associates, not friends. Our relationship has been a simple loan transaction, similar to a bank loan. Because of your unfortunate luck at the casino, you owe us quite a bit of money. From the goodness of our hearts, we have allowed you to pay it back in installments. Which, up to this time, you have been very punctual with. I would rather keep our relationship as such—strictly business. Changing that would be disrespectful."

Johnson wanted to say something about the disrespect paid his pinky finger, but he thought better of it.

"Now, the explanation, please."

"My benefactor was actually late in supplying me funds, but I did receive payment this morning, so there is no problem. I can write you a check this minute," Johnson said, anticipating that the reply would encourage Walnuts to let up with the nutcracker.

Instead, he intensified his grip, saying, "Have you been holding out on us? That would not be a good thing."

"No, no, no. I swear to God, we negotiated just yesterday over the phone and the wire transfer came today. There was no way to get it to you since the due date was yesterday. Why don't I write you a check right now?"

"You know we prefer cash."

"We could go to the bank. I'll make a deposit and get cash."

"I would prefer not to make an appearance at your local bank, Mr. U.S. Johnson. I tend to avoid those establishments."

"I could go and bring the cash back," Johnson suggested. "You can keep Dunham as collateral."

Joe Dunham's eyes grew wide, and he started to rise out of his chair when a very large hand pushed him back down to his seat.

"That is an interesting proposition, but one which I will have to reject. We are not interested—no offense, Mr. Dunham—in such collateral. Perhaps I could keep part of your finger here as collateral," Eddie Walnuts said as he twisted the nutcracker, pushing Johnson to his knees in agony.

"Oh, please…," Johnson managed to say.

Just as Johnson's knuckle was about to crack open in the vise, Eddie Walnuts abruptly let go, slipping his tool of persuasion back into his jacket pocket.

"I believe I have made my point, is this not correct, Mr. U.S. Johnson?"

All Johnson could do was nod his head in agreement; his mind was thanking the God he had just prayed to.

"You have thirty minutes to return with the cash. I trust that will be sufficient time, yes?"

"Sure, sure," Johnson said, rubbing his hand.

"And Mr. U.S. Johnson, the next time a payment is late, I will not be such a kindhearted man. Do you understand? I will answer for you. Yes, I know you do. Perhaps Mr. Dunham can serve us a refreshing beverage while you go about your errand."

THIRTY-ONE

EMMY Brownell and Johnny Roe were getting to know one another. They took the picnic lunch that Emmy had prepared to a large park down by the river and on a weekday afternoon, Buster had the run of the place. After lunch, Buster headed to a large clump of trees at the far end of the park, and Emmy suggested they go exploring.

"Didn't think Iowa had so many trees," Johnny commented. "This is what a California boy might call a forest."

"We're much more than cornfields and flatlands. That's what everybody thinks when they think of Iowa. If trees can get water, they'll grow. All these puppies are getting their drink of water from that river in the park. This forest goes back in here for miles."

They meandered through a large grove of black willow trees, and Emmy pointed out various species of eastern cottonwoods and silver maples. A warm breeze rattled the leaves, sounding like paper being crumpled by hand. They crossed a groomed trail large enough for a car to travel on and headed deeper into the woods. Buster kept close, looking back every so often to get a glimpse of Johnny, then bounding away.

"You and Doc seem to be getting along just fine these days," Emmy said as they walked along.

"He's got a lot of spirit, and I love the way he thinks. We seem to be able to talk about just about anything. He's a really good listener."

"Yeah, what do you two talk about?"

"Mostly women and beer. Sometimes business," Johnny said with a smile.

"What, no sports?"

"Oh, yeah, sports. I forgot."

Emmy paused, her eyebrows raised, waiting for Johnny to elaborate.

"Uh, I played volleyball in college."

"Uh huh."

"And I own a business."

Emmy nodded. "Go on."

"And we both like women."

"Good to know. You are from California and everything."

Now it was Johnny's turn to smile.

As they ambled through the woods, Johnny began to tell her his suspicions about his bike accident. Emmy didn't interrupt as he told her what he and Doc had talked long into the night about, their ideas to find venture money and a possible way to lure another company into the plant. Johnny was on a roll, almost like he was back at work, thinking out loud about how to win a new client. The ideas flowed, his enthusiasm grew, he was in his element.

While walking up a short hill, Buster caught a glimpse of a rabbit and took off after it.

"Buster, come back!" Johnny shouted, but the dog sprinted over the hill.

"He'll be fine. What trouble could he get in out here?" Emmy reassured him. They both picked up their pace.

From the same direction in which Buster had run, a rifle shot rang out in the distance, blasting away the tranquility of the woods. They both stopped and hunched down.

"I'm going to find Buster," Emmy said as she began to run up the hill. Johnny followed as quickly as he could in his hobbled condition.

Emmy reached the top of the hill and searched both right and left for the golden retriever. No sign of him. She continued down the slope and caught sight of him, lying flat on his side.

"Over here," she yelled to Johnny as she ran to the dog.

"Oh, God, no." She sobbed as she saw that half of Buster's shoulder had been blown off by the rifle shot. The dog was shivering and whimpering in a soft, pathetic voice, almost like a child, trying to lift its head.

Johnny stopped short of the scene, a few paces away from Buster, frozen, not wanting to look, but needing to. He slumped to his knees and crawled the last few steps to his dog. Emmy tried to stem the flow of blood, but there was too much. She had one hand on his shoulder, but the dog's blood was flowing out of his withers, too.

Johnny took Buster's head in his hands and the dog, fighting for life, tried to focus on Johnny.

"Oh, pup, no," Johnny managed to whisper softly in his ear. Tears were running down Emmy's face as she methodically tried to stop the inevitable. She took the bandanna from around Buster's neck and was using it to try and stem the bleeding, but she knew it was useless.

Johnny put his face up close to Buster's, and the dog tried to lick him. But his tongue just came out and fell to one side of his mouth. Then he died.

Johnny hugged him. And he cried.

The faint sound of an engine and tires struggling for traction on a dirt road brought Johnny's head up.

He looked around, down the dirt access road, and saw just a tiny bit of dust that had been kicked up floating in the air.

"What the..." he managed to groan, his anguish gripping him, his face contorted with a combination of sadness and a loss of hope.

"The bullet," Emmy said, "I think it entered here and exited out here." She was in nurse mode, but the tears were still streaming down her face.

"Those bastards!" Johnny said through clenched teeth, gently putting Buster's head down. He stood up and started toward the puff of dust.

"No, Johnny!" Emmy yelled. She grabbed his arm, spun him around, and hugged him tightly. "They have a rifle. Stay here. Buster would want you to. I want you to."

Johnny hugged her back. In his stiffened condition after the bike crash, he knew chasing would be useless.

After several moments, they broke the embrace. Johnny could barely look at Buster.

"Now what?" he managed to choke out.

"We'll take him to my house. We can bury him in the backyard."

Johnny nodded but wasn't sure. He thought about his dog buried in the ground. In Iowa.

"No," Johnny said, gaining a little foothold on his emotions, "he needs something different. Maybe spread his ashes...over the back roads…the country roads…the highways…someplace."

"We'll figure it out," Emmy said. "Who would do such a thing?"

Johnny gritted his teeth.

"Do you think it was an accident? Maybe they were aiming at the rabbit?" she asked.

He shook his head no.

"They were aiming at Buster?"

He nodded. In his mind's eye, he saw the image of a brown truck with white letters on the tailgate.

"I'll get them for this, pup. I'll get them," he said, staring toward nowhere, the darkness returning.

THIRTY-TWO

"I need a Louisville slugger," Johnny said to the man behind the counter at a small sporting goods store called the Booneville Sports Hut.

"Well, you came to the right place," the man responded. "Got a son playing the game?"

"Nope, thinking of doing a little slugging of my own."

"Ooo-kay. Let's head over to the rack. What kind of stick you have in mind?"

"Something with a lot of power. Know what I mean?"

"Well, kind of. But you get something too big and powerful, you can't get around on the speedball."

"Yeah, well, the guys I think I'm going to face, I don't think they're so fast."

"Ah, junk ball artists, eh?"

"Real junk."

"Then I'd go with something like this," the man said, handing Johnny a 36-ounce, 33-inch length model baseball bat called the Babe Ruth special. "You know Bonds always used those little black bats, toothpicks I called 'em, tiny, only about a 31. He used to just whip them around, connect, and crush 'em. Course he was juiced so if he got all of it, it went."

Johnny hefted the bat and took a few abbreviated swings.

"Feels good, huh? Looks like you might not have the arm strength that Barry did, so maybe you want a little more heft in the club, right?"

"Sounds about right, I'd say."

"You get the right leverage behind that, turn your shoulders, pull your hips through, you might not need to make solid contact and you're still going to send it a long way. How's the grip feel? Not too fat in your hands?"

"Nope, feels solid."

"Like you got control?"

"Full control."

"Yep, that one there will do some real damage, you get a hold of one."

"Be able to crush it, huh?" Johnny said, almost to himself.

"Smash it."

"Perfect."

"Outta here."

"Before I'm outta here, I need a hat. You got a local baseball team, so I can fit in with the local crowd?"

"Sure Des Moines has a minor league club, part of the Cubs organization. And the university over in Ames is pretty big around here, too."

"What's the university nickname?"

"Cyclones."

"Yeah, I'm all over that. I'll take one."

As Johnny left the Booneville Sports Hut, he thought to himself, now all I have to do is find that brown truck with the white letters and the two yahoos inside of it.

And if the Louisville slugger wasn't enough, he still had the Shield revolver in the cleanup position, stashed in the glove compartment of the Jeep.

THIRTY-THREE

EMMY smoothed the wrinkles out of the drop cloth that covered the hardwood floor in her spare bedroom. She moved the easel away from the direct sunlight that poked through the side window. After a quick search, she found the Beethoven channel on her phone app and turned down the volume to the Bluetooth speaker. The first symphony, starting slow and melodic, provided the exact mood music she enjoyed as she prepared the paint palette.

Emmy gazed at the beginnings of a painting that was weeks away from completion. She closed her eyes and looked for the finished image that she wanted to paint. She opened them again, looked at the painting, and tried to see herself filling in brushstrokes.

Closed, envision. Open again. Close. Open. She continued the routine that she'd found helped settle her into a painting session. To see the finished painting in some far off distance and to look for the next brushstrokes that would help her get there.

Then she concentrated on her breathing, deeply drawing in, smelling the aroma of the oil paints, and trying to capture a scent of what the scene she was painting might smell like.

She'd chosen a perspective of a country setting with a narrow dirt road that meandered off into the horizon. The fading sunlight sprinkled the road in dashes of color and bounced rays off and through the tree-lined lane. A single figure, mid-stride about halfway down the road, became her focal point this morning. She decided to make the figure a woman and wondered what type of dress she'd paint on her.

Emmy knew that no matter how hard she tried to make the scene stand out, her audience would be drawn to this woman. However much she wanted the natural features—the road, the trees, the cascading sunlight, the wildflowers, the sky—to stand on its own, to offer a serenity to the viewer, she knew all eyes would return to the woman.

But now the painting showed only outlines of that setting. She'd sketched in a large tree on the right and decided that an autumn timeframe would help her experiment with falling leaves and sunlight, dancing together, offering her options for color and the reflection of light that Mother Nature hadn't necessarily predicted.

She dabbled a darker brown onto the brush and laid down a base layer for the tree that she could lighten up in the coats to come. Emmy had to consciously slow her brushstrokes down as the strings in the symphony peaked to a crescendo.

But she stopped and gazed again at the spot, now just a few faint pencil lines, that would become the woman walking down the road.

Maybe put the woman in a dress, nothing too frilly, but still a dress. Maybe just above the knees to show off strong, muscled legs. Not like a weightlifter, more like an athlete, maybe a runner. And she could put a pair of worn cowboy boots on the woman. To add a bit of rugged. Not stylish new boots that some women wear as a part of a western ensemble. A sunbonnet would cover the woman's face almost completely even though she was walking away from view. Maybe one of those girly straw cowboy hats that are so popular now.

No, too much. Hard to make that look girly. Let's stick with the sunbonnet.

Emmy saw the woman strolling, taking her time. Definitely not a powerwalk. She tried to see if there was another living thing—like an animal or a friend—with the woman, but she kept coming back to the solitary figure. How could she make the posture of the woman depict what she envisioned?

What *did* she envision? To really get the woman right—to set the entire mood of the scene—she'd have to make up a story in her head about that woman's life. Where did she read that, that technique? Some famous painter had used that, or was it all famous painters? Can't stop and figure that out now. Back to the woman.

Emmy backed away four steps from the canvas for another perspective. She squinted her eyes almost closed. Then she backpedaled four more steps. She opened her eyes wide and without blinking zoned out a bit, letting the picture fade into the space in the room.

Now she approached the canvas slowly, getting right up close, closer, closer. The painting enveloped her. Her peripheral vision saw nothing else.

Back to the woman.

Was she confident? Just out for a Sunday stroll to take in the fading summer sunshine. Or was she a bit forlorn? Like she was walking aimlessly to try and figure out this problem in her life.

Maybe her best friend…her dog…had just died and she was…no, no, that was Johnny, not this woman.

Maybe her boyfriend had just broken off an engagement…no, no, c'mon, back to the woman.

Emmy decided to make her…just alone. Out on the dirt road, looking at the autumn leaves falling, contemplating another season come and gone. Wondering what the next season would bring. But with a bit of a darker mood than somebody anticipating springtime after a long, hard slosh through winter. Maybe looking without much enthusiasm at a bleak wintertime in the making when the last leaf settled. So her head would be slanted down, looking at the blanket of leafy color, not up, at the sunshine. Luckily, she didn't have to draw her face. Emmy couldn't figure out how she would have ever done that.

She went back to the dark brown color for the tree and added in just a little more black.

Thirty minutes later the doorbell rang.

"How'd it go? You were gone a long time," Emmy asked Johnny as he entered her front door.

He nodded but couldn't quite find the words to express himself. And he didn't want to start crying. Again. He'd cried enough for a while. He inhaled a deep breath and let it out slowly.

"You want to talk about it?" she said, barely audible, almost a whisper. She wasn't sure she wanted to talk about spreading Buster's ashes.

"I just drove around out in the country till I got lost. It musta been for hours," Johnny started as he looked at his watch. His eyes started to tear, and he filled his lungs again, looked away, and tried to compose himself.

"Then I saw this peaceful old shade tree on top of a small hill off some back road somewhere. I don't even think I could find it again if I tried.

"I suppose subconsciously, I don't want to find it again. I decided I wasn't going to scatter his ashes, cause…that seemed…just too…, I don't know, carefree, at the moment. So I dug a grave under that old tree, covered that urn up good, packed that soil down, said my goodbyes."

Emmy came to him and hugged him. He didn't return the gesture, so she pulled away.

"I don't know what to say," she mumbled. "I'm so sorry."

"I thought I couldn't cry much anymore. I mean I haven't cried since about halfway between here and the West Coast. I just thought, you know, that after so much emotion coming out of me, that there wasn't too much left. But I was wrong. I cried on that hill like everything that happened over the past few months…to my wife and kids…like it happened yesterday. God, it hurt all over again."

"It's good to express our emotions; I mean medically, it's good for us."

"I'm not so sure. I'm tired of it. I'm tired of all of it. I've had enough."

"If we don't let our emotions out, they kind of just fester inside of us. They eventually come out as anger, or something worse."

"Yeah, I know all that. At least in theory, I guess it makes sense. But in reality, I don't know. I sure don't feel any better right now."

Johnny paced Emmy's living room, back and forth, as Emmy stood in the middle of the room and traced his movements with her eyes.

Trying to distract himself, Johnny looked at the artwork in the room, mostly impressionistic, but some that looked very real.

"Nice paintings. I really like this one," he said pointing to a landscape.

"Thanks. I did that a long time ago."

He frowned, looking closely at the painting.

"Wait, what?" he said, staring at the bottom right, seeing the stylized *EBrownell.* "You painted this?"

She nodded, twirling her right finger all around the room.

"All of them? You painted all of these?"

She nodded again, and looked down, a little red rising to her cheeks.

Johnny walked slowly from painting to painting, studying each carefully, lost in the introspection.

After several minutes, he stopped and looked back at Emmy, who hadn't moved. "They're beautiful. You're very talented."

She smiled and shrugged one shoulder.

"No, really, you are. I'm not kidding. I know a little about this stuff. Do you sell a lot of these?"

"Not really. I've given some away, and I tried a booth at the craft fair one year. But mostly I just paint cause it…relaxes me, I guess."

Johnny stood in front of one painting, an old, dilapidated barn he thought he recognized. He studied the way the colors overlapped and as he took a step back how they changed almost right before his eyes. One step closer to study the brushstrokes, one step back to see their power.

"Amazing," he said, in a whisper.

"Sometimes when I've had a really hectic day at the hospital, like one crisis after another, I come home and just paint. I used to spend a lot of evenings with my parents, but when they moved to Florida…," her voice trailed off.

After a couple of seconds, she continued, "And then I broke the engagement off with…oh, never mind. It doesn't matter now. Anyway," her hand was now moving like a painter's, making imaginary brushstrokes in the air. "I find it soothing. I can get a little lost in each painting like I'm in another world. I don't mind feeling alone that way." Johnny noticed she looked down at her feet and she grimaced slightly.

The two stood on opposite sides of the room, Johnny moving from picture to picture, Emmy frozen in place.

Finally, Johnny broke the silence, in a voice barely recognizable to himself, "I feel so all alone. All the time."

"I know," Emmy said.

"I've lost my wife, my kids, my business, my purpose…even my dog."

"You must have lots of friends, probably all over the country, and family, too, right?'

"Doesn't seem like it."

"You have friends in this town, you know."

"Yeah, who besides you and Doc?"

"Sometimes two's enough. At least it's a good start."

"A good start to what?"

"Well, starting over, I guess."

"What do you mean, starting over?"

"I don't know, I'm just…saying. If you have to start over, Booneville isn't such a bad place."

"Emmy, I've only known you for a few weeks. It's not like I can start something here with you…"

"No, no, no, no…I'm not saying anything like that! Really, I'm not! C'mon. I'm just saying that you've made a connection here in this town. Something's happening. I don't know just what, but I can tell that you're…connected, that's the best word I can think of…you're doing something here that makes sense. At least that's what Doc says."

Johnny nodded, knowingly. "Well, I didn't mean that it could never happen, you know."

"What…could never happen?" Emmy asked.

"Something. I don't know. Just something."

"Something with Booneville?"

Johnny shrugged.

"Or something with…me?"

Johnny looked up and found her eyes but was too afraid to answer.

"Something, though. Imagine that."

THIRTY-FOUR

FOR the next week, after dinner, Johnny borrowed Doc's Volvo and meandered through Booneville looking for the brown truck. Johnny suspected that his Jeep may be closely associated with him now and he wanted to be more inconspicuous. He had a map of the city, and each night he circled several blocks, starting in the center of town near City Hall and worked his way out clockwise.

He would stop in small shopping centers, park the car for thirty minutes or so and watch traffic. He drove by the bowling alley, Lucky Strikes, and made sure to check down back alleys and small apartment complexes. Booneville was a typical mid-Western town that had seen its city center deteriorate in the past several decades and expand outward like spokes from a wagon wheel. One spoke led out to the interstate, another to a manufacturing plant to the west, several more along country roads that now saw development happen in the form of new homes, a few townhouses, and small businesses.

He didn't exactly know what he was going to do if he found the truck. Maybe see who was driving it. Follow it to see where the owner lived. Confront the driver. Take the baseball bat that he'd bought at the local sporting goods store and beat the crap out of the truck or whoever drove it. Whatever happened, at least he was prepared. The Shield was tucked into his jacket pocket, and his new Louisville slugger was lying in the back seat.

As he drove, Johnny kept the radio off because he wanted to think. He kept reviewing in his mind the incredible amount of change in his life over the past five months. Sometimes it overwhelmed him, the sheer pace of change. It seemed he barely was able to take a deep breath to gain some clarity about one change before another hit him like an unsuspected tsunami. First the accident, then the funeral. Followed by abandoning his business and wandering through the country. Then the bike accident, the betrayal of his wife. Then Buster. And somewhere in all that, Emmy Brownell kept sneaking into the narrative.

For one of the first times in his life that he could remember, he wasn't able to compartmentalize what was happening. He'd always been able to separate work from home, love for his wife from love for his kids, fun time from work time. Now all elements of his life blurred together. He noticed sitting in the car that he couldn't see a path forward. He couldn't think about next month or next year.

He tried to focus on what was right in front of him. He touched the gun and felt its cold metal. He looked at the baseball bat and saw the etched trademark and the script signature. He ran his hands over the worn cloth interior just to feel the texture. He sniffed to see if he could catch a whiff of Doc somewhere inside the car.

Focus now, focus here. Let the future take care of itself. But his mind kept drifting to the past.

On this Thursday night as Johnny rehashed Sam's incredibly intricate scheme to leave him, he pulled into the parking lot of a bar named Smokey's. About fifteen cars were parked haphazardly in the half-full lot. A neon sign with the bar name in red script hung high on the concrete block building. Several neon beer signs lit up the windows but other than that, not much decorated the outside. This was a drinking bar, Johnny figured.

He looked at his phone; it was 10:17 p.m. He parked at the back of the lot and waited. More vehicles pulled into the over the next ten minutes, so he assumed the crowd was still building. Maybe Thursday night in Booneville was party night for the locals.

Then he noticed a brown truck pull in. He only could see the front of the truck, not the tailgate, as it parked facing him. Two men jumped out of the truck. Both wore jeans, short sleeve shirts, and baseball caps. They laughed as they walked into Smokey's.

Johnny pulled his hat down low on his forehead, got out of the Volvo and walked toward the back of the truck.

FORD, in white letters on the tailgate. He'd found it.

Johnny knelt down beside the truck and unscrewed the cap on the air valve on the left front tire. He took a coin from his pocket, applied pressure to the valve and let all the air out of the tire. He would need some time once the two men returned to the truck to get a good look at them and maybe even engage them in conversation.

He slipped back into the Volvo to wait.

At 11:50, the two men walked out of Smokey's. One man had his arm around the other's neck and playfully mimicked like he was punching him in the stomach. Then they broke the embrace and shadowboxed each other. Johnny noticed that they easily lost their balance when they tried to move their feet quickly. Good, he thought, they're drunk.

They slid into the truck, started it up and slowly began to leave the parking lot. Johnny hoped they weren't too drunk to notice the flat tire. At the edge of the lot, the truck stopped, and the driver got out. He circled the truck until he finally saw the tire. He shook his head. The passenger exchanged some words with the driver and then began to laugh. The driver flipped him off.

Johnny exited the Volvo and grabbed the Louisville slugger, clutching it closely alongside his right leg. The Shield was in his left jacket pocket. He slowly approached the truck. Johnny had pulled his hat down tight over his eyes and had slipped on sunglasses. Luckily, a nearby streetlight illuminated the parking lot so he could see where he was going. He walked right up to the driver as the passenger was getting out of the truck to help fix the flat. Neither expected trouble. Johnny did.

"What you lookin' at, boy?" the driver asked Johnny.

"Got a flat, huh? Too bad," Johnny replied.

"Brilliant, Sherlock, want to help us fix it?"

"Nope. Especially considering I'm the one who gave it to you."

"Huh?"

"Let me ask you something," Johnny said, not giving the driver time to think too much about the last confession. "You boys like bicycles?"

"Bicycles? Nope, we like trucks."

"How about dogs? You like dogs?"

"What? What're you talking about?" the passenger said.

"You know, dogs, puppies, man's best friend. You like dogs?"

"Man's best friend is beer," the driver said with a crooked smile, "Don't like cats, don't like dogs."

"So then you probably don't like golden retrievers either, right?"

The passenger's look changed, his mouth falling open. He looked more closely at Johnny, squinting like he was trying to figure out in his alcohol-fogged brain where he'd seen him before.

At the same time, the driver recognized Johnny. He began to sneer and nod his head slowly.

"Don't like them golden retrievers one bit," he said. "He went down like a rock, didn't he? You both were pretty easy targets."

He smirked at Johnny. But he didn't notice the Louisville slugger.

"That was the hanging breaking ball I was looking for," Johnny said as the driver got a confused look on his face.

Johnny went down in a semi-crouch, gripping the bat with two hands and turned quickly in a circle and with power, 180 degrees to his left. Building bat speed every inch of the way, he cocked his shoulders and pulled his hips through. Before the driver knew what hit him, Johnny leveled the ash bat with a powerful force into his right kneecap. It sounded like the last blow of a hammer driving a nail into wood. An otherworldly scream gushed out of the driver as he fell to the ground, landing face-first on the asphalt and chipping off both front teeth. The passenger, blankly staring as his fallen partner hit the pavement, reacted slowly.

But Johnny didn't. Wasting no time or sympathy, he immediately whirled the bat back to his right, and fueled by anger and adrenalin, he spun 360 degrees and aimed the Louisville slugger at the head of his second target. The passenger got his right hand up in front of his face just before the bat arrived. That probably saved his life. The impact broke four bones in his hand and left a bump the size of a tennis ball in the middle of his forehead, and he collapsed beside the truck.

By now, the driver had vomited, his cursing and screaming bombing the parking lot. Johnny knew he had to leave, but the darkness in him lingered. He would have liked a couple of more swings. He walked quickly back to the Volvo, threw the bat into the backseat and exited at the opposite entrance to the lot. As he left, several bar patrons had reacted to the screams and were walking toward the Ford truck. None noticed the Volvo.

"Two for two, Buster. Two hard smashes, solid contact. Crushed 'em both," Johnny said.

THIRTY-FIVE

JOE Dunham burst into the office of U. S. Johnson and was about to say something when Johnson waved his arm, motioning that he was on the phone. After several minutes of a one-sided conversation with U. S. doing most of the talking, he slammed down the receiver.

"That Strasbaugh is one pain in the ass," Johnson said. "If I knew another lawyer that I could trust, I'd fire his ass today."

"We got bigger problems," Dunham said.

"Yeah, that's what you say. I say that butthole is asking a lot of questions about money and employee stock options and when his shares will be vested. Pissing me off. How much of this company does he own anyway? Like a half percent?"

"Exactly a half percent."

"He's getting mighty uppity for a half percent. Just cause he's a lawyer."

"Like I said, we got bigger problems," Dunham repeated.

"Like what?"

"The Bettcher boys were admitted into the hospital last night. Pretty beat up."

"Drunk again I suppose. Got in a fight, did they? What does that have to do with us?"

"Maybe payback."

"Payback? From who? From No-W? Give me a break. Little advertising wussy doesn't have it in him."

"That's what you say."

"Have you talked to them yet?"

"No. Jim is still in surgery, and Earl got his clock cleaned, and he's still out of it. I plan to head over there this afternoon when I can get some time alone with them after their wives leave."

"Those two are married? Must be desperate women."

"If it was Roe, then he's on to us," Dunham said.

"Not unless they talk, he's not on to us. He may be on to them, but he can't tie them to us. Just stay away for a day or two."

"You trust them that long to keep their mouths shut?"

"I don't trust them any farther than I could throw them. But if Roe has any inkling that we're involved, you showing up at the hospital will cinch it for him. Just stay away. Call them if you want to talk with them?"

"The cops are going to start asking questions, you know."

"Yeah, well, those boys say anything and they cook their own goose. After all, they were the ones that ran No-W off the road and killed his dog, we didn't do it. They'll keep quiet. They're not geniuses, but they're not complete idiots either."

"Just the same, I want to know if it's Roe."

"So what if it is?"

"He'll be trouble. He already is trouble," Dunham responded.

"What are you so worried about? We got Eddie Walnuts climbing up our butts and now Strasbaugh asking all sorts of questions. What we need to do is keep our eye on the ball. We get the money. We close the plant. We get out of Dodge. Forget No-W! Forget him!"

"Just so you get the money. Then I'll forget him."

"I'll get the money."

Dunham wanted to say, "That's what you say," but he kept it to himself.

THIRTY-SIX

EMMY Brownell stopped outside Room 117 of Parkside Hospital and began replacing the paper nametag in the slot beside the room number. Patients' names that occupied the rooms were printed on small sheets of paper, presumably, Emmy thought, so visitors—and doctors and nurses—could easily find the patient. The idea probably came from that efficiency expert the hospital had hired last year. Emmy thought the hospital should have increased salaries for nurses or hired more nurses so that the hospital's service would be better, but that wasn't how efficiency experts thought. They always wanted to cut big expenses and instill little extras to give the impression service was better.

The nametag read: JIM BETTCHER and EARL BETTCHER. Back again, huh boys, she thought.

As she was pushing open the door to the room, she overheard Earl Bettcher loudly say, "It was that same son of a trucker on the bicycle! I know it was him!"

When Jim Bettcher saw Emmy enter the room, he shook his head vigorously and motioned with his hand to silence his brother. Emmy pretended she didn't hear but the bicycle commented registered with her.

"Well, gentlemen, what are we in for this time?" she said with a smile on her face as she headed for the chart at the end of the first bed as Earl hung up the phone.

Jim's leg was in traction, pointing upward at a 45-degree angle.

"It's my leg, Sherlock Holmes," he said to her in a deadpan tone.

"Well, yes, I can see that now that you mention it," Emmy said as she read the chart. "How's it feel?"

"Like it was blown apart."

As she looked at Earl, she grabbed his chart.

"That's a pretty nasty looking bruise you have going there, Earl.

How's your head feel?"

"Horrible," Earl said.

"How long's it been, Emily?" Jim asked.

"Since your last medication, let me see here…?

"No, no, I meant the last time we seen you?"

"In the hospital? Let's see, I guess it was…what, all those stitches in your hand? Last summer?"

"Naw, I think it was the tetanus shot when I stepped on that nail."

"I suppose you're right, Jim. You both visit us so often here at Parkside, all the visits tend to run together."

"I know what you mean, girl," he said.

"So, I don't mean to pry," Emmy said, "but what happened to you boys?

"Accident," replied Jim, quickly so Earl wouldn't say anything.

"Accident?"

"Yeah, I tripped comin' out of the bar and fell on my knee. Earl here tried to save me and cracked his head on the…uh, truck."

"On the truck?"

"Yep. Kinda caught the mirror direct on his forehead."

"Helping you?"

"Yep. We kinda both lost our balance."

"I'd say."

"Yep. It was bad," Jim said.

"Still is bad," Earl interjected.

"Anybody else around? That may have…helped you…or seen anything of what happened? You know, it might help with the diagnosis," Emmy probed. She wanted to hear more about the bicycle man.

"Nope," Jim replied. "Nobody there but us two."

Earl nodded his head in agreement but abruptly stopped when the pain erupted. He held his head perfectly still.

"When do you think we'll be getting out of here?" Earl asked, not moving.

"Well, that's up to the doctor, but from the looks of you two," Emmy said, "it'll be a few days. For you, Jim, maybe a little longer. I haven't see the X-rays, but from what the chart says, that kneecap…that you fell on…will take a while to heal."

"Yep. It was a bad fall."

"Real bad," Earl chimed in.

"Say, how's the food around here?" Earl asked.

"Not bad," Emmy said. "Maybe even pretty good."

"I can handle pretty good," Earl said.

"Hey, Emily," Jim interrupted, "I'm pretty rank. You still give those sponge baths in here?"

"Nope. We had an efficiency expert tell us we had to discontinue those."

"Why's that?"

"Uh, something about misspent use of staff time…something like that," Emmy answered.

"That's too bad," Jim smiled at her, through his chipped two front teeth.

"Yeah, real bad," Earl said, holding two fingers to his nose, but not moving his head in the slightest.

THIRTY-SEVEN

"I told you never to call me, Mr. Johnson," Cheng said as he answered the phone.

"Yah, I know, and I'm sorry about that, but I haven't heard from you in a very long time," U.S. Johnson answered, trying to sound humble.

"What you want, Mr. Johnson, I very busy."

"Well, I just wanted to know when the next payment should be expected. Seeing as you are a little late, I mean not like it's a big deal or anything. I was just wondering."

There was a long silence and no response from Cheng.

"There will be no more payments," he finally said in a monotone.

"What?! What are you talking about?! That wasn't the deal," exclaimed Johnson. "You've only got the mechanical drawings."

"Now, there is a new deal," Cheng replied.

"What do you mean, new deal?"

"The new deal is that there is no longer a deal."

"What are you talking about? A deal is a deal."

"No, no longer."

"What about the software? You don't have the software and you can't run all those robots without software."

Johnson heard Cheng breathe deeply over the line.

"I have had twenty of my fellow countrymen working for months to develop the software. I would estimate that now my software is far superior to the software you have to sell me."

"No way is it better! The deal was that you wanted the whole thing. Drawings, mechanicals, bill of materials, software. It's a bundled package. You can't make it work without the software."

"I believe you are mistaken. I believe we will make it work and make it work even better than you have made it work," Mr. Cheng replied in a rather snooty tone it seemed to Ulysses Johnson, who at this point in the conversation was beginning to lose what little cool he had left.

"That's…that's…horse droppings, Mr. Cheng. We had a deal. And in this country, a deal is a deal."

"I not in that country."

"What does that mean?!"

"You smart man, Mr. Johnson, you figure it out."

"What I figure, Mr. Cheng, is that you are trying to cheat me. That's what I figure!"

"You figure correctly."

"So we…we…we won't close the plant on September first! So…there!"

"At this point, we do not really care. We have what we want," Cheng said.

"What?! What?!"

"You smart man, Mr. Johnson, you figure it out."

"I'll sue your ass, Mr. Cheng! Take me for my word, I will sue your sorry ass, sure as my name is U. S. Johnson!"

"Yes, you do that. You find lawyer that will take this case. I sure there are plenty of lawyers in your country looking for work. You have a whole country full of lawyers, don't you? And then you tell them what the deal was. Then you tell them we are a respected Chinese manufacturing firm and that they will have to deal with the Chinese government first. Then you prepare yourself for the amount of money the lawyer will need just to begin case. I believe in your country you call that retainer. Do you have that kind of money, Mr. Johnson?"

U.S. Johnson was gripping the phone hard and grinding his teeth. Snooty freaking Chinaman.

"Well, do you, Mr. Johnson?" Cheng repeated, allowing the words to penetrate.

"Screw you," was all Johnson could say through clenched teeth.

"No, I believe it has been you, Mr. Johnson, who has been screwed. Royally, as I believe they say in your country," Cheng commented as he began a slow, mechanical laugh.

Then he hung up. Johnson threw the mobile phone across the room, and it shattered against the wall.

THIRTY-EIGHT

EMMY and Johnny sat on Doc's porch enjoying a beer as the late summer sun began to set. The evening was warm but not humid, a relief to Johnny who, over the past week, always felt like he needed another shower. No wonder so many people lived in California—no humidity.

"We've had a couple of interesting patients at the hospital this week," Emmy said as she looked down the street in front of the house, making sure not to make eye contact with Johnny.

"Do tell."

"The Bettcher brothers. Know them?"

"Don't think so, no. What happened to them?"

"Not quite sure, but it looks like they ran into a real buzz saw."

"You mean like a real saw or some whirling dervish?"

"Nooo, not a real saw. But I'm not sure what a whirling dervish really is."

"It's a buzz saw! Without the saw part."

"Great, that clears that up," Emmy said after a short giggle. "Anyway, it looks like they were beat up, but nobody can find out anything about it."

"Uh huh."

"So, you didn't hear anything about it?"

"Don't really read the papers around here."

"Well, I just thought you might know something, that's all."

Johnny leaned in close to Emmy and looked her directly in the eye. "Why do you think I might know something about it?"

She held his gaze and almost forgot the question.

"Uh, they mentioned a 'bicycle man' when they thought I wasn't listening."

"And…."

"And...that this bicycle man might have something to do with how badly they were...buzz sawed."

"And..."

"And...you ride a bicycle. Used to. Before you got hurt."

Johnny rose from the rocking chair, stretched his back and his neck, and walked to the end of the porch and back. He looked at Emmy, deciding how much to tell.

"You don't have to tell me anything if you don't want to," she said as if reading his mind.

How does she do that, he wondered? He took in a deep breath and let it out slowly.

"Or you can tell me because you want to tell me, or you need to tell somebody. And we'll keep it our little secret."

"Like doctor-patient confidentiality?" Johnny said.

"Something like that. Or just man-woman...secret telling."

Johnny smiled at her comment. "You don't know much about me, Emmy. I'm not sure how much you want to know. Or how much you should know."

"You told me about your wife and kids."

"Yeah."

"So what could be more personal than that?"

"A few things."

"Like I said, it's up to you."

"Not sure I want to incriminate myself."

"You don't trust me," Emmy said, looking hurt, her eyes getting wide.

"I don't know you that well."

"I made you a bath. And shampooed your hair. That should count for something."

Johnny had to smile. Then he turned serious. "They were the two that killed Buster."

"What! How do you know?"

"Okay, now you have to trust me, I know. Positive."

"Then they deserved what they got."

"There's more. They were the same ones that ran me off the road when I was on the bike."

"You didn't tell me you were run off the road. You said something about running off the road by yourself."

"I said there were a few more things you didn't know."

"What happened?"

Johnny told her the whole story of the encounter out on the country road and the brown Ford truck. After, her mouth tensed up, and her hands were balled into fists.

"Then you should have taken a baseball bat to those bastards!"

Johnny smiled and nodded his head.

Emmy's eyes grew wide, "A baseball bat? Really? No, you didn't!"

"I did."

"Good for you! Well…except for the fact that you almost killed them." She made a face with a big grimace like she'd tasted something bad.

"Got what they deserved."

"An eye for an eye, huh?" Emmy asked.

"Don't judge me. I did what I had to do."

"I'm not judging you. Well, I guess I am. I'm just saying there may have been a better way."

"Like what?'

"Like, I don't know. But I'm pretty sure taking a baseball bat to somebody is assault with a deadly weapon."

Johnny looked at her like he didn't know her.

"It's just that it's a small town, Johnny. There are no secrets in Booneville. At least not for long."

"Now I'm not sure I should have told you."

She came next to him and touched his arm. He almost pulled it away. Almost.

Finally, he said, "I know it was a horrible thing to do, Emmy. Looking back, I hardly recognized myself. Did I really do that? But I couldn't help myself. When I saw them and…thought about Buster…it just brought out something in me that I couldn't control. Or maybe deep down, I didn't want to."

"Like I said, it's our secret. I won't tell a soul. But now what? Do they come after you with a baseball bat? Or something bigger?"

"I gotta find out why they're after me. Doc and I have a theory."

"And…?"
"And…do you want to hear it?"
"Yes, but I may need another beer."
"Or two. It's a pretty wild theory."

THIRTY-NINE

NORM Boswell methodically filled three coffee mugs from the pot on his kitchen counter. One mug said *Thank you from United Way: it brings out the best in all of us.* He set two of them in front of Doc and Johnny, who both had settled at the small Formica topped table in Boswell's kitchen.

"Norm, how long have you been head of operations at the plant?" Doc asked. He knew the answer, but it was a way to get the conversation rolling. He and Johnny had asked to talk privately with Boswell, but they really didn't know where they were headed. More like a fishing expedition.

"Almost seventeen years. It's a good job. I like it, and I'm pretty good at it," Boswell answered.

"You pretty much know everything that goes on out there, right?"

"Well, I wouldn't say that. Ulysses is still the boss. I'm sure there are things he does that I don't know about, especially on the financial side of things. But if it happens in the plant, I probably know about it."

"You get along okay with the boss?" Johnny asked.

"Yeah, fine, he's a hard man to get to know, that's for sure. Tell me, gentlemen, what's this all about? You said on the phone you had some suspicions. About what?"

"About what's been going on at the plant. About things that maybe you don't know about, but should," Doc said.

"Like what?"

"We haven't nailed it down yet, and it's mostly just a theory. But we think that there's more going on out there than just what they're telling everybody, that business is really bad," Johnny explained.

"You ready to share that theory? Is that why you wanted to talk with me?" Boswell asked.

Johnny looked at Doc. They didn't have a game plan for this talk.

Johnny was looking for assurances that Boswell was on their side. Doc nodded.

Johnny got up from the table and poured himself more coffee.

"Sure," he finally said as he leaned against the countertop.

"We think that the business isn't just dying. We think somebody's killing it. On purpose," Doc said.

"Why would somebody want to do that?"

"We have no idea."

"Got any ideas who is killing it?"

"A few suspicions only."

"Ulysses?"

"Maybe."

"Dunham."

"He's probably involved."

"What do you want from me?"

"I know a few operations guys," Johnny began, "and they're all really good detectives. It's their job to figure out what's going on with whatever they're managing. A lot of times, they have to dig to find the root cause of a problem. Are you a good detective?"

"Never thought of it that way, but I suppose I am, sure."

"Then get your magnifying glass out and start snooping around."

"What am I looking for?"

"Something that doesn't make sense. Something out of the ordinary. Something you have never seen before. Actually, I have no idea, I'm just guessing."

"Well, if you set those parameters, I can recalculate my perspective," Boswell smiled at both of them.

"We're not saying you should neglect your job. We have no authority out there, you know," Doc Enbright said. "We don't want you to get into any trouble."

"What kind of trouble could I get into?"

"We're just saying, that's all," Johnny said.

"Trouble with Ulysses? I'm always in trouble with Ulysses. Either I'm not doing my job, the employees aren't doing their jobs, or they're not doing them fast enough or efficient enough. I'm always on his hit list. He doesn't scare me. He's mostly bark, not a lot of bite."

"But dogs that get pushed into a corner might bite with a vengeance, especially if they get pushed too far."

"Maybe. I see your point. I'll be careful."

"This is trouble you don't need. I can tell you that," Johnny said.

"Heck, it seems like we're in a lot of trouble right now. And it is my job to investigate trouble in the plant. May even be in my job description."

"Just be careful," Doc said.

"Careful is my middle name, Doc. You should know that by now."

"A lot of things I should know by now. But it seems the older I get, the less I know."

All three contemplated that reality as they sipped their coffee.

FORTY

DOC strummed a pencil on his one knee and bounced his other foot off the ground. Johnny kept cracking his knuckles and stretching out his neck muscles by rotating his head back and forth. They sat in the lobby of Bantz Ritter Dawson, one of the largest venture capital firms in Kansas City. They'd driven the three hours south this morning for the 11 a.m. meeting with Ryan Ritter, one of the partners. After several phone calls and what Johnny might have classified as badgering, Ritter had agreed to give them an hour.

In the week since the appointment had been made, Johnny and Doc had been busy boys. Doc had gathered the needed information, and Johnny was in charge of the Prezi slides and presentation materials.

Johnny had crafted the fifteen slides and focused them on people and capabilities. He'd featured Norm Boswell and two other, long-term plant managers, one in quality control, the other in engineering. And he had printed out bar charts that listed each employee and the length of employment at the facility. The capabilities list was strong on engineering, software, and manufacturing and was a compliment to a twenty-page report that listed each piece of equipment in the plant, with maintenance records and depreciation spreadsheets. He'd also gathered biographies of the top twenty employees; Johnny wrote each and had a color photo embedded in the document, which had been blown up to poster size and mounted on foam boards. On-time delivery, quality control, OSHA audits, and a half dozen other pertinent manufacturing data were also professionally charted, enlarged, and color-coordinated. Every time Doc picked up something from FedEx Office, he was amazed at Johnny's ability to make difficult information easily readable and understandable.

Johnny got about three hours of sleep a night for the past week because he knew he only had one shot with the VC firm and he'd needed to do his homework. He found that advanced manufacturing was the single largest business sector in the state of Iowa at over $27 billion for the last year on record—three times that of farming. He even uncovered a full page ad in a clean energy magazine with the headline: *America is outsourcing its manufacturing to Iowa,* sponsored by the state's economic development department. But he still needed the VC money. All the residents of Booneville, Iowa, combined couldn't come up with enough cash to try to revamp U.S. Johnson Controls into a brand new company. If Johnny could attract enough VC money to transition the plant to another product, the state would kick in enough incentives in tax breaks to get through the first year or two. Maybe the state would even help them refinance the building.

Of course, Johnny didn't own the company or the building. Ulysses Johnson owned both. But nobody at the plant had seen Ulysses for two weeks, and even though Johnny and Doc suspected something had happened, he didn't want to let on to Ritter that the owner was MIA.

Ryan Ritter was about thirty-five years old, Johnny guessed, as he met them in the lobby. He dressed like Don Draper of the TV show *Mad Men.* His hair was tightly cropped at the ears and longish on top, slicked back. He flashed a warm smile, but Johnny sensed it was guarded as they shook hands and he led then to a large conference room. Johnny asked for two minutes to set up his presentation, and Ritter and Doc went to find coffee. When they returned, Johnny had his MacBook laptop connected to the conference room projector, his posters standing at attention around the room, and a small robot stationed on the table. Ritter's eyes betrayed his outward cool. Johnny had seen that look before. Ritter was impressed but didn't want to show it.

"We have a short presentation, Mr. Ritter, fifteen slides," Johnny began. "But as you can see from the documentation I have scattered around, I'll let your interest in whatever you want to talk about dictate the direction we go. But I think you're really going to like this presentation. May I begin?"

"Sure. It's your hour," Ritter said with a faint smile.

Johnny grabbed his iPhone and flipped to a special app. He aimed the phone's camera at the laptop and took a photo. The app sent the photo to the robot, and it reared its artificial-looking hand, more like a mechanical skeleton than an actual hand. The hand moved toward the computer. Ritter leaned in to take a closer look.

The Prezi presentation was in sleep mode and as the robot moved to the computer keyboard, one finger outstretched from the hand and lightly touched the return button. The presentation sprung to life and Ritter actually let out a small laugh.

"How'd you do that?" he asked Johnny.

"We'll get to that. It's called 'vision-guided robotics.' It's one of our specialties."

"Forget the presentation. I want to know how that works."

Johnny had set the hook, fish had bitten, now it was time to begin to slowly reel him in. Johnny had done this a thousand times before. He was the master at setting the stage and leading a prospect to the close.

"It's a little more complicated than this, but here's the gist. In vision-guided robotic applications, a camera is used to locate a part or a destination for the part. Then the coordinates are sent to the robot to perform a function, like picking or placing a part. In manufacturing, the parts don't have to be perfectly staged or stacked; they can just be loaded randomly and the robot finds them, orientates them, and places them. We'd already programmed this robot in a pretty simple task of finding the return key on the laptop and plunking it with one of its fingers."

"So the camera is the key?" Ritter asked.

"It's part of the process. Cameras are amazingly precise and inexpensive now. Every smart phone has a better camera today than you could buy ten years ago. And they're lightning fast. So the camera takes the picture, relays it to the robot, who finds the part from the photo, and you're off and running."

"So basically it just speeds up the manufacturing process."

"That and a whole lot more," Johnny continued. "For instance, you can now do a visual inspection of parts during the manufacturing process instead of relying on visual inspection at the end. In semiconductor wafer manufacturing, for example, new machines are incorporating vision with motion control to detect minor imperfections in the freshly cut chips and to intelligently adjust the cutting process to compensate for the imperfection. That dramatically increases yield in manufacturing. And it happens during the manufacturing process, not after, so you can make adjustments and keep on manufacturing. It's a brave, new world."

"Cool. Now, what's that got to do with me?"

"Thought you'd never ask," Johnny said. Then the robot hit the return key again, and the next slide appeared.

After twenty minutes, Johnny had only one slide left, the close. He sat back in the chair and let the information sink in with Ritter. Doc hadn't said a word since they'd returned from their coffee quest.

"Alright, let me see if I have this straight," Ritter began. Johnny knew the technique. Ritter would recite back the pluses and minuses of the presentation and Johnny would have a chance to counter or add to each.

"You've got a well-oiled manufacturing facility in Booneville. You have tenured, experienced engineering, software, QC and manufacturing personnel. Sophisticated robotics, vision guidance and a long history of solving manufacturing problems for customers. So that only leaves one question…"

"What do we need the money for?" Johnny interjected.

"Exactly."

"We need more than money. We need a product to produce. Maybe I should say *more* products to produce."

"Huh? I thought you said you have twenty years' worth of customers."

"The world is changing. We need to change with it. We want to manufacturer one product, for one customer. Prove the manufacturability of the product. Perfect the manufacturing process. Then help move it to the large scale production if that's the destination of the product."

"You mean like a contract manufacturer?"

"No. There is too little profit margin for those companies. More like a prototype manufacturing company. We make the first ten or hundred or thousand of the product. Prove that it can be manufactured. And more. We do so many custom jobs now that our strength is really in helping companies streamline the manufacturing process. We can take out some of the fat for the OEM."

"That would seem to be a short term solution to your problem. If there is a problem. You produce the product, perfect the process, then the product leaves your plant. Now you need another product, right?" Ritter said as he stood to look at one of the posters.

"Precisely. We become an engineering firm, not simply an automation controls firm. Unless, of course, we do such a good job of the manufacturing that they give up the volume manufacturing contract, too."

"Again, sounds short-sighted."

"Maybe…but maybe not. You've heard a lot about how manufacturing is leaving America. We've all heard it. And the main reason is labor costs. Other countries pay low wages, and since wages are a huge part of the manufacturing costs, once America develops the product, it moves offshore because it can be produced more cheaply. Foreign competitors eventually steal, or re-invent the technology and take the business away from us. We've seen it with TVs, VCRs, autos, cameras, you name it."

"Right. So how does your solution solve that?"

"I'm not sure that it does, completely," Johnny said, standing now and animating his words with his hands and arms. "But if we can perfect the process of manufacturing a widget, let's call it, then an American company can move that widget production offshore itself, set up the manufacturing wherever labor costs are lower and continue to manufacture the widget instead of losing production to foreign competition."

"Might work," Ritter said.

"It's working now," Johnny said. "Intel perfects the manufacturing of its microprocessor, and when the price of the product starts to decline, as most all technology products eventually do, it moves the production to an offshore facility. It's just that most companies in the semiconductor industry were slow on the uptake; they didn't see the foreign competition sneaking up on them. They saw Japan but missed Taiwan and Korea. Now those two eat its lunch, for the most part. And China's not far behind."

"How do you know so much about semiconductors?"

"It's all right here in my bio," Johnny replied. "I've worked for over ten years with some of the famous and many of the up and coming tech companies in the world. But that's a long story. I'll tell you sometime over a few beers." He sat back down and waited.

"Well, Mr. Roe and Dr. Enbright, you tell a very compelling story and your hour's almost up. But you missed one important point. We don't fund companies looking for products. We fund products looking for production. Big difference."

"Maybe…maybe not," Johnny countered. "I bet you've got a product in your portfolio right now that looks good on paper, but you can't tell if you can manufacturer it and sell it at a price that you can make money. Or at least prove that the product works as you say it will. Then make money."

"Maybe," Ritter replied.

"Is it worth another hour of your time? Say next week sometime after you've had time to sift through all the paper here and talk to your partners?'

"Maybe."

"Can I call you Monday to find a time that works?"

"Maybe," Ritter smiled. "Sure. Call Julie, my secretary."

"Deal," Johnny said as he offered his hand.

"Not yet."

"But maybe is better than no."

FORTY-ONE

"I found something," Norm Boswell said in a very precise voice to Johnny and Doc. All three stood in Boswell's kitchen.

"Go on," Doc said.

"Well, I took the contrarian stance. I'm usually on the manufacturing floor looking at the process or going over the data that explains the process. That's what ops guys do. But for the past week, I've been on the computer. Just searching. I researched a lot of things, and found articles around a lot of manufacturing topics."

Johnny didn't want to hurry him along, but he wondered when he'd get to what he'd found.

"But one group of articles intrigued me," Boswell continued. "Security. Keeping the company IP safe and secure. For a manufacturing company, IP is usually engineering drawings or software. And to tell you the truth, the software we do, except for the new vision-guided technology, is pretty routine. Basic even."

Doc motioned with his hand by rolling his fingers to keep the conversation moving.

"We have an encryption system for our engineering files. They are all digitized and filed after they are encrypted. The encryption method is changed quarterly. I supervise that change myself. I use several different pieces of software to conduct the change, but there is a log that defines the encryption process, the change and a method to make sure the encryption can be un-encrypted, so to speak, so the original files can be accessed. Only two people have access to that log. Me and Ulysses."

"Let me guess," Johnny said. "That log has been accessed by Ulysses repeatedly over the past year. Right?"

"Close. Over the past two years. I went back four years when we installed the encryption process, the software, the quarterly changes, and the log. Before two years ago, he had never once accessed the log."

"Does he know enough about the software to access the actual drawings?" Johnny asked.

"Oh, yeah, he's brilliant with software. It was his suggestion to set it up this way in the first place. It took him almost a month to train me sufficiently so I could run the system. I've had a lot of experience with software over the years, and I felt like a novice in his presence."

"What drawings did he access?" Doc asked.

"Mechanical drawings of the robots. All the robots we manufacture. Even the new vision-guided ones. Basically, everything."

"If he did access the drawings, what would he want with them?" Doc said.

"Maybe he wanted to sabotage them. That would certainly kill the company," Boswell said.

"But why? What does he have to gain from that?" Johnny countered.

"I don't know," Boswell admitted.

"The only other reason I can think of was to reproduce them," Doc said.

"What for?" Boswell asked.

"To sell them," Johnny said.

"To who? And why?"

"Does it matter? Either question? If he's selling your IP, he needs money. He could be selling it to a competitor."

"Son of a bee," Doc said, enunciating each word slowly.

"Do you feel comfortable confronting him, Norm?" Johnny asked. "Pressuring him a bit. Tell him you were inspecting the encryption process and tell him what you found?"

"Maybe. I don't know what good it would do, do you?"

"No, not really. I'm just grasping."

"We could report this to the board," Doc suggested.

"That might work. At least for the few on the board that aren't beholden to Ulysses in some way," Boswell said.

"I think we need to do something to flush him out. If we are going to attract the VC's, then we need Ulysses out of the picture or at least not an obstacle," Johnny explained.

"It's his company," Boswell noted.

"Technically, you all own the company," Doc said.

"He runs the company is what I meant."

"Technically, the board runs the company, but I know what you mean."

"Then let's confront him," Johnny suggested.

"You don't confront him, he confronts you," Boswell corrected.

"Not me, he doesn't. I don't have a horse in this race. Nothing to lose. I'll confront the SOB. You set up the meeting," Johnny said, pointing to Boswell.

"It's your funeral."

"I'm done with funerals."

"He's not going to want to meet with you. Or Doc either, for that matter."

"Fine, just call me or text me when you know he's going to be in the office. Doc and I'll take care of the rest."

"I hope you know what you're doing. He's a real ball-buster. He doesn't necessarily fight fair."

"Like I said, at the moment, I don't have much left to lose."

FORTY-TWO

"**W**HAT in the world is going on, Roe?" Ryan Ritter asked even before Johnny and Doc had settled into their chairs in the VC conference room.

"What do you mean?" Johnny replied with a slight smile.

"We had you checked out. Neither one of you has any controlling interest—or any interest at all that we could find—with Johnson Controls. So what are you trying to pull?"

"We're not pulling anything. Who'd you talk to over there?"

"A guy named Dunham. He wasn't complimentary of you two. In fact, quite the opposite."

"Yeah, that doesn't surprise me," Johnny said. "We're not working for him. Did you talk to Ulysses Johnson, majority owner?"

"No, couldn't reach him."

Johnny saw a slight opening. "Yeah, Dunham's been left out of the loop, purposely. He's not an intricate part of the team going forward. We've run into some issues with him that we're not able to speak about right now, due to … circumstances," Johnny replied, trying to keep his voice even.

"So who are you working for then?"

"We're working for the company. It's employee-owned. All the employees are backing us and Ulysses is well…not quite on board yet. But he's considering it, and I'm sure he can be convinced. Especially once we bring him a product to produce."

"Yeah, well I'm not convinced."

"I can see that, but think about it. We're talking about a huge change for that company. From producing the same product for twenty-some odd years to completely changing their focus. It's not something that's going to come easy for everyone, especially the guy who runs the company and invented, for the most part, the products. It's a tough change."

"I still don't see how you two are involved."

"Doc here used to be on the board and still has the ears of those now currently on the board. He asked me to work a little with the Director of Operations, Norman Boswell. We got buy-in from many of the managers at the plant, too. We've been putting ideas together for some time now, and we're almost ready to report our findings to the board. We're not quite a stealth operation but not everyone, like Dunham, has been brought in. We didn't want to raise too many questions at the plant, get people talking and speculating. When we researched your firm, we saw the potential. Go ahead, call Boswell right now, he'll verify that we're working with him."

"What's his number?"

Johnny found Boswell's cell number on his phone and showed it to Ritter.

Ritter picked up the handset in the conference room and dialed through the speakerphone. Doc took a huge breath in.

"Boswell," he said when he answered the phone.

"Is this Norman Boswell of Johnson Controls?"

"Speaking."

"Mr. Boswell, my name is Ryan Ritter, and I'm with the firm Bantz Dawson Ritter, and I'm sitting at a table here with two gentlemen that say they are working for you. Can you shed some light on this situation?"

Norm Boswell hesitated only a few seconds, then said, "That'd be John Roe and Dr. Enbright I assume, right?"

"Yes, sir."

"What do you need to know?"

"Exactly what are they doing for Johnson Controls?"

"Mr. Ritter, was it? I don't mean to be impolite, but I don't know you personally. I recognize your firm because Mr. Roe has brought me up to date on the last meeting. But I'm not quite sure I want to tell you exactly what we're working on. Do you know what I mean?"

Ritter looked at Johnny, who noticed he hadn't muted the phone and said, "We're not out there talking to everyone about what we're planning, so we've all taken a vow of silence. Boswell's just following the script."

Boswell broke in with, "If you give me a few minutes alone with Mr. Roe and the good doctor, I just want to make sure I'm not overstepping my bounds."

Ritter considered it, but let it drop.

"That's okay Mr. Boswell. I think we can work out the details here. Sorry to bother you." Doc let out his breath, slowly.

"No bother, goodbye then."

Ritter clicked off the phone.

"Okay, I feel a little bit better now. I still want written assurances that you guys represent this company. And I want to come up and see U.S. Johnson Controls for myself—and U.S. Johnson himself."

"We can arrange that, as soon as you want," Johnny said. "But did you call us down here just for this, or did you want to talk about working with us? Cause that's the impression I got last time we were here. And when your secretary confirmed today's meeting, she let on that you had something important to talk to us about."

"Now I'm the one not sure that I want to tell you what I'm working on," Ritter said.

"Understandable. But we did make the drive all the way down here. So maybe you can talk in generalities without the specifics. It's not like we're going to take your idea and run with it. I mean we're manufacturing guys, not inventors. And we've already signed the non-disclosure form you sent us. So we might as well make good use of our time since we're here and everything. What do you say?"

"I'm thinking," Ritter replied.

"Just big picture type stuff. To see if we can do it. If it sounds like something we can do, then we bring in the engineers, the software guys, operations, and talk details."

Ritter nodded, but he still seemed unsure.

"Mr. Ritter," Doc started, "I've lived in Booneville my entire life. Been practicing medicine almost fifty years. I delivered some of those boys out at the plant and placed them in their mother's arms. Saw them draw their first breaths in this world. Mended them when they broke an arm playing baseball. I even had to help them bury a loved one every once in a while. I'd bet my life on those fellows that they could accomplish anything they put their minds to. When you know somebody your entire life, you tend to build a lot of trust in them. You've only known us a short while now, but if you just give us a chance, I know you won't be disappointed."

"I'm not saying I don't trust you two…"

"Sounds like it to me," Doc said.

"Sorry, it's just we get a little paranoid about technology around here. Okay, let's proceed. But I have to tell you, I'm going to record this conversation."

"No problem," Johnny said.

"We've been working with a group out of Dayton, former NCR employees."

"NCR?" Doc asked.

"National Cash Register," Johnny answered.

"Right. Anyway, these guys have put together a prototype of the next generation ATM. We think it can be big business. Most all of the ATMs out there now are on their last legs. Poor security is the biggest issue, but most all of the current technology is going to be outdated in the next five years. These guys think they have the solution."

"Competition?"

"We're sure NCR is working on something, but they've had terrible cash flow problems, and their R&D budgets have been slashed. We've been funding the Dayton gang for two years, and we're impressed with the technology. But the market window is tight. We need to manufacture a limited run and get them in front of the one particular bank pretty quickly. If we can secure the next generation, then it will be a very lucrative deal. Eventually, we may be able to sell the technology to other banks. If not, it's money down the drain."

"Why not just go to a contract manufacturer?"

"A couple of reasons. One, we want to keep the technology in house. But more importantly, the team we funded is in for the long haul. They want to control manufacturing and build a global manufacturing brand. They have more products that could be developed out of this technology. They don't want to just develop the intellectual property and sell it to other manufacturers. They want to create manufacturing jobs, too. But we may be forced to take it to contract if we can't make some of the deadlines."

"What's the timeframe?" Johnny asked.

"We have California Bank and Trust very interested. We've shown them the idea, even simulated some of the technology, because we've got some of the subassemblies completed and tested. But they're the biggest regional bank in the U.S., and they want to be sure we can deliver in quantity if they buy from us. And they are very hesitant to work with a start-up. Banks have to be the most conservative companies in the world. But they absolutely love the technology and the potential. I'd say we have a six to nine month window to show them we can deliver."

"Then we better make quick arrangements to get you and your team out to Booneville," Johnny said.

"Let's get it on the calendar for next week," Ritter said, opening his iPad.

How in the world are we going to do that? Johnny was thinking, as they compared calendars.

FORTY-THREE

"WHERE is Ulysses?" Stanley Strasbaugh demanded to Joe Dunham as he entered Dunham's office.

"Don't you ever knock?" Dunham said, barely raising his head to look.

"There was nobody at the front desk."

"Maybe because it's seven o'clock in the morning."

"That doesn't answer my question. Where is he?"

"He doesn't report to me, you know. It's the other way around."

"You two are inseparable. Like warts on a frog's ass. You should know where he is."

Dunham grimaced at the comparison but didn't say a word.

"I just got some very distressing news. As a member of the board, I have a right to speak to Ulysses."

"I told you. I do not know where he is. Do I have to spell it out to you? You're a lawyer, aren't you? Don't you understand English?"

"Listen, Joe," Strasbaugh continued, softening his voice, "the news I got is very bad for Ulysses, and he needs to know that the board has been given the details of some actions that are very incriminating."

"Like what?"

"I'm not in a position to reveal those to you."

"Just tell me the general direction of the accusations."

"No, I can't do that."

"Fine, then why don't you just leave?"

"Joe, this is an employee-owned corporation. I've got an obligation to inform the employees."

"I'm an employee. Inform me. Then I'll inform the rest of the employees."

"You know it doesn't work that way."

"Well, for as much as the employees own, it should work that way."

"We own a substantial part of this company. It's a partnership. And I own part, too, don't forget that."

"You never let me forget it."

"And you never seem to understand the term partnership. It's a legal term, not something to be tossed around haphazardly. It carries with it obligations, responsibilities."

"Everything is a legal term to you. Warts on a frog's ass is probably a legal term to you, right?"

"Funny."

"No, it isn't funny, Strasbaugh. You own a crummy one half of one percent of this company, and you come in here acting like the King of England. I haven't seen you work a day in your life for this company, not counting golf games with the board of directors. So why don't you take your stuck up ass, warts and all, and get out of my office so I can get some work done."

Stanley Strasbaugh was not used to being talked to this way. His face flushed and he noticed perspiration beading on his forehead. A corporate lawyer, he was not a litigator comfortable in the courtroom. He exhibited intelligence but not necessarily a quick retort. Joe Dunham continued to look at him, with eyebrows raised in a what-are-you-still-doing-here attitude and Stanley Strasbaugh couldn't think of a single thing to say.

He turned to leave. Then he thought of something. "If you see Ulysses, tell him it's urgent I talk to him."

"Urgent. Got it. Get out."

Strasbaugh slammed the door as he left. *There, that should show him who's boss*, he thought, not quite believing it.

FORTY-FOUR

"**H**AVEN'T seen hide nor hair of Ulysses in well over two weeks," Norm Boswell said to Johnny. They stood outside the plant under a shade tree.

"And that's unusual?"

"He always tells me when he'll be gone. Doesn't always mention where he's going. But he always, always, calls me every few days. He just can't let it go, even on vacation. I don't think it's that he doesn't trust me, he just seems to live and die with this place."

"So why did you call me?"

"Well, I know you're planning to get those venture guys here soon, and I figured they'd want to talk to the boss, right?"

"Right. Have you checked his home?"

"Yep. Drove over there myself yesterday. His car is gone. Everything looks locked up tight."

"Maybe he's traveling for a while."

"It's just very strange for him not to call or email me."

"Any relatives you could check with?"

"I don't even know where his wife is these days. I haven't seen her in four, maybe five years. He has a sister over in Kansas City, I think, but I don't know how to reach her. I mean I could check with HR to see if anyone else is listed on his next-of-kin form, but I doubt it. Ulysses wasn't big about completing that kind of paperwork on himself, just employees."

"Did you ask around the plant? Anybody else heard from him? How about our buddy, Dunham?"

"I did inquire, and nobody's seen him either. Something's…not right."

"I suppose you ought to let the board know, don't you think?" Johnny offered.

"Suppose so."

The two men were both lost in thought as a small breeze meandered through the shade tree.

"Maybe you could put on your investigative hat again," Johnny said. "Can you get on his computer, check his email, his browser history - things like that - to pick up a trail?"

"That might be a breach of protocol."

"Might be. Your call."

Norm Boswell bit his lower lip as his analytical mind ran through a list of possible consequences.

"In the meantime, I can talk to Doc and ask him to start calling the board. Chances are the board would approve a little snooping on your part as the next step. Want me to suggest that to Doc when he makes the calls? He could survey the board and get a tentative buy-in to approve. That would take you off the hook."

"That'd work."

FORTY-FIVE

DOC assembled a majority of the board of directors of U.S. Johnson Controls the following day. Four of the six members of the board—minus Ulysses and the local banker who was on vacation in Florida—munched on doughnuts and coffee in the conference room at the plant. No one seemed to want to take control of the meeting and call it to order; that had always been Ulysses' job.

Johnny whispered to Doc that he should suggest that Stanley Strasbaugh, board secretary/treasurer and the highest-ranking member present, start the meeting. Doc relayed the message to Strasbaugh.

"All right, all right, everybody, let's take a seat and start this meeting," Strasbaugh shouted over the various conversations in the room. "I guess we need to talk about what's going on."

After the men settled in, all eyes turned toward Stanley Strasbaugh, still standing at the head of the table. He wasn't used to being the center of attention, and he quickly looked down at his legal pad full of notes, avoiding all eye contact and flipping pages on the pad. He'd been up late the night before sketching out questions to ask.

"I suggest that we forego formalities," Doc said. "Throw out Roberts' rules for the time being and get down to the business at hand."

"Doc, you are not an official member of this board anymore," Strasbaugh said, "and you really shouldn't even be here. This is a board matter. And who are all these other people I don't know and why are they here?" he said, waving his hand around like he was swiping at flies.

"Stanley, you're right, of course," Doc said in his most melodic bedside manner, "I don't have any right to even comment at an official board meeting." He looked purposely to everyone around the large, mahogany table, making eye contact and offering a slight smile. "And I appreciate you not kicking me out the door. I'll certainly acquiesce, Stanley, to let you run the meeting. No problem. If you'd like me to introduce my guest, I'd be happy to do that."

Strasbaugh contemplated that offer for a second. He wasn't a man to jump into uncharted territory easily. "Fine," he managed to say, although it came out clipped and defensive, accompanied by his ever-present frown. Not being a courtroom lawyer, he'd never mastered the ability to keep his feelings from infiltrating his face.

"Thank you, Stanley. Gentlemen, this is John Roe," Doc began, remembering the script he and Johnny had rehearsed the night before, "president of Troubadour, a San Francisco based public relations and marketing firm. He's a close friend of mine, although a fairly new one, who has taken a keen interest in U.S. Johnson Controls, mostly because I've been badgering him to do so. Again, if I've overstepped my boundaries, I apologize."

Doc didn't pause long enough to let Strasbaugh object or interrupt. "Mr. Roe has an extensive background working with manufacturing companies and the list of his clients from Silicon Valley is certainly impressive. Not a lot of household names but all on the cutting-edge of technology and all successfully competing in the global marketplace. He's been gracious enough to spend some time with Norm Boswell over there and others at the plant. He's doing this all pro-bono, hasn't asked for a penny. Let's just call him a 'friend of the company.' I've requested he be present at this meeting only as an observer, which is certainly within the scope and guidelines of the board's bylaws. Gentlemen, Mr. Roe."

Johnny smiled, gestured a small wave with his hand, and nodded hello as acknowledged everyone at the table. Most nodded back, but nobody said a word.

"Okay, well…okay, let's proceed," Strasbaugh stammered, looking at his notes. "It's come to the board's attention that Ulysses is…how would you say it, missing I guess is the right word. Norm, could you bring the board up to date, since you're the highest ranking employee of the company present here today?"

"Sure, but there's not much to report," Boswell began. "We haven't had contact with Ulysses in twelve full days. No calls, no emails, no contact whatsoever. I drove by his home and knocked on the door but no answer. I called a few of his friends, but nobody had knowledge of his whereabouts. I checked the country club, talked to the golf pro—

nothing. Oh, and we haven't seen Joe Dunham in about a week."

The report hung over the group like an impending thunderstorm. Nobody said a thing and wondered when the lightning might strike.

"What's this mean for business?" Strasbaugh asked.

"Business as usual, almost," Boswell answered. "We have orders to fill although sales have been very, very slow. Manufacturing is running, sales is working overtime to fill the pipeline, customers are—as far as we know—happy and content."

"Is this unusual, that U.S. is…not here?" another board member asked. He was a local builder and developer.

Boswell again explained, as he had to Johnny and Doc, how very unusual the events of the past few days had been. He emphasized Ulysses' hands-on approach to managing the business, but he didn't tread into his investigation of the possible breach in security of the company's intellectual property.

"And Norm, can you explain all these reports that each of us received yesterday? I've had some time to review them—don't know if everyone has or not—but I didn't have time to study and digest them," Strasbaugh said.

"Stanley, if I may interrupt," Doc said, "I had a chance to talk to each member of the board, at least the four that are here, yesterday. I didn't review the documents, but I did give you all a bit of background on the possibilities that Mr. Roe has uncovered for us."

"Fine, we're getting to that. Are you saying that the reports are not relevant to each of the discussions—about U.S. and about the venture capitalists?"

"The reports simply convey a snapshot of the business right now," Norm Boswell said. "And I think they are relevant to both discussions. They show sales slipping, manufacturing slowing down, and shipments in a serious trend downward."

"So you're saying that U.S. is to blame for this? Or his absence is to blame?" Strasbaugh asked.

"Yes…and no," Boswell replied.

"I don't know if we have time right now to try and assign blame or not," Doc said. "I think the bigger issue on the table is the upcoming visit by the venture capital firm. I know Norm is working on several angles to try and locate Ulysses but with or without him, this meeting with the venture folks is going to happen and we have to be prepared."

"Wait a minute, wait a minute," a flustered Strasbaugh said. "We don't know where U.S. is; we don't know where Joe Dunham is."

"Nobody should even care where that guy is," Doc said, losing the tone of bedside manner.

Strasbaugh's eyebrows shot up. "What?"

"Sorry," Doc offered, "but we've had our differences. I'm sure he's an asset to this company, but he rubs me the wrong way."

Johnny gave Norm Boswell a slight nod, encouraging him to jump into the conversation.

"Let me answer Stanley's question, as best as I can right now. I've been doing a little investigative work in Ulysses' absence, trying to dig into the reasons some of those figures in the charts have been slipping. I've uncovered some…discrepancies, let's call them. We think, err, I think that Ulysses has had a hand in something—hard to tell exactly what at this moment—that perhaps have caused those numbers to decline. It's too early to tell, and it's nothing the board has to be concerned with now because I'm still digging. It may take a while. And I agree with Doc, the bigger concern on the table is the meeting with the venture capital firm."

"Well, I suppose we can table that discussion about Ulysses for right now, but I reserve the right to come back to it later," Strasbaugh said in his best lawyer banter, emphasizing the point with a raised hand, finger pointing skyward.

"Maybe Mr. Roe can fill us in on the venture visit, he's the expert," Doc said.

Strasbaugh nodded slightly, still flummoxed a bit by his leadership role.

Johnny stood. "Please call me Johnny. I almost don't know who you're talking about when you say Mr. Roe."

He then proceeded to paint the picture of how venture capital worked and how it might just work for the plant. He told of the meeting and research he and Doc had gathered at the university, the data he'd uncovered about new start-ups and monies invested in the Silicon Prairie and the work he'd done to find a venture firm like the one due to visit in two short days. He never mentioned Boswell's discovery of tampering with the mechanical drawing files or their suspicions, which were only that, suspicions. Johnny stuck to a positive path, a way to transition the plant into the future of manufacturing in America, a way to ensure that the plant stays relative–and keeps jobs in Booneville–for the foreseeable future.

He talked just long enough to hold the room's attention, but he didn't get lost in facts and figures. He then walked to the corner of the room and duplicated the motion sensor demonstration with the robotic hand and the computer that he'd done at the venture capital office. Again, everyone smiled when the robot found the keyboard. He concluded with a short glimpse of what the visit might entail. Then the room fell silent as he sat down.

"Well, thank you, Mr. Roe…er…Johnny," Strasbaugh said, "but to tell you the truth, I really don't know what to do with all that information. It's a lot to absorb."

"Yes, I know," Johnny acknowledged.

"It seems like you've done your homework."

"Yes, I believe so."

"So what do we do next?"

"I know the venture firm would like to see a show of support from the board. Especially in light of the circumstances–whatever they are–surrounding Mr. Johnson. Perhaps if the board voted to proceed with…a green light, let's call it…for Norm Boswell and the rest of the management staff to proceed with the visit, to represent the company, to put some ideas together and then come back to the board with findings. They wouldn't make any quick decisions and wouldn't have the authority to commit to any long-term arrangements."

"That seems logical," Strasbaugh said.

"It's really just a fact-finding visit by the venture firm."

"I suppose it makes sense to continue, now that we've gone this far."

"It does to me."

"Would the board need to be present during the visit?"

"It depends. I really don't know how this board works. Some boards are very knowledgeable about their business, others not so much so. They work at a higher level, advising ownership and management in more strategic matters."

"We're more like the latter," Strasbaugh said. The others around the table nodded vigorously in agreement, all checking their calendars trying to come up with an excuse of why they probably wouldn't be available for the meeting.

"Then maybe a simple introduction of the board—whoever can make it—at the start of the meeting. I can explain that you're all busy men, that you've given management the approval to proceed, then you can probably leave."

Everyone nodded, again checking calendars.

"I really don't like to do this without Ulysses," Strasbaugh cautioned.

"Ulysses is not here," Doc countered.

"I wish I knew where he was."

"Don't we all, don't we all."

FORTY-SIX

RYAN Ritter arrived early the following day at 6:30 a.m. and just sat in his car for the next fifteen minutes, watching. He was mostly a numbers guy, with an accounting degree from Washington University in St. Louis and an MBA from Stanford. In any venture deal, the numbers had to make sense, at least to a degree. At some point in time, a company has to be profitable, has to make money. For all the companies like Google, Facebook, and Twitter that couldn't show a profit for years, and even though they eventually did, most companies can predict when the technology, the market, and the product will coincide to generate cash and, hopefully, profit. It's only a small percentage of companies that hit pay dirt by going public; most languish just to find an audience and turn positive cash flow. Venture capitalists know the numbers game. And not just the spreadsheet numbers. They know that any deal to fund an idea is a crapshoot. Some companies turn that idea into gold; many piss away the money and move onto the next idea—or out of business. Ritter knew that ideas were plentiful, and that success was the bull's-eye that most entrepreneurs missed.

He also knew that Johnny, if he was any kind of leader at all, would have the plant ready for today. He would have prepped the entire management team what to expect, what to say, and especially what not to say. The maintenance crew would have worked late the night before spiffing up the facility. Ritter had talked to several execs who'd admitted spit-shining the presentation room, cleaning the whiteboards, polishing the conference table, and even using a small, portable vacuum to freshen the carpet. So, he knew that the plant would be putting its best foot forward; it would be ready.

But any venture capitalist has to be able to judge people, too. Maybe even more than numbers, people make ideas work, sometimes even when the idea seemed farfetched or ill-conceived. At Stanford Ritter had studied the trajectory of FedEx when it was still named Federal Express. It was literally a textbook case now, filling pages and pages of case studies for an idea that was panned from the beginning and destined to fail. The entrepreneur in this case, Fred Smith, had conceived of an idea to compete with the Post Office to deliver packages and overnight letters. Fly them all into a hub, Memphis, segregate and distribute them back out, and deliver them in a day or two. Preposterous his grad school professor said. Won't work. But somehow, someway, it did. Smith had filled a demand he wasn't even sure existed—and changed the way business was done.

Ritter viewed U.S. Johnson Controls as a crapshoot, too. He didn't think the idea was sound and wasn't sure they could perform as advertised. But he also knew that if you didn't do your due diligence as a VC, if you didn't know the numbers and the people, you never had a chance to hit the jackpot. Just another day in his life, almost like looking for a needle in a haystack, and hoping that the needle was made of gold instead of steel.

So Ritter camped out in the parking lot with a large coffee and just observed. He wanted to see if employees were anxious to get to work or if they dragged themselves into the plant. He looked to see if they took pride in their environment—if the outside of the plant was well-maintained, grass mowed, flowers growing, parking lot swept. It was a small indicator of success, and it might not make any difference at all in the long run, but Ryan Ritter searched for any signs that would turn the odds in his favor, to make the crapshoot not such a long shot.

Ritter spotted Johnny Roe enter the building a little before seven. Ritter liked Roe, liked his enthusiasm, his intellect, his experience. And even though he thought Doc Enbright was way too homespun for business, Ritter liked him as well. But Ritter also knew he didn't have to like them, that it didn't matter how he felt about them personally. He'd worked with many an entrepreneur that he didn't like; the lot could be brash, full of themselves and dictatorial. Traits of the breed.

The late summer day blossomed into a gorgeous Iowa postcard. The grass was green, the flowers lush, the air clean and pure. It might just be a good day after all, Ritter thought. A good day to find that elusive jackpot. He climbed out of his BMW, slipped on his suit coat and headed into the plant.

His mood quickly changed.

When he was ushered into the conference room, he expected to meet the president and owner of the business, Ulysses Johnson. Instead, he was surrounded by the board of directors, Roe and Enbright. He met Stanley Strasbaugh, but the man seemed nervous and flustered. Strasbaugh explained that Johnson was away on business. Ritter understood the rigors and demands of business travel but wondered why they hadn't set up a Skype call with Johnson as a means of introduction. He'd made it pretty clear that Johnson was a key to this visit.

All of the directors on the board said a quick hello, introduced themselves and made excuses as to why they couldn't stay longer. They all seemed anxious to leave. Not a good sign.

Strasbaugh quickly turned the meeting over to Johnny Roe and Norm Boswell, and they summarized what the morning visit would entail. Pretty standard stuff—charts and graphs to tell the story of the plant's manufacturing, a tour, meet and greet with several managers, and a Q&A back in the conference room.

As he toured the facility, Ritter was impressed with its capabilities and its people. Like a well-tuned automobile, the plant ran smoothly on all cylinders. At least from what he could see. He asked tough questions, and the answers didn't seem canned or rehearsed. Employees answered honestly and candidly. If Norm Boswell didn't know the answer, he didn't try to make something up to impress Ritter. He admitted he didn't know something when he didn't. But most of the time, he knew.

Ritter spent several hours talking with the men in R&D. It wasn't a big group, only three engineers. He got the feeling that although they were mainly hardware guys who spent most of their time on the mechanical drawings of current customer projects in production, they showed creativity, too. Like most engineers they thought in a linear fashion, first things first, from A to B to C to D. But when Ritter jumped out of sequence to ask a question, they followed his thinking and asked more questions before answering. To Ritter that meant they first relied on their training as engineers but had the capacity to think outside the box and create new solutions to new problems.

Ritter ranked the plant's automation as first-rate for a small manufacturing facility in the middle of Iowa. Of course, that was their strength, and he expected to see top-of-the-line equipment. The software engineer and his associate acted nerdy, but Ritter was used to the type. He could discuss generalities with them and ask intelligent questions, especially after so many discussions with the former NCR people making the new ATM machines. Ritter led the software engineer through a series of inquiries to gauge his intellect, his speed of picking up new ideas, and his ability to quickly grasp a concept. A bright engineer, an asset to the team, Ritter concluded.

Next, Ritter spent time in the machine shop. He knew enough about manufacturing to know that the machine shop was a small but vital component. They were usually profit centers, charging big fees to make prototype parts to fit into new manufacturing lines. But they also showed the ingenuity and resourcefulness—the creativity if you will—of the entire operations. Ritter judged the machine shop at Johnson Controls as top-notch, maybe even close to top of the line.

Norm Boswell surprised Ritter. He resembled many operations guys he'd met in the past—knowledgeable, versatile, determined, focused and well-liked by his employees. But Boswell had a leadership quality that was sometimes missing from ops guys. Some simply followed directions from company presidents and didn't rock the boat, didn't make waves. Get the product out on time with high quality. Boswell spoke his mind and wasn't afraid to take the role of plant leader. Ritter respected that but wondered if Boswell had that forced on him by the absence of Ulysses Johnson.

Just after one o'clock in the afternoon, Johnny found Ritter on the manufacturing floor.

"Why don't we take a short break, for sandwiches in the conference room," Johnny said.

"Thanks, but no thanks. I really don't eat lunch often. Plus I have some more to do here, and then I need to get back to the office."

"It would give us a chance to answer a few questions."

"I'm getting most answered already. I'll let you know if I have more."

"Okay, your call."

"I'll find you when I'm finished."

At three-thirty, Ritter ran out of questions. He said quick goodbyes without giving much indication to Johnny and Doc if he had found the answers he was looking for. He said he'd be in touch in a day or two, once he'd had a chance to talk to his partners. Johnny couldn't decipher whether that meant he was intrigued or had lost interest.

Ritter left the parking lot, heading his BMW south toward Des Moines. On the drive back to the office, he let the feeling in his gut percolate. Maybe after a long drive and time to think, he'd be able to figure out what bothered him about U.S. Johnson Controls.

FORTY-SEVEN

"**WE'RE** going to pass," Ritter said to Johnny right after phone call pleasantries had been exchanged.

"What?"

"Yeah, well, there just seems to be too many holes to fill."

"What's that mean?" Johnny asked as Doc craned his neck to hear over the speakerphone.

"I liked the staff, the facilities, the technology. But management level expertise seemed to be lacking. I liked Boswell. Even his leadership. But this venture needs much more. We're passing."

Johnny's mind spun. He knew when a client was this adamant that they rarely changed their minds. But he couldn't let it go without a fight.

"Needs more what?"

"Leaders, Johnny. More than just management. Leaders."

"But you're going to bring in your own leaders, aren't you? The guys that invented the technology. I've worked on these projects before; you always bring in your guys."

"Our guys are technologists. They have a great idea. They don't know all that much about running a business."

"C'mon, Ryan, don't feed me that. I know you have a guy in mind already to run this business. I don't know who he is, but you wouldn't have gotten this far in the process without hand-picking someone you know, someone you've worked with before, to bring in, to take charge. It's how you guys work. Even if you loved the leaders at Johnson Controls, you're gonna bring in your own guy anyway. You have too much to lose."

Ritter didn't say anything.

"Isn't that right, Ryan?"

"Most of the time, yes."

"If it isn't the leadership at the plant, what is it?"

More silence.

"Listen, I know you don't owe us an explanation. And we're big boys, so whatever your final decision, we'll live with that and move on, but there's something you're not saying, and I'm real interested to know what that is."

"It's Johnson himself," Ritter finally admitted. Johnny winced; he knew deep down that that answer was coming.

"I still haven't met the man, Johnny, and he owns the company. I like you, I like the idea, I like the facility, and I think your guys out there could make this happen. But my partners keep asking me one question. Is the owner one hundred percent behind this? And I can't answer that question."

Now it was Johnny's turn to be silent.

"And I don't have time to find the answer either," Ritter continued.

"I see," Johnny said, his eyes closed tight.

"I'm sorry, I wish it had turned out differently."

"Me, too."

"You'll pass along my thanks to your whole team?"

"Sure."

"Maybe we'll have a chance to work on another project in the future."

"Yeah."

"Take care, see ya."

"Bye." Johnny clicked the phone off. He stared at Doc, closed his eyes, and let out a deep breath.

"Now what?" Doc asked.

"No clue. No clue at all."

FORTY-EIGHT

EVERY fifteen minutes or so, a car slowly snaked its way along the street, slipping past the front porch of Doc Enbright's home. The puttering of car engines and the occasional bark of a neighborhood dog were the only sounds that cracked the silence between Doc and Johnny. Johnny slipped into a funk and answered Doc's questions with little more than grunts and shrugs. Over the past hour, Doc had quit asking. They were on their third beer.

Emmy Brownell danced along the sidewalk, slowing her stride as she approached the porch. Neither man smiled as she placed her foot on the lower step of four that led to the big welcome mat at the front door. Doc waved half heartedly from the cushioned rocker and Johnny nodded his head from the porch swing. *Uh oh*, thought Emmy.

She sat down on the top step, slightly turned toward the two men. They both were slumped into their seats, either extremely comfortable or a bit drunk. Emmy wasn't sure which.

"Want a beer?" Doc asked.

"Sure, I'll get it," Emmy said.

"In the back porch frig."

As she returned, Emmy commented, "You've got that stocked like you're expecting a party."

"Or a wake," Doc said.

"Which is it?"

"The latter."

"You want to talk about it?" Emmy asked, aiming the question toward Johnny.

Johnny looked at her and let out a long, slow breath, wanting to capture some words with the air as it escaped his lungs but finding none. He took another breath in and held it for a beat or two. "Sure," he finally said, opening his mouth to continue but shutting it again without offering anything.

"We got a call from the venture people," Doc said. He shook his head and took another swig.

"Bad news, huh?" Emmy asked.

"Yeah, basically they said they weren't interested."

"Well, the crappy thing is," Johnny said, "they actually were interested. A lot, I think. But without Ulysses, they just weren't going to pull the trigger."

"It's a done deal, no hope of resuscitation?" Emmy asked.

Johnny smiled at the medical term, saying "To put it into your lingo, flat lined."

"DOA, huh?"

"Asystole," Doc chimed in.

"A what?" Johnny asked.

"Brain-dead. Medical term."

"Dead as a doornail," Emmy whispered. "Err…whatever that means."

"I think it means the nail got hammered," Johnny said, "which at the moment seems the appropriate response to the day."

"I'll fetch the next round," Doc said, slowly rising from the chair and stretching his back. "You ready?" he asked, pointing to Emmy.

"Uh, sure?" she responded, having it come out more like a question than a statement.

As Doc swung open the front porch screen, Johnny said to her, "Try to keep up."

"How many am I behind?"

"Several."

"You boys had dinner yet?"

"Nah, that tends to soak up the alcohol, diminishing its effectiveness."

"I see."

Over the next several hours, each took their turn making a beer run to the back frig and offering an analysis of the plant's predicament. Johnny flowed from idea to idea, but when he reached the point where he suggested that they collect recyclables and turn them into parking lot wheel stops—and got "what are you talking about" responses from both of them—he shut up. Doc offered stories about several of the men and women at the plant and how he'd treated them, omitting the actual illness, confidentiality he claimed. Emmy simply encouraged the talking, somehow surmising that at least they weren't holding it all in and figuring maybe they'd hit upon something that might actually work but quickly realizing that they just needed to vent.

Doc stopped venting after five or six beers, and nobody was counting anyway. Johnny slowed down after eight or so. Emmy had trouble keeping up.

When she got up to go to the bathroom, Johnny got her attention and held his index finger to his lips, shushing her and nodding toward Doc, who was now comfortably sleeping in the rocking chair. She nodded and opened the screen door slowly. It creaked more loudly than she expected, like a door in a horror movie. Her eyes went wide in mock fright, and she suppressed a giggle. Johnny clasped his hand over his mouth suppressing one of his own.

When she returned, she noticed Johnny had his left foot clamped on the front of the rocker and was doing his best to keep up the rocking rhythm Doc had established before he nodded off.

She leaned close to Johnny's ear and whispered, "Let's see if we can gently wake him and get him to bed."

Johnny signaled her the A-OK sign with his right hand.

"I get the message," Doc said, opening one eye. "You two want to be alone. And besides, I'm way past my limit. With ideas and beers."

Emmy helped him up and walked with him toward the bedroom, making sure that in his condition he didn't bump into any furniture or walls. They shuffled slowly to the back of the house, barely missing the bookcase at the front of the hallway and the table just inside Doc's bedroom door.

"I can take it from here, darlin'," Doc said, kissing Emmy on the cheek and closing his door. She noticed that he smelled like her grandpa.

As she returned to the porch, her right foot hit the bookcase. Luckily, her tennis shoe absorbed the blow, but it knocked her a little off balance. *Whoa,* she thought, *how many beers have I had?*

Johnny had moved from the front porch to the living room, plopping himself at one end of the leather sofa. Emmy joined him but sat at the other end.

They began to talk about anything other than the events of the day or the manufacturing plant. Johnny got up and fetched two more beers, but Emmy only took a rare sip as they chatted. Several times they laughed out loud and when they realized it, they both put their fingers to their mouths, indicating they shouldn't wake Doc, and then started to giggle. Gradually, Emmy inched closer to Johnny, so they didn't have to talk so loud.

As the conversation lulled and the alcohol dulled, they sat on the couch looking at each other. Emmy had on a white cotton blouse with the two top buttons undone. Johnny caught his gaze drifting toward the peek of cleavage. He thought of his dead wife and both kids. For a second, then they were gone.

He reached out with his right hand and unbuttoned the third button. Then he stopped, his gaze never leaving her blouse.

Emmy swallowed hard. But her hands stayed at her side. She was looking at his hand on her buttons.

He reached for the next button, but she gently grabbed his hand.

"Wait," she said. "I can't."

FORTY-NINE

"WHAT happened last night?" Emmy asked as she leaned closer toward Johnny, across the booth from her in the restaurant.

"You don't remember?" he asked back, a little surprise in his voice.

"No, I mean yes, of course, I do. I wasn't that drunk."

"Oh, good."

Yes, it really was, Emmy wanted to say, but she resisted. As she was about to rephrase the question, breakfast was delivered. Eggs and bacon for Johnny, oatmeal for her. They delayed wading into deeper conversation as they began to eat. Emmy didn't want to press the matter and waited for Johnny to say something. Anything actually.

"I'm sorry if I took advantage of you," he said finally.

"Is that what you think you did?"

"No, I guess not. But I wasn't sure."

"You didn't."

He just nodded his head, but his eyes softened, almost smiled.

They continued to eat in silence for another few minutes. As the conversation was about to begin again, more coffee was served. Johnny ordered another glass of water.

"It's not that I'm not attracted to you," Emmy almost whispered.

"I didn't think that. I don't actually know what I was thinking," he said, looking away.

Now it was her turn to nod, a relieved look on her face.

Johnny gulped down his second glass of water. Their eyes didn't often meet across the table, but when they did, each smiled. "I don't know what it all means, Emmy. I'm having a little trouble figuring that out."

"I wasn't asking that."

"Yes, you were. And you have a right to."

"Maybe."

Emmy knew her hair must look a bit mussed and she wore little makeup. She caught him staring, raised her eyebrows in a silent "what?" and tried to suppress a bigger smile.

Finally, she asked, "What? Do I have oatmeal on my chin?"

"It wasn't sympathy, was it?"

"What? You mean like did I feel sorry for you and let you…start something? Like that?"

"Yeah, I guess."

"Sorry to tell you, but it never crossed my mind."

"Your mind was a bit fogged by the beer."

"Maybe a bit but not as much as yours."

"Yeah. Sorry…"

"How bout we just slow down a bit and talk…a little more," she said, her face flushing with color.

Johnny let a small smile spread across his face as he reached over and wiped a bit of oatmeal from Emmy's chin.

FIFTY

NORM Boswell finished filling Johnny's cup, placed the pot back on his Mr. Coffee, and sat in his favorite chair at the dining room table. Doc stood by the stove.

"I asked to see you both," Johnny began, "because…I guess…well, I'd like to figure out where we go from here."

"Why don't we start by determining what we know so far," Boswell said. "If we can assess where 'here' is, we might be able to chart a path…to somewhere."

"Okay, what do we know?"

Boswell said, "Ulysses is gone."

Doc said, "Dunham is gone. Good riddance."

Johnny said, "VC money is gone. At least with Ritter."

"Business is off," Doc said.

"Way off," Boswell corrected.

"And we don't know why," Johnny added.

"Well, we have a clue," Boswell said.

"Oh?"

"Seems that Ulysses wasn't being very cooperative with sales. He balked at discounts, tried to increase pricing, beyond reasonable levels. Not approving standard terms and conditions, dragging his feet making decisions. I got that out of the sales guys. He was really making life difficult for them all."

"Huh," Johnny said. "So, it sounds like he was trying *not* to win orders. Very strange. Did he understand the sales process? How to win business?"

"Definitely. More time than not, sales would take him along to close business. He was very good at that," Boswell said.

Johnny shook his head. "Okay, what else do we know?"

"Somebody, probably Ulysses, accessed the IP, the mechanical drawings," Boswell added.

"Definitely Ulysses," Johnny corrected.

"How's that related to what's been going on?" Doc asked.

"Let's speculate. If the mechanicals were actually accessed for a bad reason," Johnny started, "which we don't know for sure, then we can assume that Ulysses sold the IP. Why else would he access it?"

"He didn't make changes or upgrades. We know that," Boswell said.

"If he sold it, and he got something, like cash for it," Doc added, "maybe it's in the safe in his office."

"Doubtful," Boswell said.

"Yeah, I know, but maybe there's…something…a clue, I don't know, in there."

"Possible I suppose."

The three men sipped coffee, silence spreading over them like fog creeping in from the ocean, seeping up alleys and side streets, blocking visibility.

Johnny paced. He was comfortable with silence because he knew from silence came ideas.

"That's all we know? That can't be all we know," Doc said.

Johnny put his hand up, to say wait, something's coming. He kept it raised for several moments.

Then it came. "Bettchers," was all he said.

"What do you mean?" Boswell asked.

"Somehow they're involved."

"Why do you say that?"

Johnny told Boswell the story of his encounter with the Bettcher boys. Most of the story. He left out the part about the baseball bat.

"Is the one still in the hospital?" Johnny asked.

Doc said, "Emmy will know."

Emmy, Johnny thought. *Focus, focus. Get your mind back in the game*, he said to himself.

"Are you saying they know something we don't know?" Boswell tried to confirm.

"I guess I'm saying that since we don't have much else to go on, I'd sure like to know what they know," Johnny said.

"They may not react well to seeing you," Doc said to Johnny.

"True. Why don't you pay them a visit?"

"How am I going to get them to talk?"

"You're a doctor, use your bedside manner. Besides, from what I hear…and from what I know…they're not the sharpest tools in the shed. Might just need a little coaxing or a little distraction. Try to get to the truth somehow. While you're working on that, Norm, why don't you start working on getting into that safe?"

"Truth. Hmm," Doc said. Then an idea came to him, out of the silence.

FIFTY-ONE

"**H**EY, Doc, how are you?" Emmy said, cradling the cell phone between her shoulder and left ear.

"Oh, yes, Emmy, hello. Are you at work?"

"Nope. If I was, I wouldn't be answering my phone. New rules over there since you've been gone."

"I see."

"I'm just folding laundry. What's up?"

"Do you, by any chance, know if Jim Bettcher is still in the hospital?"

"Why the sudden interest in Mr. Bettcher?"

"Johnny and I are working on a theory, that's all. Trying to get a little more information about what's going on at the plant. We thought Bettcher might be able to shed some light on the subject."

Johnny, Emmy thought. *Wait, what was the question? Was there a question?*

"Oh, yeah…I suppose that's possible. But no, Jim was discharged a couple of days ago."

"Oh, too bad. I wanted to talk to him."

"Well, he's not going far. With that leg, he's pretty much confined to his home. You could find him there, I'm sure."

"I don't have any medical reason to see him, and if I just show up out of the blue, he might get suspicious."

"Want me to go with you?" Emmy offered. "I'm sure he'd be happy to see me. He always is, if you know what I mean."

"I suppose I do. Sure, that might help. You free this afternoon? About three?"

"Yep."

"Great, I'll pick you up, a little before."

On the short drive over to Jim Bettcher's home, Emmy and Doc caught up on Booneville current events and hospital news. Two old friends chewing the local fat. Finally, the conversation came around to Johnny.

"How are you two getting along?" Doc asked.

Emmy frowned and turned down the corners of her mouth. "I'm not really sure. He's still in a lot of pain, emotionally, and I don't think he's even ready for something like 'getting along'."

"How's that make you feel?"

Emmy blew out a long breath. "Sad, I guess."

"Sad for him? Or sad for you?"

"Oo-o. Hadn't really thought about that. In that way."

Doc leaned closer to the dash so he could catch Emmy's eye as she drove. "What do your girlfriends think about all this?"

"What girlfriends?"

"Well, isn't this what girlfriends talk about? Men, I mean, mostly."

"Ah, well, yes, I suppose. But I don't have too many girlfriends."

Emmy continued driving through the neighborhood looking for the address. Doc sat back and stared out the passenger window.

Finally, he said, "You need some girlfriends. And I think I know just the place to find some."

Emmy pulled the car over to the curb. Looking at Doc with raised eyebrows, she said, "Oh?"

"I know where…some girls…ladies…gather regularly. I'll introduce you."

"Well now. Okay. That might just work."

"So what's the game plan here?" Emmy asked Doc as they continued down the street and pulled into the Bettcher driveway.

"Sodium pentothal."

"What? Truth serum? You have truth serum?"

"Well, no, not actually."

"Say what?"

"I'm simply going to use the power of suggestion with our dear Mr. Bettcher. I'm going to inject him with a little saline solution traced with just a teeny amount of codeine."

"Okay…I'm still not following you."

"Well, I'm surmising that Mr. Bettcher will not know he hasn't received the actual truth serum. Thinking that he has may induce him to tell the truth. Like a placebo effect."

"You think that'll work?" Emmy asked.

"I do."

"Is that even legal?"

"I'm pretty sure…I don't know."

"Don't you think that would be something you'd want to know before the actual injection?"

"No."

"Doc, are you listening to what you're saying?"

"Emmy, I know the Supreme Court, in all their illustrious ramblings over the past fifty years, has declared that sodium pentothal confessions are not permissible in a court of law. Threw them out in the '60s as I recall. Fine, I understand. But nowhere have I read or heard that placebo injections to mimic the effects of sodium pentothal are…illegal…or unethical…or in any way counter to our Hippocratic oath."

She looked at him with a raised eyebrow, overemphasizing her skepticism. "Really?"

"Besides, I'm retired. What are they going to do, take away my license? Big whoop. You, on the other hand, may have something to lose. If you'd like to back out, no hard feelings. Just get me in the door, and you can take off. I can call you when I'm ready to leave."

"Now, don't get all huffy on me. I never said I was backing out. I'm just thinking this through, that's all."

"Well, don't think too hard. After all, that's what we're counting on for Mr. Bettcher."

"What?"

"That he won't think too hard about it. And from what I'm told, that won't be a problem for him."

Jim Bettcher slowly opened the door and saw Emmy Brownell staring back at him. She smiled broadly.

"Emmy? That you? What…?"

"Hi, Jim, how are you? I just came by to check up on you. Can we come in for a sec?"

"We?" Bettcher asked, craning his neck around the door as Emmy moved past him into the house.

"Hello, Mr. Bettcher," Doc said, extending his right hand, "I'm Dr. Enbright. Nice to make your acquaintance."

Bettcher returned the handshake, pivoting on his crutches as Doc continued into the hall.

"Jim, please sit down," Emmy said. "You'll probably be more comfortable back in your chair." The recliner looked like Bettcher had spent the better part of every day since he was discharged from the hospital in its embrace. A small TV tray was alongside the chair and was crammed with bottles of medicine, a box of Kleenex, the TV remote and several unidentifiable items. The tray resembled the rest of the living room Emmy noticed with a quick glance. Trash, old magazines, beer cans, and many dirty dishes littered the living room.

"Yep, just might do that. Not real comfy standing up," Bettcher replied as he struggled to get back to the chair. He looked very unsteady, either like he couldn't get the hang of using crutches or he'd taken too many medicinal crutches. He eased himself down into the chair as Emmy grabbed the metal sticks, placing them against the far wall, considerably out of his reach. Bettcher never noticed, his gaze affixed to Emmy.

"What again do I owe the pleasure of this visit to?" he asked.

"Doc Enbright and I are just out seeing some patients, making a few house calls, that's all," Emmy replied.

"I didn't know docs and nurses did that kind of thing."

"I'm retired," Doc said. "And it's Emmy's day off. It's just a goodwill kind of thing we do for the community. You know, give back, pay it forward, that kind of thing."

The look of confusion on Jim Bettcher's face indicated that he had no idea what Doc was talking about, but he said, "Well, alright then, good for y'all."

"Mr. Bettcher, please tell …" Doc began.

"Hey, Doc, just call me Jim." His voice came out a little too loud for normal conversation.

"Of course, Jim. Tell us how your leg is feeling," Doc continued.

"Well, it still hurts mighty bad, Doc, I don't mind telling you."

"That's certainly understandable. It's only been…"

"…a few weeks," Emmy finished the sentence.

"A few weeks," Doc said, "so certainly the healing process is still progressing along. You know, the healing often hurts more at the beginning stages. Don't you agree, Jim?"

"For sure, still hurts, I know that."

"And have you been attending your physical therapy sessions regularly?"

"Sure thing, Doc. They came here the first few times, but now Earl has to pick me up and take me there."

"How have they been going?" Emmy asked.

"They ain't doing much with the leg yet, just sort of keeping the rest of me moving a bit. Said they can't work on the leg for…can't remember. A while at least."

"They're right," Doc said. "You need to let that kneecap heal for a few more weeks. To let the bones knit together. Then they can start to work on the flexibility."

"Have you been taking your meds like a good boy, Jim?" Emmy asked, smiling.

"Got my stash right here," he replied, pointing to the cache on the TV tray.

"And are they working okay for you, Jim, or do you think you could use something more powerful every now and then?" Doc inquired, knowing the answer before he even asked. He looked at each container, checking the description of the medication.

"More powerful, you say? Don't suppose that could hurt, don't ya know." Jim Bettcher actually licked his lips in anticipation.

Doc had settled into the couch adjacent to Bettcher's chair. He reached down to the floor and picked up his small black bag. "I have a little something here in my bag that I'm authorized to administer if the situation arises," he said, reaching into the bag.

"The situation has arisen," Bettcher stated with a distinctive nod of his head. Both Emmy and Doc smiled.

Doc withdrew a large needle from his bag.

"Whoa! That's a monster!" Bettcher said, his eyes bulging.

"Oh, Jim, I've seen you take bigger ones than that many times at the hospital," Emmy replied, beginning to roll up the sleeve on his right arm.

"Really, bigger?"

"Many times. Unless, of course, you don't think you need something to take the edge off the pain?"

"No, no, I'm not backin' down. I just won't look, that's all," he said, looking away as Doc swabbed his triceps.

"Little prick," Doc said, letting Bettcher know what to expect. Emmy turned her head, trying not to laugh.

"Oh boy, yeah!"

After a few seconds Doc slid the needle out of the arm and quickly returned it to his bag. "Now that didn't hurt much, did it?"

"No pain, no gain, eh Doc? No problemo."

The three exchanged small talk about the weather, sports, beer and hunting over the next ten minutes or so. Doc wanted to make sure the codeine did its job. Jim Bettcher slowly slid farther down into his recliner, and his speech became even slower than when they'd arrived. Doc had checked with Emmy before they arrived to get an estimation of what medications Bettcher was likely taking. They both agreed that the small dose of codeine would do no harm. Emmy only hoped that Bettcher wouldn't fall asleep before Doc got to ask any questions.

"How are you feeling, Mr. Bettcher?" Doc asked, returning to his more formal voice.

"Sweet," Bettcher replied, not noticing the change in the doctor's tone.

"Are you feeling relaxed?"

"Absolutely."

"Very well, then I'd like to begin."

"Begin? Begin what?" Bettcher asked, suspiciously looking at Doc.

"That wasn't a painkiller I gave you, Mr. Bettcher. It was sodium pentothal. Truth serum."

"Huh?"

"And even though I'm a retired doctor, I'm also working for a private investigator who's looking into some nefarious happenings around Booneville lately."

"Nefarious?"

"Just sit back and try to relax. You have little if any control over what is about to happen. In fact, it's a proven medical certainty, that even if you tried to lie about anything in your answers to the questions I'm about to ask, that it would be virtually impossible, medically speaking, of course," Doc said.

"What're you talking about?"

"The sodium pentothal. The truth serum. It takes away the inhibition, the inclination so to speak, to tell lies. It's a proven fact. It's really an intravenous hypnotic medication, a psychoactive sedative you might say, that reacts in the brain to render the victim—in this case, you—incapacitated. You have no choice but to tell the truth. Got it?"

Bettcher nodded, looking like he didn't believe or couldn't understand what he'd just heard, but too zonked out to care much. He looked at Emmy for some solace, but she just nodded her head, indicating that everything the good doctor had said was true.

"Ain't ya gonna hook me up to one of them machines?" Bettcher said.

"What machines?" Doc countered.

"Them lie detectors."

"Not needed. I don't need to tell whether you're lying or not because I know that with the truth serum, you can't lie. Now, the first question. Please tell me your name."

"James Earl Bettcher."

"And your brother's name is…" Doc wanted to know.

"Earl James Bettcher," Bettcher said, straightening up a bit in his chair. Emmy bit her lower lip.

"Your occupation?" Doc continued.

"Painter. Like in house paintin'. Not like in picture paintin'."

"Home address?"

"Here," Bettcher said, pointing with his finger to the floor beside him.

Doc was stalling, and he let the last answer pass without asking for clarification. Now he ventured into what he'd come for.

"Have you ever met Johnny Roe?"

"Met like in sayin' howdy or like in a more formal way?"

"Either."

"Then, no."

Doc furrowed his eyebrows. Emmy's eyes grew large, and she had to look away.

Emmy entered into the questioning, "Do you know who Mr. Roe is? He's the bike man."

"Oh, yeah, I know that dude."

"How do you know him," Doc asked.

"Me and Earl was paid to follow him," he replied.

"Who paid you?"

"Well, Dunham actually gave us the money…."

"But…?"

"But what?"

"But who supplied Dunham the money?"

"U.S."

"Ulysses Johnson?"

"Yep. Him."

"Why?"

"Why what?"

Now it was Doc's turn to bite his lower lip. "Why do you think he was paying you money to follow Johnny Roe?"

"We asked Dunham that but he didn't say. Only said somethin' bout he was stickin' his nose into business that weren't his own. Said we was supposed to scare him off."

"How?"

"How what?"

Doc could only stare straight ahead. "How were you supposed to scare him off?"

"Like let him know somebody didn't want him around. Scare the livin' bejesus out of him, random like, but not so random that he didn't know it was meant for him."

"What did you do? To scare him?"

"Ran him off the road on that bike of his."

"That was you?"

Bettcher nodded his head, smiling, "Me an' Earl."

Emmy asked a question, "What else did you do to scare him?"

Bettcher looked at her like either he'd forgotten she was there, or he wondered if she was allowed to ask questions. He didn't respond.

"The dog?" she whispered.

Bettcher hung his head and drew his hand slowly across his mouth. "I didn't want to do that," he said in a soft, childlike voice. "He made us."

Emmy's eyes turned hard, and she clenched both fists. Trying not to lash out verbally, she blurted a loud guttural sound, coming out as a deep grunt. She had to turn away.

Doc steered the questioning back to Dunham and Ulysses, "Why do you think Joe Dunham and Ulysses wanted to scare Mr. Roe?"

"He said somethin' about the plant but didn't give no details," Bettcher replied, searching his brain, trying to remember if he ever knew any details.

"Relax. Try to think back. Can you remember anything at all about the plant?"

Jim Bettcher was feeling no pain, and he started to yawn repeatedly. He really couldn't remember what Dunham had said or even if he had mentioned the plant. He sighed heavily, knowing he couldn't tell a lie.

"Mr. Bettcher," Doc said, shaking Bettcher's arm to rouse him. "Let me repeat the question, what was going on at the plant that wasn't Mr. Roe's business?"

Jim Bettcher remembered his instructions well and smiling broadly said, "Doc, I cannot tell a lie. I have no idea whatsoever!"

FIFTY-TWO

"**W**HY are we stopping here?" Johnny asked. Emmy had pulled her car over to the curb in front of an abandoned building with a large parking lot.

"That used to be the drive-in restaurant. When one of us girls could get a car, we'd all pile in and come here. It was a real hang out place."

"Hang out, like you mean a pick-up place?"

"No, not really. Just boys and girls hanging out together. Flirting. Boys in one car, girls in another. You know, high school type stuff."

"Well, we have those Sonic drive-ins in California."

"This was just a mom-and -pop restaurant. A family ran it. Best French fries around."

"Were the waitresses on roller skates?" Johnny asked.

"Roller skates?"

"Yeah, like in the movie *American Graffiti.*"

"No, just tennis shoes."

"What happened to it?"

"I suppose the big chains, like McDonald's and Burger King, finally found their way to Booneville and they just couldn't compete."

They sat in the car listening to a soft rock radio station, both lost in thought. Emmy's mind drifted to the past and high school, Johnny's to recent events. Fleetwood Mac sang a rollicking little number.

After a while, Johnny said, "Maybe I should've used the gun on the Bettcher boys instead of the baseball bat. I could've made them talk."

"Wow, way to change the subject and kill the mood."

"Sorry, I've just been rehashing the whole thing. Seems there could've been a better way to handle that."

"Shoulda, coulda, woulda. But didn't."

"What?"

"You just don't seem like a shoulda, coulda, woulda kind of guy to me, Johnny. More like a 'what's next' kind of guy."

"Yeah, you're probably right."

Emmy reached over and slipped her hand under his. He squeezed it but didn't look at her.

"I didn't mean that it's bad to look at the past to figure out what you could have done differently. We all do that. It's perfectly normal…" she said.

"…in situations like mine?" Johnny finished.

"I didn't mean that."

"Yeah, you did."

"Okay, maybe a little I did."

"It just seems like life was perfect there for a while, and now everything is so…I don't know…screwed up," he said, staring at nothing through the windshield.

"Nothing is ever really perfect in the world. We just look at things and most of the time we simply miss the imperfections. Rose-colored glasses and all. God overlooks our imperfections all the time."

"I suppose," he agreed, shrugging his shoulders. *There's that reference to God again*, he thought. *Where's God been through all this?*

"I mean it's good to overlook small imperfections, right? If every time I looked at your weird-shaped ears and commented how dorky they were, eventually you'd take offense, am I right?" she said.

"What's wrong with my ears?"

"Nothing, silly. That's not the point. Nobody's perfect. We all have our flaws. Yours just happen to be sticking out both sides of your head."

He turned toward her, his eyes wide open in mock surprise. "Enough with the ears."

"Kidding!"

They sat there, holding hands in the silence. Finally, Johnny said, looking directly at her, "I'm not looking for perfection."

"Good, I'm not perfect."

"I didn't mean that."

"Yeah, you did."

"Okay, maybe a little I did," he admitted.

"All men look for perfection in women, Johnny. It's their nature. Perfect body, perfect hair, perfect teeth, great personality."

Johnny knew what she meant.

"But nobody is perfect. Some better than others, some not."

"And some look perfect for a long time, then it all turns to junk."

"Like your wife, huh?"

"Yeah. Like her." He massaged the thumb pad on his other hand. He wanted to punch the dashboard, to let the anger out, just a little. He could feel his breath quicken, and he took a deep breath to suppress it all.

"But you produced two perfect children, didn't you?" she asked, leaning close, in almost a whisper.

"Yeah. We did."

Again, the silence closed in on the car.

"Why are you showing me sites like this around Booneville?" Johnny eventually asked.

"I don't know. Maybe to give you a little taste of life in Booneville."

"It's way different than San Francisco. I know that."

"Different as in distinct, not like in bad, right?"

"Distinct, yeah, very distinct."

"Like your ears."

"Enough with the ears."

She smiled, trying not to laugh. So did he.

"I don't know if it's me. Booneville, I mean."

"What do you mean?"

"When I set out on this journey, I never expected to be here."

"Where did you expect to be?"

"I don't know."

"Then how do you know it wasn't supposed to be here?"

He shook his head, "I don't."

"Maybe God wants you here for a reason."

"Like what?"

"Don't know. He didn't tell me."

"This business at the plant isn't over, you know. Maybe you still have a part to play in that," Emmy continued

"In what?"

"In whatever happens."

"What can happen? We've pretty much used up all our options."

"Maybe, maybe not."

"You referring to something specific? Because if you are, I'd like to hear about it. I'm all out of ideas."

"No, nothing specific. It's just that people around here don't give up so easy."

"I'm not giving up."

"I know. I didn't mean that. I meant that people around here are…I don't know…maybe resourceful is the right word. They'll just keep working at something till they find a solution. It doesn't have to be like something sudden or earthshattering. Sometimes we just march along, trying different things, till we hit on the one thing that works. Not like plodding, we're not plodders. We're workers. We work at something till…it works."

He smiled at her analogy and shook his head like he understood. "Got it."

She squeezed his hand a little harder. "Wanna see the water tower?" she asked.

"Oh, could we? Be still my heart."

"It's the daring side of me. We used to climb to the top of it and look out at the whole countryside."

"I didn't know you had a daring side."

"There are a few things you don't know about me. Guarantee it. But daring, well, I guess I'm not too daring. Mostly we'd climb up there and just sit and talk. Some of us would look out and try to envision a future far away from Booneville. I suppose we all thought about that at some point. And many of my friends moved away and never came back. But I never saw myself living anywhere but here. So that's one thing you now know about me, but they're lots more things you don't. So there."

"What, like you've had plastic surgery to repair ugly ears?"

She howled. "You need to work on your comebacks a little, Johnny Roe. They're weak!"

"Your mother's weak!"

"My mother's dead," Emmy said, her face suddenly clouded and concerned.

"Oh, jeez, I'm sorry, I didn't mean…."

Her face exploded in a huge smile and her eyes lit up. "Gotcha!"

Johnny closed his eyes, shook his head, and tried not to smile.

FIFTY-THREE

ULYSSES Johnson slumped in the chair. At first glance, he seemed relaxed, almost lethargic. Not quite a smile on his face, but certainly nothing that would resemble discomfort to the outside observer. Except maybe the left side of his face. His cheek was swollen, and the swelling was both creeping up to his left eye and discoloring it a bit. Upon closer inspection though, Ulysses didn't look so good. After all, poor boy had been in that particular chair for almost thirty-six hours.

Eddie Walnuts entered the room. Having just been refreshed from a short nap, a little breakfast (ham and eggs), a shower and a shave, his thick, curly hair was slicked back, still damp from the shower. Even in his weakened state, Ulysses could smell the cheap cologne before Eddie Walnuts entered the room. He had slipped on a freshly starched shirt and was just attaching the second cuff link. He always wore a shirt with cuff links. If it was good enough for all the presidents of the U.S. of A., it was good enough for Eddie Walnuts. When somebody pointed out the Barrack Obama never wore cuff links, Eddie simply pointed out that he probably shouldn't be president anyway, since his birth certificate was obviously a phony. Eddie loved conspiracy theories and could talk endlessly about the impossibility that Lee Harvey Oswald could have gotten off those four shots in Dealey Plaza and actually hit anything smaller than the side of a building much less the side of the head of John Kennedy. Don't get him started.

Ulysses Johnson had sneaked into Atlantic City the week before. He figured he was safe on the East Coast. Eddie Walnuts and his thugs were strictly Vegas guys when they ventured out of Chicago. They never went to the slums of Atlantic City. Wouldn't be caught dead there. And Ulysses had an urge. It seemed to grow much bigger once that dirty chink Mr. Cheng had told him no more payments were coming. And Ulysses had to find a way to pay back some of that debt he owed. *Maybe my luck will change.* That had become his mantra: *maybe my luck will change.* He chanted that on the plane to Jersey almost the entire way until the "maybe" had been lost somewhere over Ohio (or maybe it got lost in those four bourbon and gingers) and the phrase now rattling around in his head was—*my luck will change.*

And for the first couple of days, for the most part, his luck was better than usual. He won. A lot. For almost twenty-four hours after he entered the Lucky Seven Casino, he won consistently, almost three out of four hands of blackjack at the $200 table. But once he stopped—he had to, he was almost falling asleep at the table and nodding off was seriously hampering his concentration—his luck changed when he returned to the tables after a nap and some dinner. Like guacamole dip that one day looks green and fresh and the next looks brown and bad. And luck that can be described as guacamole gone bad is never good. He stopped after another six hours and estimated that he was still up about five grand. He sat at the bar and had a beer, contemplating a return to Booneville with his winnings.

As he talked to himself about the pros and cons of more gambling, he caught a glimpse of one of Eddie Walnuts' goons out of the corner of his eye. *No way. Nooo way.* How could he know Ulysses was in town? Maybe it was a coincidence; maybe the goon was after another gambler. Ulysses tried to sneak out the side entrance of the casino, but in hindsight, that was probably what they were waiting for. Inside the casino, Ulysses could have called for help, he was safe. Outside, he became a sitting duck. They quickly shoved him into a car and left Atlantic City, heading west.

Eddie Walnuts was riding shotgun, and Ulysses was in the middle in the back seat, between goon one and goon two. Aviator sunglasses masked the driver, dressed in all black. They were in some type of Lincoln limo as far as Ulysses could tell. The car left Atlantic City in the early evening and except for a few bathroom stops, drove eight hours directly to Pittsburgh. Eddie spoke softly into his cell phone for the first few hours of the trip. Halfway across Pennsylvania, it was decided not to return to Chicago but to stop in the Steel City.

Now Ulysses sat in the chair, which was in an office of a nondescript warehouse in the Three Rivers district. Not too far from the sports stadium down at the juncture of the Monongahela, the Ohio, and the Allegheny rivers.

Ulysses was a bit delusional. Maybe Eddie and the goons were just sweating him out. Trying to make him talk, although he'd said just about everything he could possibly say to bull them into thinking he was going to pay back the money. Ulysses was pretty good when it came to spreading the bull, and for the first twenty-four hours or so, he laid it on pretty heavy. Not too heavy, but just enough to keep them going—and believing. But as the second day wore on and he began to lose strength, he'd begun to fade. The goons had provided meals to everyone except Ulysses; he had gotten only water. Even to himself, his talking now made little sense with only hints of clarity.

Eddie Walnuts nodded into the mobile phone, grimly, then hung up.

"Boss says we're to cut our losses and get back to Chicago," he said to nobody in particular.

Goons one and two had no reaction. Ulysses, however, took notice.

"What does that mean?" he asked. "You're letting me go?"

"Wishful thinking," Eddie replied.

"Then what?"

"Must I spell it out?" Eddie said.

Ulysses nodded.

"The boss believes he has received all of the debt that he will ever receive from you, including the five grand you relinquished in Atlantic City. That particular fact does not make him happy."

"I told you—" Ulysses continued.

But Eddie held up his hand to stop him.

"We no longer believe what you say, Mr. Johnson. But all is not lost. There is still a victory at hand for us."

"Like a win-win situation?" Ulysses said, a look of hope creeping into his eyes.

"No, actually, more like a win-lose. We win, you lose."

"What do you mean, lose?"

Eddie sighed, "Oh, how the desperate hold on to any faint hope. We gain respect. You lose your life. Simple, actually. And brilliant in its depth."

Ulysses, now fully awake, grabbed the chair in a death grip.

"You can't kill me," he whispered.

"Do tell," Eddie inquired. "And why is that?"

"If you do, you'll never get your money…" Ulysses stopped, hesitated a beat or two, and continued, "…back."

"Seems the boss has lost interest in getting the remainder of his investment back. Like I said, he would like to exit the agreement and cut his losses."

"Exit the agreement?" Ulysses asked, almost to himself.

Eddie sighed even more heavily this time.

"We're gonna fry your ass and make an example out of you to all the rest of the loser assholes who owe us money!" Eddie shouted, momentarily losing the composure he so prided himself on. "That clear enough for your sorry ass?"

He took a deep breath, recomposed himself, and began to decide how actually to kill Ulysses Johnson. For all his hype and threatening, he actually didn't really enjoy the physical job of taking another life. But he couldn't ask goon one or goon two; and after all, he did have his reputation to uphold. He contemplated for a minute or two.

"Okay. I've decided. I will shoot you in the back of the head two times from close range. Then we will dump your body outside the stadium, leaving your wallet and phone in your pocket. It will not look like a robbery but rather, as the vernacular says, a hit. Word will leak of your demise, and if we're lucky, even gather momentum on the World Wide Web. Then we will use that digital information to let others know, those indebted to us in any number of ways, that we only have so much patience." He nodded approvingly, liking his own plan, and seeing no flaws.

Ulysses fainted or passed out. Eddy began to maneuver Ulysses in the chair. He grabbed a couple of loose bath towels and situated them just so.

"There. Don't want to get my newly cleaned shirt all bloody now, do I? Let's commence," he said, before abruptly stopping.

"First, I want a souvenir."

FIFTY-FOUR

THE package arrived in Joe Dunham's office mid-afternoon with his other mail. It was one of those medium-sized rectangular boxes with the distinctive red-and-blue markings from the post office. Hand addressed to him, but the return address had no name, just a city, Chicago. For a reason he couldn't pinpoint, Dunham had a knot in his stomach, and bile bubbled up in his throat. He set the box at the corner of his desk and went through the rest of his mail.

The box kept beckoning to him.

He reached into his desk drawer and grabbed a pair of scissors. He sliced the clear tape that held the box together. With the scissors still in thumb and forefinger, he used the blades to lift the box's flap. Bubble wrap surrounded what looked like an eyeglass case inside. Dunham hesitated. He had a bad feeling about this.

He removed the bubble wrap and looked for any indication of who sent the package, like a note or a return address. Nothing. Only the script logo of Eddie Bauer embossed on the brown leather case.

More tape wrapped around the eyeglass case. Too small for a bomb, Dunham thought. His heart rate slowed a bit, thinking that maybe he'd misplaced a pair of shades somewhere and somebody was mailing them back to him. But he still had that bad feeling.

He used the scissors to slice through the tape but didn't open the case. He thought he smelled something odd, like bad cheese.

The phone rang, and he answered it, never taking his eyes off the case. When the call ended, he got up from his chair, walked around his office, and took a couple of deep breaths.

Without picking it up, Dunham finally gripped the case and separated the two sides. It snapped open, and he saw more bubble wrap, loosely surrounding something inside. He used the scissors to flip the wrap away.

As soon as he saw what was inside, Dunham swallowed a gag and felt his stomach lurch. But he didn't toss. He quickly shut the case and returned it to the box. He reached into his desk, found his tape dispenser, and wrapped the box back up as best as he could.

He paced his office and thought about his next move. Whatever he did with the box was the least of his worries. Eddie Walnuts was definitely the most of his worries. Dunham sat at his desk and looked at his hands. He flexed all of his fingers several times, extending them out, then making a fist. He gingerly grabbed the box, and as he opened the door to his office, he almost bumped into Norm Boswell who was poised to knock, his hand raised in a fist.

"Not now," Dunham said. Boswell was left frozen, his fist still in the air.

Dunham headed toward Ulysses' office, and using his key, opened the locked office and closed the door without making a sound.

Even though he knew Ulysses hadn't been seen or heard from for days, his paranoia made him look around the office to make absolutely sure it wasn't occupied.

He approached the safe, searching his mind for the combination as he knelt in front of it. After it clicked into his rather distracted brain, he spun the dial and grunted as he opened the heavy door.

He found the stack of small bills Ulysses always kept on hand.

Just then, unexpectedly, a pang of guilt showed up. Dunham almost didn't recognize the feeling. For ten seconds he thought about Ulysses. They'd been friends—well, not exactly friends, more like…what were they to each other?—for over five years. He wondered if Ulysses had lost any more fingers. Was he hurt? Did he need help? Where was he? Was he even alive?

The ten seconds evaporated. He snatched the bills and replaced them with the box. If he was still alive, he might want the box back. Ulysses often bragged about how he could always get his hands on five or ten grand when he absolutely needed to. From the size of the wad in Dunham's hand, he figured it was closer to ten.

Fair trade, he thought.

He closed the safe, locked the door to the office as he left, and hustled to his car.

FIFTY-FIVE

"**W**HAT in the world is Ulysses going to say when he returns and finds his safe broken into?" Stanley Strasbaugh demanded to know, directing his question to Norm Boswell. Huddled in Ulysses' office, they both concentrated on the man hired from Des Moines to open the safe. He had maneuvered a large drill to the front of the safe but hesitated when he heard the question, waiting for any final approval. Once you drilled a safe, there was no turning back.

"If he returns," Boswell countered.

"Well, if he returns, all manner of chaos will break loose," Strasbaugh said in his lawyerly manner.

"I'll take full responsibility," Boswell told him.

"No, he'll blame the board. He'll blame me. I know it."

"Settle down, Stanley. We'll say you weren't even here. You can actually leave if you want to. That's fine. Like I said, I'll take the heat."

"No, I'm staying."

Boswell kept his eyes on the man with the drill. He nodded towards him, an indication to proceed. "Besides, he'll fire my butt. You got nothing to worry about," he finally said.

The drill whirled into action, the sound penetrating the entire office like the shock of a sudden fire alarm.

Johnny, Doc, and a few other managers at the plant stood at the back of the office. The more Johnny saw Norm Boswell in action, the more he liked him. It took some stones to go into the boss's office and crack open his private safe. If Ulysses were indeed alive, Boswell was probably right. He'd be canned, and it wouldn't be pretty. Bold on Boswell's part, Johnny thought, and a little daring.

"This could take a while," the safe-drilling man said. "Got to get past that cobalt plate and find the wheel pack. It's not a top of the line model, so this shouldn't take all that long, maybe a half hour or so. I'll let you know when I get it open unless you want to stand around and watch. Which could get pretty boring. Boring, ha, get it? No pun intended," he said, his right hand doing small circles, mimicking the motion of the drill.

Nobody laughed. Norm Boswell advised everyone to return to the conference room.

During a lengthy conversation about the future of the plant, drill man stuck his head into the conference room.

With thumb and forefinger holding his nose, he said, "Something died in there. Pee-uuu!"

"What are you talking about?" Strasbaugh said.

"I got her open, and as soon as I cranked the door, the smell 'bout knocked me down. Don't know what it is and I'm not too keen on finding out. Anyway, the safe door is open. I'm done here."

They all scrambled out of the room and headed back to Ulysses' office. As Strasbaugh held back, Norm Boswell approached the safe. He had to turn his head to the side as the stench hit him hard. He edged down into a crouch, looking into the safe, trying not to breath in the bad air. He observed papers and files, a hard drive, and other miscellaneous items. Boswell reached in and extracted a jewel case, set it on the desk, and without much deliberation, opened it. Money clips, a few silver dollars, a couple of men's rings, a small plastic bag with what looked like loose gemstones. But nothing that smelled bad.

Then he spotted the eyeglass case with tape. It looked like it had been previously opened since the tape had been sliced. As soon as he brought it out of the confined area of the safe, the power of the stench hit the entire room. Boswell looked around like he wanted to grab a pair of gloves to open the case, or a pair of oven mitts, or something besides his bare hands, but when he saw everyone in the room looking at him, he fought through the urge. He took in another deep breath. Turning the case toward the room, he opened it with a slow, audible creak demanding attention. The smell made his eyes water.

"What is that?" Strasbaugh asked, backing away another step or two and holding a handkerchief to his nose.

"Looks like a finger," Boswell answered, rather nonchalantly. "With a tiger's eye ring."

Everyone in the room, with the exception of Johnny, gradually realized exactly whose finger they were looking at.

Finally, Boswell expressed what everyone was thinking. "Ulysses' finger. And his ring."

Stanley Strasbaugh had to suppress a gag and almost everyone, Doc excepted, took a few more steps away from the desk.

Doc leaned in to take a better look. Through the plastic wrap and the discoloration of the digit, he couldn't see it well, but remarked, "Whoever did this was rather crude about it. Definitely not a professional job, if you ask me."

"Depends on what profession you are talking about, Doc," Johnny said.

"What do you mean?"

"In some cultures, they cut off the hands…and I suppose, fingers…of thieves. So they aren't tempted to steal again."

"Jesus, you don't think we're going to find his whole hand in there, do you?" Strasbaugh croaked from the back of the room.

"Doesn't look like it," Boswell said, leaning in for another peek. "That's pretty much it."

"What's the card say?" Johnny wondered.

"What card?" Strasbaugh shouted.

"The one on the inside of the case."

Boswell leaned in close without touching the card. "It says, 'Mr. U.S. Johnson has paid his debts. Paid in full.'"

"He paid his debts with his finger? Is that what that means?" Doc asked.

"Or more," Johnny said.

"More than his finger?"

Johnny nodded.

"Why in the world would Ulysses keep his own finger, assuming it actually is his finger, in his personal office safe?" Doc wondered aloud.

"Maybe like a receipt. A receipt that he paid his debt…in full," Boswell guessed.

"Who else had access to this safe?" Johnny asked.

"Not me," Boswell answered. "Nobody else I know, except maybe…Dunham."

"What're you saying?" Doc asked.

"I'm not saying anything," Johnny responded, "but it won't be hard to find out if it's actually his finger."

"Let's assume that it is," Boswell said.

"Then maybe somebody else put it in there."

"Why would they do that?"

"Maybe Ulysses couldn't."

They all stood around, pondering questions that had no answers.

Finally, Johnny said, "Something tells me Ulysses isn't coming back."

"Unless it's piece by piece," Norm Boswell said.

FIFTY-SIX

IN what had become quite a normal afternoon for them when Emmy wasn't working, she and Johnny walked the streets and roads of Booneville. It helped Johnny stay in decent shape as his injuries from the bike crash healed. Walking seemed to do him good; being with Emmy seemed to make him feel good.

As they strolled down a tree-canopied avenue near Doc's house, Johnny's cell phone buzzed. He checked the number before answering and saw that it was his partner, Walt Mathews. Maybe he should take the call.

"Walt, what's happening?"

"Johnny, long time no talk to, bud. Where in the world are you, Waldo?"

"Iowa. Long story."

"Yeah, I got bits and pieces from Wacker. Not much. Do you have him sworn to secrecy or something?"

"Something like that. What's up?" Johnny knew that this just wasn't a social call. Something in the stiffness of Walt's demeanor perked his antenna to what might be the reason.

"We need to talk."

"You sound like a woman, and I hate it when a woman says that to me." Even when he said it, Johnny winced a bit. Too much recent history, too much Emmy close by. Too much something; he couldn't put his finger on it.

"Yeah, I know, but we still need to talk some things out, you know?" Walt said, his tone showing resignation.

"I suppose you're right. I owe you more than you've been getting. You want to schedule something or do it now," Johnny said, looking at Emmy, who gave him a "sure, don't mind me" look.

"You kind of sound busy. Maybe we can do it late today or early tomorrow?"

"Either is fine with me, but tell me what it's about so I can prepare a little, okay."

"It's about the company, our company."

"Why, what's wrong?"

"Nothing, really. No, no, we're doing fine. And I thought you didn't want to talk about it now."

"Maybe I do. Maybe a little."

"I just think we need to talk about the future, that's all. Like what your plans are, how they include or don't include us, what happens to us? Things like that."

"Sounds like a planning session, a brainstorm."

"Definitely. And it'd be nice if some of the staff were involved, too. At least at some point."

"Yeah, probably a good idea," Johnny agreed. "Let's talk, you and me, first thing in the morning, to get our ducks in a row before we bring in others. Man to man. That'll give me the rest of the day to do some planning, thinking…stuff."

"Stuff? When did you fall off the technical jargon wagon, dude?"

Looking directly at Emmy, Johnny replied, "Iowa does that to you."

Emmy mouthed the words "don't blame me" to Johnny and he laughed.

"I suppose you get up with the roosters or hens or whatever they have in Iowa and I've got a busy day tomorrow, so how's about we talk early? Is seven my time too early for you, you cornhusker?"

"That's Nebraska, dude. And seven works fine. Call me on my cell."

"Later."

"See ya," Johnny said as he clicked off his phone.

"Trouble at home?" Emmy wanted to know.

"No, I don't think so. That was my partner, Walt. I guess he and the others at our company are wondering where the heck am I and what the heck I'm doing there."

"And they don't know the difference between Iowa and Nebraska?"

"Right, probably couldn't pick out either on a map."

"So what's the planning and thinking you need to do between now and tomorrow?"

"Alright, I'm keeping track," Johnny said with a smile, "That's three questions. You only have seventeen to go."

"Good to know," Emmy replied as she grabbed his hand and they continue their walk. After a few minutes of silence, Emmy asked, "If I ask the same question again, does that count against my twenty questions?"

Johnny chuckled, "No. I'm sure Walt wants to know if I'm ever coming back. Knowing him, he's figured out how to run things pretty smoothly. Maybe even figured out how to replace my creative side."

"Shudder to think," Emmy said.

"Yeah, I know. But we always hired good people. Maybe somebody's emerged."

They continued down the sidewalk, avoiding the uneven sections that had been lifted up from invading tree limbs. *Step on a crack, you break your mother's back.*

"Anything I can do to help you think and plan?" Emmy finally asked.

"Like what?"

"Like tell you how I feel about you."

They had stopped and turned toward each other. Johnny looked into Emmy's brown eyes.

"How do you feel?"

"I'm not sure."

"That's honest." He pulled his eyes away and looked down the sidewalk.

"How do you feel about me, Johnny Roe?"

"Does that matter? In how you feel about me?"

"It shouldn't, should it?"

"Boy, don't ask me. I guess it shouldn't, but I know that it does, sometimes."

"How do you feel, Johnny?"

"I don't suppose 'I asked you first' would be a good reply right now, huh?"

"Well, you would be right about that, I suppose. Okay, here goes." Emmy gathered herself and took a deep breath. Before she spoke, she waited almost a full minute. "I like when we're together. I look forward to being together with you. No, look forward…is the wrong phrase. I…feel kind of empty when we're not together. Like…I miss you, terribly. It's a longing, like an ache, a good ache and I can definitely feel it, right here." She pointed to her heart. Tears started to pool in her eyes.

"I like when you touch me, even if it's just holding hands. Even though you don't do it often…and I understand that…when you do reach for me, it…thrills me, it warms me, it…settles me in some way that is kind of hard to explain."

Johnny just nodded but didn't know what to say.

"You're funny, and you make me laugh. Sometimes I laugh at things you said a day earlier. Not like I didn't get it the first time, but that it's funny all over again."

"It's a gift." Johnny shrugged.

"And when you kiss me, I lose track. I lose track of where I am and what I've been doing. I can't even hardly think. I don't want to think. I just lose myself in that kiss somehow. I lose part of myself to you. I…it's like I become part of you a little bit. Or you a part of me, I don't know. And as I think about that and actually say it out loud, that's a little scary to me. I don't know if I've ever felt that way about anyone, ever. And I don't know what to do with it. Except say it out loud. That helps."

Emmy inhaled again and tasted the fresh air, the trees, the grass, the everything of Booneville, Iowa. Her face was radiant, her eyes sparkled, and Johnny noticed.

He leaned in to kiss her, but she backed away a little. "Oh, no, big fella. No more sugar until you at least give it a shot." Lowering her voice to just a whisper, she said, "Tell me how you feel."

Johnny mimicked her deep inhale and said, "That's fair." He let go of her hand and circled the section of sidewalk where they'd stopped. Twice, he started to talk but couldn't find the words.

"I'm not so good at this," he admitted.

"Just practice. Just say how you feel."

"I feel good."

"Could you be just *slightly* more definitive?"

"Good about you. But…don't know what that means. I like being with you. I think about you all the time. When I'm deep in thought about something totally different, you pop into my mind. I think you're beautiful. Those eyes, wow. And I know I'm holding back from you, backing away. Every time I start to examine my feelings, something gets in the way. It's like a roadblock, a wall. It's big and tall, and most of the time, I can't even get around it…or see over it…. I can't explain it, I can't even tell you what it is. It's just there, and I smack into it all the time. I'm sorry, I'm so sorry."

The pools of tears in Emmy's eyes were now little streams, dripping down her cheeks, landing on her blouse. She didn't even notice them or try to wipe them away. She reached out and pulled Johnny close, hugging him. She didn't let go. Through a snuffle, she said, "You actually are very good at this."

"I can't say that I love you, Emmy. It's not in me right now."

"I'm not asking you to."

They held the hug, closely, full body, tight. Finally, Johnny lifted his head back. "Can I kiss you now?"

"You'd better."

FIFTY-SEVEN

NORM Boswell had called the staff meeting the day before. No board members, no Doc, no Johnny, just his managers. He called them his managers but not all actually reported to him. He was just the director of operations, so technically Sales, Customer Service, Accounting and Marketing weren't under his command. But Norm Boswell had always invited those managers to sit in when appropriate on facility and operations meetings and frequently they had. He'd been able to build a cohesive team that way, knowing it was always good to have everyone in the company listening to the same sheet of music even if they played different instruments.

For the past several weeks, he'd been dissecting the business from every possible direction. He'd been using what Johnny had said were his detective skills. And he was ready to discuss with the team what he'd found.

He had arrived early that morning and personally cleaned the conference room. It was pristine; he didn't want anything to interfere with the discussion. He'd learned that trick from Johnny. So he'd cleaned the whiteboard and tray that held the markers, conference table, and even vacuumed the rug. Large, white Post-It sheets, two foot by three foot and too big to be called sticky notes, stuck to the walls. He wanted to write down ideas and have people see those ideas so they'd generate more ideas. If you let a thought percolate on the back burner but still within sight, it could boil into something interesting. He'd even stopped at the local office supply store the night before and bought two new sets of markers in different colors.

As the team gathered early that morning, nobody grumbled, even at seven o'clock. They knew this meeting was important. A lot was on the line—maybe the company's future—and Boswell had done a good job of prepping them all on its importance in the days leading up to the meeting.

Cell phones were turned off, not just silenced.

After the coffee was poured and the staff grabbed a bagel or some fruit, Norm Boswell launched his PowerPoint presentation. He knew to make it short and to the point, especially this early in the morning. Each manager had supplied a one-page summary to Boswell the day before, so in fifteen minutes he was able to give a quick snapshot of where the company stood. He let each manager spend no more than sixty seconds reviewing their department's slide, and only clarification questions were allowed during the review. Boswell knew that if there was any gold to be discovered, it wasn't going to be in the details of the review. Old mine shafts can sometimes lead to new veins of gold, but digging down the same old tunnels usually just leads to more dirt.

Once all the reports had been completed and Boswell had finished his review, he set the guidelines for brainstorming. *There are no bad ideas, let's just get all ideas down on paper, for all to see. We can expand upon the good ideas later.* Everyone in the room knew that Norm Boswell had a system for voting for the best ideas. People would actually walk around the room and "star" good ideas with a marker. You only got so many votes, so you had to make them count. Vote for the two best ideas. More rules: always keep comments positive, and nothing personal should be hashed out. This wasn't a bitch session and personality conflicts or discussions would not be tolerated. Take it outside after the meeting, be adults. Boswell would control the brainstorm by introducing new topics, and he always started the discussion with the topic of money.

Josh, the Accounting manager, had discussed concerns about cash flow in his slide, so they started there. Ideas were plentiful. Boswell laughed internally when the Customer Service manager even suggested they cut out coffee and fruit at meetings. He had to admire her *cojones* and didn't want to let her know that he'd paid for the coffee and fruit served this morning out of his own pocket. Good idea, he'd said.

He switched topics and marketing was next up. Sales numbers were down but at least lead times for product delivery had shrunk. The Marketing manager suggested that they publicize the fact that now their lead times were half of what the competition was offering. Everyone liked that idea, especially if Marketing could accomplish it without spending money. The Marketing manager wondered out loud how that was going to happen, but that was his problem to solve, not the group's.

Boswell shifted topics often, simply by announcing new parameters: What if money was no concern? What if you could institute one new idea in your department? What if you knew we'd be out of business in six months if we didn't change something? How could we increase business immediately? How could your department cut expenses by twenty percent?

When the Sales department was on the hot seat, finally good news emerged, like sunshine breaking through rain clouds. Boswell smiled broadly when the Sales manager, Jackson Smith, announced that he'd personally taken three unsolicited phone calls in the past two weeks from prospective new customers that looked extremely promising. Jackson had devised a very detailed way to evaluate possible new business and, to cut to the quick for everyone in the room, he pegged these possibilities at over eighty percent. Most new business entered his matrix below twenty percent, especially if they were interested in the newest technology. And these three calls were all about vision-guided robotics, their newest. None of the three would divulge how they came to hear about U.S. Johnson Controls for this technology, but that wasn't too unusual in this global marketplace. It was too early to tell what the final sales estimates might be, but it had been a long time since Norm Boswell had seen such enthusiasm from his Sales department. The news lifted everyone's spirits, and from that point on, tough choices were easier to make about things that had to change. Boswell made a mental note to keep on top of this and bring Johnny Roe into the loop on the topic.

After two hours, they had voted on some of the good ideas they could implement starting that day: workers would be encouraged to use unpaid time off to decrease payroll; facilities would delay scheduled maintenance for thirty days; health care plans would be re-evaluated yet again; no raises would be given for six months; sales would decrease travel expenses by ten percent however they could (hello, red-eye plane flights); no more overtime without consensus approval; Marketing would shift from paid advertising to unpaid sources (organic search was all that came to mind, but they'd have their own brainstorming tomorrow); Sales would implement a phone campaign to contact all existing customers, yet again; and the list went on.

Boswell took a picture with his phone of all the large sticky notes that surrounded the room. But he also planned to transfer the actual sheets to his office walls. Another good idea might emerge just by looking at them again. He knew the meeting was productive—ideas flowed, decisions were made, and spirits were lifted. Sometimes just doing something was better than doing nothing, even if that something was difficult to do.

FIFTY-EIGHT

"**G**OING somewhere?" Doc asked as he leaned into the room Johnny had been using since the bike accident.

A half-packed suitcase on the bed and clothes scattered about the room indicated an upcoming trip. Sunlight filtered in from the side window, illuminating a section of the faded chenille bedspread. The sparsely decorated room held only a queen-size bed, an old antiquey looking dresser with an attached mirror, a wooden rocking chair with a frayed seat cushion, and a floor lamp. Hardwood floors were barely hidden by a Navajo blanket substituting for a rug, faded along the side of the room where the sunlight invaded daily.

"Little trip back to San Francisco."

Doc nodded once and raised his eyebrows, anticipating more from Johnny. None came, so he probed more.

"You coming back? Or should I wash the sheets and towels?"

"Definitely coming back. I'm even leaving my bike here and the car. Emmy's driving me to the airport in Des Moines this afternoon."

"Good. Good, then."

Johnny sat down on the bed as Doc settled into the rocker.

"It's a company visit, mostly. The people that are running our business need me to poop or get off the can, pardon my French."

"No offense. It's a good analogy. Made up your mind which it is yet?"

"No, not really. They seem to have some ideas of how things could work so I said I'd fly back and listen. That's all."

Doc slowly worked the rocker. "If you don't mind me saying, I've noticed an uneasiness in you lately. A restlessness. Ever since the venture boys declined our offer. You getting restless?"

Johnny thought for a moment or two before answering. "Yeah, I suppose. When I left, back...when it all happened...I didn't know where

I was going or even why. Just needed to get away."

He laid back on the bed, grabbed a pillow, and propped himself up on one elbow, facing Doc.

"And I sure didn't see myself ending up in Booneville, Iowa. No offense."

"None taken. You know, I didn't see myself ending up here either."

"I thought you were born here."

"I was, but when I went to med school, I always thought I'd end up in a big city. Ended up going to Case Western in Cleveland. Maybe it was Cleveland that cured me of big cities, but after a while, I ended up longing for the life of a small town. So I came back here and set up my practice."

"I'm not sure I'm longing for that life," Johnny thought out loud.

"I can understand that. Not always a lot going on here. It takes a bit to settle into the pace of small town life. We often see folks move here from the bigger cities, wanting to slow down their lives. They retire or try to set up a little bed and breakfast or a coffee shop or something. Sometimes, not saying all the time but sometimes, folks just can't get the hang of slowing down. They miss the fast-paced life, I guess. Me, once I was in that life, I found it didn't suit me too well. I suppose I could have adapted to it. But my rhythm is slower, the rhythm of everyday, the rhythm that God gave me you might say. It's…measured. More Harry Bellefonte, less Harry Connick, Jr."

"Got it."

"And nothing is forever, you know. Just because you spend some time in Booneville doesn't mean you're going to spend the rest of your life here. God says 'this too will pass,' not 'this too is forever.'"

"Didn't know you talked to God so much."

"Got more time to do that, now that I'm retired. Course, I found time even when I wasn't. Maybe Boonville living gives you more time for that."

"I never had much time for that," Johnny said, looking to some place that he couldn't quite see.

"A lot of folks don't. I'm not saying that's good or bad, just saying it works for me."

The side window was open, and a gentle September breeze wafted into the room, bringing with it the faint scent of freshly cut grass.

Breaking the tranquility, Doc asked, "How long are you going be gone?"

"I left the return trip open-ended. Maybe a week or two. I'd like to say hello to a few friends, visit a few old haunts, tie up a few loose ends."

"I bet you're going miss Booneville when you're gone," Doc said, a smile slowly spreading across his face.

"Maybe. You might be right."

"Know you're going to miss parts of Booneville."

"Yeah, like what?"

"Me, fishin', maybe female companionship."

Johnny smiled and nodded his head, looking directly at Doc.

"I've seen those googly eyes you've been making toward Miss Brownell."

"There we go with googly again."

"Yessiree, googly, indeed."

To change the subject, Johnny asked, "What's going on out at the plant these days?"

"Heard they have some new business on the horizon if they can close it. That vision-guided robotics you were showing Ritter. Got some folks out there excited, I think, although they're hiding it pretty well. Too soon to tell, but it might be something."

"Who's running things?"

"Norm Boswell is taking charge. Heard they're making a few changes. Cutting back where they have to, getting lean and mean."

"Lean and mean is usually a good thing. As long as they don't get too lean or too mean."

"He likes you, you know, Norman. Always says how much you opened up in him something that he really hadn't noticed."

"He's a good guy. I could see him running that place."

Doc had never thought about that and let it settle in a bit to his thinking. "Hmm, might not be a bad idea."

"He's got all the tools and a lot of the right people."

"What's he missing?"

"Don't know. Most ops guys just need to learn to take charge and make decisions when they get promoted. Maybe that's all he needs, the opportunity."

"And a little help on the marketing and PR side of things?"

"What? Like me? I didn't seem to help much with Ritter and the venture boys."

"Don't sell yourself short. Maybe that whole exercise opened up some new thinking out there."

Doc let the rocker settle. "I remember the time a new chiropractor moved to town. First we ever had here. Thought he was a crackpot. Just cracking bones. But then he began to show me how to relieve chronic pain in a few of my patients. We started talking regularly, comparing notes. He taught me a good deal about the nerve systems in the spine. Opened up some new thinking for me. We were good friends for thirty years."

"What happened to him?"

"His wife died. Moved closer to his kids, out in Oregon, I think. We lost touch. But my point is just opening a door to new thinking helps. Gotta have somebody opening those doors."

"I understand what you mean. It's just that door opening isn't too…I don't know…just doesn't seem real important to me."

"Depends what door is opened, now, doesn't it?" Doc replied, a twinkle in his eye.

Johnny laid back on the bed, two pillows propped behind his head. As Doc continued the rhythm of the rocker, silence came over the room, both men lost in their thoughts.

After a few moments, Doc asked in a quiet, contemplative voice, "What do you fear in life, John?"

"Fear? Like how?"

"What keeps you up at night? What gnaws at you, maybe even makes you uneasy?"

"I don't know, the usual stuff, I guess. Money, death, loneliness. Never thought too much about it."

"Bull. We all think about it. Hard to avoid."

"I suppose," Johnny admitted.

"Me, I don't fear death," Doc continued. "And I've seen more than my share. Some folks fight it till their last breath. Some are pretty much petrified of it. When they see it approach, they just … freeze up, can't make a decision. Death takes away all their thinking, totally locks them up. They virtually stop functioning."

"I can understand that I guess," Johnny said.

"Others, when they know they're going to die, become serene. They're not fearful, at least they don't appear to be. It's not like they give up, but they don't run away either. Maybe it's a religious thing, like they expect to see heaven, God, Jesus."

"What's your point? You trying to convert me?"

"Nah, that's not my job. Believing in something you can't see is hard for most folks. But it's not impossible."

"I've done some things I'm not proud of," Johnny said. "I'm not sure God would forgive me for some of them."

"Pretty sure there's nothing that unforgivable."

"You positive?"

"Nothing I can see in the Bible. Maybe you ought to give it a gander sometime."

"There you go, trying to convert me again."

"Well, ha, no. I mean I'm always willing to talk about God, don't get me wrong. But my point is that some people run away from their fears and some don't. They either run toward them or embrace them some other way."

"It's like those folks who fear being sick," Doc continued. "Some of them were so afraid of being sick, it's really hard to heal them. That fear grips them, engulfs them, like a cocoon. If you always have that fear, that feeling, that prickling, it can overwhelm you. Like people who aren't content in life. You know those types?"

"Sure," Johnny answered.

"They seem to be always searching for the next best thing. Sick people always want the magic bullet. Heal me instantly, doc, they say. Life as it is, even with a little pain or illness, isn't enough for them. They always want something more. Something that's perfect. They're never satisfied. You know, most illnesses will take care of themselves on their own with just a little bit of help from someone like me. Half of my practice was *do no harm*."

"You mean like hypochondriacs?"

"No, that's only the extreme. But if you know there is perfection out there, whether you call that God or heaven or…that's just how you live your life, you can let go of the trying to be perfect, the searching. You can let go of the fear. But until you face that fear or face the fact that perfection already exists in your life, you always just keep searching. You're never satisfied. And if you're sick, you never heal."

Johnny nodded but kept silent.

"You don't seem like the kind of person who runs away from his fears," Doc offered.

"Seems like I've been running a long time now," Johnny said.

"Yep."

"Sometimes it's hard to embrace your fears."

"Yep."

"Sometimes you don't even know what you're afraid of."

"Amen."

"You trying to tell me to embrace my fears rather than running away from them?" Johnny asked in a low voice, almost a whisper.

"Nah, you'll figure it out."

"I don't know that I'm done searching."

"A lot of folks are like that. Some keep searching their whole life. And they never find what they're searching for. They never completely heal."

"You put it that way, it sounds pretty terrible," Johnny said, lying back on the bed, staring at the ceiling.

"Like hell."

"Doc, sometimes I don't know what I'm searching for, but I don't think it's God."

"Oh, it's not hard to find God. What's really hard is to let Him find you."

FIFTY-NINE

THE United flight approached the Bay Area from the north. Johnny knew that eventually it would bank to the right, out over the Pacific Ocean, and fly into the San Francisco Airport from the west. He wished the plane had taken another flight path. He always enjoyed the trip up the valley from the south, Silicon Valley, high-tech haven. But with major airports in San Jose and Oakland and minor ones scattered in between, air traffic was busy now. He'd have to be content with just remembering those valley clients, not actually seeing the buildings from the air. And even though he could usually pick out a few actual companies on the ground, some had probably moved to bigger digs by now or gone out of business. Life in the valley.

Johnny usually opted for an aisle seat, but on this flight, he sat by a window. Better to reminisce if you could actually see the landscape, and this was a flight—and a trip—for reminiscing. He'd been gone for almost five months now, and he was ready to go back. Not back to this life, but back to see if he still wanted this life.

As the plane advanced toward SFO in that freakish flight path along the ocean, timing its landing as close to the end of the runway as possible, passengers never saw the landing strip until a few seconds before touchdown. It could be unnerving if you'd never experienced it. But it was old hat to Johnny, and he was lost in thought. He sat wondering why he wasn't excited to be home and why he was dreading the next week or so.

Walt Matthews met him at the curb, and they settled into the short drive up the 101 into downtown San Francisco.

"You've lost a little weight," Walt said as the conversation waned after its initial boy vs. boy banter.

"Yeah, maybe a little."

"And you seem to have some new artwork adorning your face in several places. You alright?"

"Stitches, I'm told by a very reliable source in nursing, make you look more manly," Johnny said.

"Yeah, you do look more like a hockey player now, that's for sure."

"Just lucky I have all my teeth. So, what's the agenda for tomorrow?"

"We need to be at Troubadour at nine. I scheduled a two-hour meeting with everyone, but the rest of the day is open. We'll play it by ear."

After another few minutes, Walt asked, "You sure you wouldn't rather stay at my place tonight? It's on the way and a shorter commute in the morning."

"Nah. I got some sleep on the plane, and there are a few things I want to catch up on at home, so I'll be fine. I appreciate you being my taxi tonight, but I'll call Uber in the morning. No need to pick me up."

Johnny was pretty sure he wouldn't be getting much sleep the rest of the night. Too many memories.

"Hey, you alright? You look a little pale. You feeling okay?"

"Not really. I'm feeling…very strange," Johnny replied as he noticed his heart was beating much harder than usual and perspiration had begun to creep from his scalp down the back of his neck.

They had pulled up in front of Johnny's home, an updated Victorian in the Pacific Heights neighborhood. It was dark and, to Johnny, a bit foreboding. His heart rate increased, and he hesitated before getting out of the car.

"You got a key?"

"Nope, but I can get in through the garage. Luke texted me the new code."

"You want me to come in, stay a while?"

"Nah, I'm good. Gotta do this sometime." He took a deep breath. "It looks good, doesn't it?" Johnny asked, not wanting to get on with it quite yet.

"Yeah, it does. What did you do, repaint?"

Johnny nodded, "Luke had some touch-up done, not a complete paint job, mostly just the trim. And we had the outside cleaned. Not quite sure how they do that or what they use, but it does kind of sparkle, huh?"

"Looks really nice," Walt said. "Like its ready to go on the market to sell."

Johnny didn't respond.

As Johnny grabbed his suitcase from the trunk, Walt walked up to him and gave him a hug. Not the usual shoulder-to-shoulder bro hug. The first real hug the two had ever shared. It took Johnny by surprise, but he quickly settled into it.

"Welcome home, Johnny."

"Thanks." But no "it's good to be home" followed.

"Let me know if you can't sleep. I got a bottle of bourbon at home that just might help. I'll bring it over."

"Will do. See you in the morning. And Walt, thanks for being such a good friend. I appreciate it. I do, man."

"Sure," Walt whispered, but he didn't make a move to leave.

Johnny noticed the hesitancy and said, "You want to hug me again or something?"

"Nah, I'm good."

"Okay, then, get outta here."

Walt waved as he got back in his car and drove away. Johnny stood in front of the house and looked up at it. It was a small Victorian as Victorians went. He and Sam had purchased it early in their marriage with help from her folks and put a lot of sweat equity into it before the kids arrived. They'd had it repainted on the outside, being sure to follow San Francisco's strict guidelines for Victorian homes. They'd toned down the color combo a bit, but Sam wanted to include pink in the pattern somewhere, so some of the trim was painted salmon, Johnny's choice for a compromise color. Luke had left it when he'd had the touch-up completed.

The one-car garage faced the street, and Johnny pulled his phone out to remember the intricate access code Luke had sent him. He punched it into the keypad, and the door began to rise. When it was fully open, Johnny willed his legs to move, but they wouldn't. He looked around the dimly lit garage and saw some familiar things, like bicycle wheels hanging from the walls, the mini-fridge in the corner, and lots of boxes everywhere. Boxes he suspected held things he didn't want to see. All he had to do was step around them and enter the house.

Nope, legs still not working. He realized he didn't want to relive what was in that house. He didn't want to see Carson's room; he didn't want to experience the emptiness of Cameron's room or the TV den where they watched all those Disney videos. He didn't want to see how his bedroom, now devoid of Sam's belongings, looked or felt. *No thanks, not ready for any of that.*

He re-entered the code, and the door slowly descended. He hit the app for Uber on his phone and spent the night at a nearby Marriott.

SIXTY

THE cab dropped Johnny off the next morning at the corner of Third Street and Market, about three blocks from his office. Former office? Current office? He didn't know what to call it. He wanted to slip into that little coffee shop he liked so much and grab his usual latte and a muffin. The guy behind the counter didn't recognize him, and there was no "Want your usual?" response like he'd expected.

He found a seat outside on the street. The morning was foggy but not too bad by San Francisco standards. Traffic in the street was sluggish, but foot traffic on the sidewalks was hectic. Like pinballs flowing in opposite directions, pedestrians were bouncing off one another. In this business section of town, people had places to go. Johnny could pick out the tourists in the crowd; they would exit their hotels, look up at the skyline, then try and find their bearings, usually a street sign, then dare to step out into the flow.

A little before nine, as Johnny was finishing his muffin, ready for the short walk to the office, his phone buzzed with a text from Emmy. It read: *Can you see any trees right at this moment?*

Johnny smiled but didn't have to look up or down the street. His answer: *Only in my dreams.*

Emmy replied with a smiley face.

The walk to the office took Johnny past Moscone Center, the city's largest convention complex. The strong wind flapped the high flags on the poles that rimmed the front of Moscone. Even though they were at least thirty feet in the air, he could hear the flapping. Johnny turned left at the Mexican restaurant and walked down Howard Street, past The Thirsty Bear, a local brewery and restaurant. Decent food, small plates, great beer. As he stepped into the lobby of the building that housed Troubadour and other small businesses, he noticed the digital sign on a flat screen beside the unmanned front desk.

Welcome home, Johnny Roe.

Nice touch, he thought with a smile.

As he exited the elevator on the third floor, Carrie, the receptionist, let out a little squeak scream and rushed over to hug him. The hug lasted longer than a hello hug, long enough that Johnny felt a bit uneasy, but it gave time for the rest of the staff to gather. He hugged almost everyone with the exception of a few of the guys who forced the guy hug on him— a handshake with the right hand and a shoulder hug with the left.

After lengthy hellos and back slaps, a small round of applause, and a few pecks on the cheek, a smaller group consisting of Johnny, Walt, and a few managers headed to the conference room.

Walt had prepared a short presentation about the business, and Suzanne McLean joined him at the front of the room, improvising as Walt flipped the slides. It wasn't overly practiced or staged, and the two worked well together. Not quite finishing each other's sentences, but doing a great job of not stepping on each other's toes.

Impressed on the state of the business, Johnny let the team know it. Sales had slipped a bit after he'd left, but everyone had done a good job rebuilding the backlog, mostly with smaller accounts as Johnny had advised. They'd lost a few key staff members to other agencies, and at first, they hadn't hired replacements. Then as sales picked up, they hired a key account manager. Suzanne had taken the lead in Sales and Marketing, but as far as Johnny could tell, nobody had stepped forth to assume Creative leadership. The team approach in that regard seemed to be working, at least for now.

After a short break, Walt dismissed the other managers and he, Suzanne, and Johnny settled into Walt's office. *Nitty gritty time.* The three sipped coffee and exchanged glances, but nobody seemed eager to start the conversation.

Finally, Johnny began. "Okay, I guess it's my turn. Where do I start? When I left five months ago, I just pointed the car east and took off. No plan, not much purpose other than to get away for a while. I missed all of you, but I didn't miss the work. I was too…distracted I guess, too…heartbroken." He took a few extra seconds to compose his emotions and thoughts.

He continued. "I hadn't taken a vacation since…well, since never in this way. I had few commitments, no schedule, an open slate, and an open road ahead of me. At first, I was lost. Didn't know where I was, didn't know where I was going. To some degree, I feel the same way now, at least at times. Like last night…I couldn't even go in my house. I was so afraid of where that might lead that I didn't chance it.

"But in other aspects of my life, I am more…settled, I guess, is the right word. I may never fully recover from the loss of my children, but…other losses…will eventually be easier to bear, I realize now. Without going into too much detail, I'm at least on the road to recovery." Johnny seemed to be stuck at this point, and he fell silent.

Suzanne couldn't stand the silence and asked, "When will you be coming back to work?"

"I'm not sure," Johnny replied.

Walt dug deeper. "Not sure when you're coming back or not sure if…?"

"Either."

Johnny rose and looked out the window. The fog was almost completely gone now, and the sun cast shadows throughout the city, half in sun, half in dark.

"I know," he continued, "that the elephant question in the room is where does that leave us?"

"We'll give you more time. You know that. It's your company."

"No, Walt, it's our company. And now, it's probably more your company than mine. I think…and I'm just talking out loud here…you should develop a plan to assume full control of the company."

Walt sat back in his chair, his eyes revealing both shock and surprise. "Wow."

"We were all hoping you'd come back, Johnny. We need you here. It's not the same without you," Suzanne said.

"I've thought about that a lot, Suzanne, especially the last two months. Once I began to be able to think again, creatively speaking, I would lay awake at night and try to picture myself in that office, doing that job again. But that office and that job were hard to separate from…all that made up my life at that time. It was like trying to enter my house last night. It was that life, my past life, and I've been trying to forget that ever since I left. Somehow, I need to forget it. I need to…move on."

"How are we going to move on without you, man?" Walt said in a low, melancholy voice.

Johnny shook his head, but as he looked at Suzanne McLean, he didn't see the melancholy. He saw the gears turning.

"In some ways," Johnny said, "it may be the best thing for you all. I bet you've considered the fact that I may not return and you've come up with ways to cope if I don't. I could help with the succession plan, but it's probably better that you develop the plan without me. It'll be your plan then, not mine."

"So now it's definite?" Walt moaned. "You've gone from not sure to definitely not coming back? Jesus." He stared off into space, to a place in a murky future.

"Sort of sounds like that, doesn't it? I hadn't verbalized that before. I just saw how well you were doing without me and realized that you're doing a great job, that's all."

"We hyped that up a bit," Walt admitted. "Sometimes it gets depressing. Without you, I mean."

"You complete me? Like that?" Johnny said with sincerity.

Walt averted his eyes but managed to say, "Yeah, something like that."

"It is difficult at times without you, Johnny," Suzanne said. "Your enthusiasm is hard to match. Your ideas are spot-on; that's hard to duplicate. And you're the best closer I've ever seen. The business suffers without you. You have to know that."

Johnny wanted to tell them about the suffering he'd been feeling. The suffering of not knowing, of not understanding, of loss beyond explanation. The searching, the healing. But he let it go.

After several silent moments, Suzanne offered a suggestion. "Listen. How about we don't announce anything to the staff. They seem pretty happy right now, now that you're back, Johnny. Give me and Walt a couple of weeks to figure things out. Put a plan together. Okay?"

"Yeah, sure, that makes sense."

"And if you change your mind," Walt said, "at any time, just…come back. Just come back."

"Are you going to be in town for a while?" Suzanne wanted to know.

"Yeah, probably at least a week. Why?"

"We can tell the staff you're just getting things together at the house. I suppose you won't be coming to the office, right?"

"Probably not."

"Well, then give us a week to come up with a plan."

"Sure, no hurry."

"And I agree with Walter. Come back if you change your mind. I know that's not really my job to say that. But it's how everyone feels, I know."

"Thanks." But to Johnny, it didn't feel like that was going to happen.

SIXTY-ONE

JOHNNY met Luke Wacker at a trendy restaurant just off Union Square that evening for drinks and dinner. Even though they had 6:30 reservations, the place had begun to fill up, and they had to wait fifteen minutes to be seated. Johnny had requested a quiet table in the back, but the noise level was still cranked up from the crowd.

He hadn't gotten a text from Emmy since that morning, and although he wanted to reach out to her, he hesitated. Let things run their course, he thought.

After an Anchor Steam beer, Luke asked, "How's the place look? Pretty good, huh?"

"Uh, I haven't been there yet. I stayed at the Marriott last night."

"You want to go out after dinner. I can show you what I did. If we keep it kind of technical, maybe it'll be easier," Luke said in an understanding tone.

"Yeah, we should. Good idea."

The two enjoyed a dinner of fish, veggies, and a salad. Luke polished off a few slices of sourdough bread, and then they got down to business. "Okay, give me a two-minute recap of where we stand," Johnny asked.

"It's all on this sheet," Luke said, handing Johnny a one-page printout. "This doesn't cover all the investments but offers a summary. You've got the detailed reports in your email. It's a net worth summary; assets and liabilities, although the only liability you have right now is on the mortgage and it's only about $300,000. Not bad in today's world."

"What's the property worth?"

"I suspect about $1.5 mil, maybe a bit more. Home prices are skyrocketing right now, and although I personally think the peak has passed, the right properties are bringing in big offers, and sometimes, multiple offers. Why, are you thinking of selling?"

"Maybe. Just curious."

"Well, with a little staging, it would be ready to put on the market. It's been cleaned top to bottom and most of the rooms…are pretty bare. Like we talked about, you know?"

"Yeah, I know. Go on."

"We did the touch-up painting, replaced the rear sliding door, got the carpet cleaned, and then did the major cleaning. We could paint the interior if you wanted. Maybe do something a little more neutral. Less color. That might make it more desirable."

"It's fine for now." Johnny was distracted, doing the calculations in his head, but Luke had read his mind.

"If you sell it for, let's say, one and a half and the commission is five percent, pay off the mortgage, and you can walk away with just over a million. Easy."

"Nice. Thanks."

"That could buy a nice spread in, er, Booneville, Iowa, huh?" Luke asked.

"If I was looking there."

"You aren't?"

"No, I'm not."

"None of my business?"

"No, it is your business. I'm just not ready to buy more real estate at this time. What's a stager going to cost?"

"We might be able to include that in the commission. I've heard of properties selling for as low as four or four and a half percent. I've got a few buddies in the biz. I could check it out."

"Okay, do it. And get it staged. I'll trust you on the cost. Run it by me if you want, but I'm not too concerned, even if it runs a grand or so. It needs to be done."

Luke was taking notes directly into his iPhone.

After he'd finished, he swiped his phone and brought up the investments. "Are you still satisfied with the risk levels in the investments?"

"Yep, unless you've found something without risk," Johnny said with a smile.

"Wishful thinking."

"Okay, one more thing before we head out to the house."

"Shoot."

"You know that pub over by the Hilton on Geary? The Irish place, Lefty O'Doul's? I think I'll need a couple of pints to get primed for this visit."

"I love my job," Luke said, leaning in to be heard over the clamor.

SIXTY-TWO

STANLEY Strasbaugh delicately fondled the ornate wooden gavel he had borrowed from one of his judge friends. He felt its power as he leveled it down on a small piece of wood he'd brought specifically for that purpose.

"The Board of Directors meeting of U.S. Johnson Controls will now come to order," he said, rapping the gavel several times. All that was missing from the introduction was a formal *hear ye, hear ye.* All board members were present and accounted for, and several "interested parties" as Strasbaugh had them designated were also in the room, including Norm Boswell, Doc Enbright, and other key managers at the plant.

"We will suspend discussions about old business for the time being. Well, actually, this is probably old business and new business both. For the purposes of this discussion and the official meeting notes, let's call it new business," Strasbaugh declared, motioning to the secretary taking notes. She responded back with a nod.

"Stanley," Norm Boswell said with a gentle tone, "I recommend we forego the ritual of Roberts Rules for a minute and just talk like regular folks here. We all know what's going on and the board just needs to make some decisions and set some direction for the company."

"We just need to take notes so that we're covered," Strasbaugh said, pointing his finger in the air.

"That's fine," Boswell said. "Debbie, if you have any questions whether something that is discussed needs to be included in the notes, just let us know, alright? We can refer to parts of a discussion without noting every detail. This isn't court, and you're not a court reporter, got it?"

Strasbaugh did not particularly like that comment, but it was said with so much compassion that he didn't want to voice a complaint. "I suppose the first order of business is to talk about how the board sets a course for the future," he offered.

"Pardon my interruption, but that seems bass-ackwards to me," Doc said. "This board at times has taken an active approach to governing, but for the most part, its job has been to support Ulysses. Now there is no Ulysses. And nobody to take over for Ulysses. So maybe that's where we should start."

Strasbaugh frowned visibly at Doc's interruption, but he saw quite a few heads bobbing in agreement, so he declared, "If everyone thinks that's a good beginning, I open the floor for discussion."

"Stanley, what do the bylaws say about succession?" Norm Boswell asked.

"Actually…" Strasbaugh said, fumbling with his notes, looking for a copy of the bylaws, "…I read that last night…and couldn't find anything reviewing the manner to which a successor would be named in light of…what's happened. Perhaps we should designate a committee to look into the matter and come up with both recommendations and a proposed addition to the bylaws in this regard."

"That's a great idea. I propose you and George head up that committee," Boswell said, motioning to a reluctant George at the end of the table. "How about one month. Does that give you enough time to report back to the board?"

"Well…I suppose…" stammered the return from Strasbaugh.

"But in the meantime, I also propose we move forward. I think we need to elect an acting president to run the day to day here and make immediate decisions. Since we are employee-owned with board supervision and there is nothing in the bylaws about replacing the CEO, then what's to prevent us from adding the position of Acting President?" Boswell said.

"Well, legally, I'm not sure if we can do that," Strasbaugh mumbled.

"Okay, fair enough. Why doesn't your committee also investigate that and let us know. But, and this is a huge but, we need to make some vital decisions now about the direction of the company. And that's not going to work if we always have to assign a committee to look into the legality of things."

"Aren't you functioning in that role for the most part, Norm?" Doc asked. "As an acting president?"

"No, actually I'm not. I'm functioning in my job as Director of Operations. I have no authority in finance, human resources, and marketing. I simply run the operations of the plant."

"What else needs to be done at this point?" A question came from George.

"Well, for instance, I'd like to work with the bank to renegotiate the loan on the building. Sometime in the last five years that payment ballooned and it's a real killer on our cash flow. Also, we need to make some tough decisions in HR, layoffs, forced time off, things like that. I have no authority under the current structure to do that. Those are two major situations that need to be addressed, and immediately, I might add."

"Oh…" George said, averting his eyes from the rest of the board.

"I move that we take nominations from the floor for the position of acting president," Doc announced.

"You can't do that. You're not a board member," Strasbaugh said, his brow furrowed.

"Then you do it," Doc demanded back.

Stanley Strasbaugh considered his options. As a very minority owner in the company, he had a stake in the decision. And although he craved the power that an acting president may have in this situation, he was not a stupid man. He wanted neither the authority nor the consequences of running this company, not at this time, not without Ulysses.

"Okay, okay. I open the floor for nominations and discussions for the position," here Strasbaugh motioned to Debbie to start taking notes, "for the position of acting president of U.S. Johnson Controls, Incorporated."

"I nominate Norm Boswell," Doc said in a loud voice to the group.

"Dammit, Doc, you cannot do that. You are not a member of this board," Strasbaugh said.

From the back of the room, generous George offered rather meekly, "I nominate Stanley Strasbaugh."

Doc managed to contain himself with only a resigned nodding back and forth of his head.

"Well, that is flattering. Thank you, George. But I must decline. I'm quite busy with my own practice right now, and we have several big cases that may be coming onto the docket in the not too distant future. I couldn't possibly do it. So please delete my name from the list."

"We don't have a list," Debbie managed to say in a squeaky voice, clearing her throat as she did. That managed to break the tension, and a few in the room laughed.

"I'm sure I can at least ask a question. Who would like to be nominated? That's not against the rules, is it?" Doc asked, glaring at Strasbaugh.

"It's not who wants it, Doc. It's who's best qualified," George said, proud of himself.

"Maybe it's the same person," Doc said, looking at Norm Boswell.

"I'll do it," Boswell said in a firm voice. That quieted the room. "And I'm probably the most qualified. At least at the present time under the current conditions. If the board wants to set up a search committee and go about finding a leader, that could take several months or more. I'm just saying, I'm available."

"Will somebody on the board, for the love of God, nominate Norm Boswell?" Doc said.

Stanley Strasbaugh saw both a way out of the situation and a way to be a hero if Boswell succeeded. "I will. I nominate Norman Boswell." *Now it's my idea, for the record, the official record,* Strasbaugh thought. He motioned for Debbie to include that in the notes.

"All in favor?" Doc asked.

"Dammit, Doc," Strasbaugh scolded. "Other nominations?"

Nothing.

"Discussion?"

None.

"All in favor?" Doc whispered.

Strasbaugh relented, "All in favor?" he said in a louder voice.

All said aye.

"Opposed?"

Nobody said a thing.

"Approved! Swing that gavel, Stanley," Doc demanded.

This time, Strasbaugh did as he was told.

SIXTY-THREE

LUKE and Johnny exited the cab in front of the Victorian with bellies full of beer. Whatever beer Doc Enbright had stored in his mini-fridge in Booneville, Iowa, paled in comparison to cold draught beer made in the San Francisco Bay area. The two had sampled several favorites and almost had worked their way through the series of fancy tap-handled brews at O'Doul's.

"Are you sure you don't want me to come in with you?" Luke asked. "I could take some notes if you need it."

"Nah. It's getting late. If I see something that needs to be done, I'll let you know. And I think…this is probably something I need to do alone. At least for now."

"You're the boss. Call me tomorrow, okay?"

"Sure. Thanks, Luke. I mean it. Thanks for all you've done for me."

"Like I said, I love my job." He jumped back in the cab, and it drove slowly away.

"Déjà vu, all over again," Johnny said out loud to himself, remembering last night. The same scenario, the same cold, damp sidewalk, the same foreboding home. But he had an advantage over last night that propelled him into the house and past the sentinel garage boxes. He had to pee like a drunk racehorse.

As he threw his suitcase on the bed, Johnny noticed how familiar his bedroom felt. He saw the clock radio on the nightstand, now dormant, undoubtedly unplugged. In his mind, he heard the many times he'd awakened to the low musical sounds of an easy listening station, audible only to him, so low that Sam wouldn't stir.

The stack of books on the stand was straightened; the magazines that had been there, mostly Forbes and Kiplinger's, had been removed. The same pictures held their positions on the wall surrounding the high-ceilinged room, almost like they were staring down from a balcony to the bed. The two dressers with their glass-topped shields were shining, upright, and proper, just the way Sam would have wanted. But the room had a sterile feel to Johnny. No newspapers on the floor, no sweatpants slung over a chair, no kids' toys anywhere. Didn't feel much like home anymore to him.

As Johnny was about to look into the newly castrated closet, he noticed his phone and a missed call from Emmy. The phone call had come in several hours earlier and, mixed with the din of a crowded restaurant and pub, had gotten lost in the evening. She hadn't left a message. He glanced at the clock on the table out of habit—no time there—and then at the top of his phone. 11:37. With the two-hour difference between here and Iowa, he knew Emmy would be asleep. He decided a text would be better.

Sorry I missed your call. Too late now?

Wow, how impersonal can I get? Not even a 'talk to you tomorrow' or 'miss you.'

As Johnny opened the closet door, he expected half his life to be gone. The half that was Samantha. He had seen the closet in his mind all the time since he'd left. His half of the closet full with clothes, Sam's half completely empty. But Luke had done his job well. He had spread out Johnny's clothes to fill almost the entire closet. Pants on hangers, usually crammed together in a small section, had been expanded over two sections, each hanger about an inch apart from the next. His shirts occupied the top section and hung straight and true, with room to breathe. Sweaters stacked on a single shelf before now had space to take up several shelves. All the shoe racks, mostly Sam's, now held Johnny's shoes. The built-in dresser, with drawers of different sizes, was now empty, new shelf paper the only remnant.

He wandered into Carson's room. The clothes were gone from the closet, but the room still held the essence of his son. A few soccer trophies stood tall on the shelf above his bed. A photo of him and his sister at Disneyland, the two of them sandwiched around Goofy, smiled at Johnny from the dresser top. The stuffed teddy bear stood in anticipation of a return hug among the pillows on the bed.

As he meandered down the hall, he decided to just close the door to Cameron's room. He wasn't quite ready for that memory lane stroll.

Several of Johnny's friends had recommended that he simply sell the house, without ever returning to see it again. But one dear old aunt who had called him several weeks after the funeral had warmly advised him to return again and capture the good memories the house held. She had walked him through an exercise over the phone where he ventured into each room in anticipation of remembering the good times and storing them in his mind. No remembrances of bad times, dark memories, or sorrowful lapses; just stay on the right side of positive.

Johnny spent the next two hours in a daze of days gone by. He laughed out loud in the kitchen when he remembered Buster getting into the birthday cake and spreading it all around the floor. They spent the afternoon cleaning the floor and walls, and Buster got an extended bath in the backyard. He cried when he remembered how excited Cameron had been after her first-grade dance recital. His aunt had told him that when he finally did revisit the house to let the tears flow, and he followed her instructions every time the ducts drained, which was often. As he saw the outside basketball hoop, barely seven feet high, he smiled as he remembered the time he had yelled at Carson from the bench in a YMCA league game to grab the rebound after a missed foul shot. His son was the only third grader who moved when the foul shot clanked off the rim, and he swished a five-footer to win the game at the buzzer. In the bedroom, Johnny got aroused as he reminisced about long, leisurely Sunday mornings spent in that bed before kids.

After several hours, he settled onto the living room couch, the beer and the long day finally catching up with him, sending him off to dreamland.

His cell buzzed him awake, and he searched for it on the coffee table in front of the couch. It was seven o'clock in the morning, and Doc was on the phone.

"Hey, Doc, what's up?"

"You sound sleepy. Did I wake you? Want me to call back?"

"You did wake me, but no, I can talk."

"Just wanted to bring you up to date on what's happening at the plant. The board elected Norm as acting president."

"Wow, the board actually did something, huh? That's great. He's the man for the job, that's for sure."

"That was yesterday, and already he's making an impact. Had to do a small layoff and something he calls mandatory time off."

"Like a shutdown. What? Like a week or two?"

"Two."

Johnny had gone to the kitchen and was searching cabinets for coffee. Nothing.

"He's also getting some very interesting phone calls from potential customers. About that vision-guided stuff."

"Great. It's the future."

"But they have no idea where the inquiries are coming from. They really haven't publicized it much."

"Could be anywhere. Once a technology is out there, people who are looking for it tend to find it."

"You have anything to do with that?"

"Me?! No. Other than the presentation we did for Ritter…hey, wait, we did put a little something on the website, but it was just a short video clip of the technology, that's all."

"Norm asked me to call you to see if you'd be interested in taking that presentation you did on the laptop to some of these customers. You know, to show them the potential."

"That's really the sales department's job. They can do that. I could send them the presentation."

"It would be better if you took them through a quick training on it, wouldn't it? Show them the details of the laptop and how to make that finger hit the right key at the right time. The presentation was fine, I mean you had it down pat, but it was really the mechanical hand hitting the laptop that sent Ritter crazy. If you could teach them how to do that, we'd have a much better chance of landing those accounts."

Johnny agreed with Doc's thinking but wasn't ready to return to Booneville just yet. "When would you want to do that?" he asked.

"Soon. Strike while the iron is hot, right?"

Right again, Johnny thought.

"John, we are in pretty desperate straits here. You know that. We need your help, or we wouldn't ask. We're proud men out here in the prairie. But this plant won't last too much longer unless we can bring in some high-quality, profitable business. We need a new direction. This may be our best bet. Our last hope."

"You're really laying it on thick here, aren't you, Doc?"

"Thick as I can. Listen, I know you've only been gone a few days and it's a lot to ask, but we wouldn't ask unless it was crucial. And I didn't mean to jump right into business without asking how your trip is going. Sorry. How are you doing?"

"It's been pretty…emotional, I guess." Then Johnny told Doc about the office visit and a room-by-room blow of the last six or eight hours. Just in the retelling, Johnny felt a sense of release, a letting go.

When he was done, Doc asked, "What's next?"

"I'm not sure. I need to come to some conclusion about the business. They made a big pitch to get me to come back. I might return for a few months to see if that'll work. I don't know; just saying that sounds…forced. About the house, I'm pretty sure it's got to go. Don't think I can stay here. Too many memories and even though most are good, I can't live…in the past…here. Need a fresh start, I suppose."

"Maybe a little clean, fresh Iowa air will help clear your head."

"Maybe. Maybe you're right. I'll book a flight. Give me a day or two to figure it out." Looking at his calendar on the phone, he said, "Maybe you can set up a meeting with Sales on Monday morning. Sound okay to you?"

"Absolutely, sure. You want me to have Emmy pick you up?"

"Uh…how about you pick me up. That way we can talk a little business."

"Hmm. Business, huh?"

"Yeah, I'm in a business mode right now, I guess." Johnny wasn't sure he was ready to talk anything but business. And he wasn't ready to talk to Emmy Brownell. Too many memories of everything in his life before Emmy Brownell were flooding over him now, like a riptide taking him out to sea. He felt like he was in a desperate fight to swim back to shore, but he was losing the battle. Sometimes he wasn't even sure which way the shore was.

SIXTY-FOUR

JOHNNY scanned the outbound flights, found his to Denver, and discovered it was running late. He calculated the time he had to make the connection in the Mile High City to Des Moines. Close. As he sat at the boarding gate at SFO checking email, he quickly got seduced into people watching, one of his favorite pastimes at airports. He noticed parents with kids, probably traveling home this Sunday; some parents were very calm and relaxed, others disheveled and tense. Businessmen wearing their Monday suits without a tie, already in the mode for tomorrow's meeting, traveling light, maybe just an overnight. Vacationers traveling home, wherever home was, from San Francisco, carrying presents and extra bags, some no doubt containing sourdough bread or Ghirardelli chocolates bought at the airport.

The gate area was packed with people going home or going away from home. Johnny felt that he didn't quite fit into either category; this was home, but it really didn't feel like it anymore. Iowa wasn't home, and yet there was a pull, like a tide. Again with the ocean and swimming, with the tide or against it. Tiring, he thought.

His cell phone buzzed to bring him back to Sunday afternoon. *Ryan Ritter?*

"Hi, Ryan," he answered with trepidation.

"Johnny, how are you?"

"Good…good. Among the wandering masses at SFO as we speak."

"Did I catch you at a bad time?"

"Nope. Flight's delayed, so I have nothing but time."

"You're back at work in the Bay Area then?"

"Kind of. Spent a few days at the office. Also trying to clean up my…uh, home. Thinking about selling it. Seems like a good time for the market. And it's really more than I can handle. Might be a good time to downsize."

"Everything I follow in California real estate indicates it's still a hot market, depending, of course, on the property and the location."

"That's what I'm hearing, too."

"How's Troubadour?"

"Running much too smoothly in my absence. Honks me off."

"Funny. They tapping into software at all? Seems like almost every deal we see these days is software. Hardware is having trouble keeping up."

"Yeah, we have new software business. But as I always say, with a nod to Steve Jobs, you can't have software without hardware."

"With the cloud, I'm just not sure how long that analogy will work."

Johnny didn't much care for "the cloud," but he let the statement pass without comment.

"How is U.S. Johnson Controls these days?" Ritter asked.

Johnny had no idea where this conversation was headed; it seemed like Ritter was probing all over the board and Johnny wasn't in much of a mood to answer every question in detail until he understood where it all was headed. "Carrying on. Trying to book new business. Why do you ask?"

"Listen, I'm just curious, that's all. Like I said when we last talked…I liked…I mean *like*…those guys. I just didn't see a way to put something together, like a deal, at the time. But it doesn't mean I've lost all interest in the technology…or the people."

Johnny wasn't buying much of this, "Uh, huh," his only response, mostly just to keep Ritter talking.

After receiving short updates from Johnny on the personnel at the plant, including Doc Enbright and Norm Boswell but no mention about Ulysses, Ritter asked, "They get some new business out there, in the vision robotics?"

"Where'd you hear that?"

"Little birdy told me."

These venture guys, Johnny thought, not willing to give anything away.

"Well, then, maybe your birdy knows more than mine. I've been away for a while."

"That's a dynamic technology, Johnny. It won't be hard to sell, especially the way you do it."

Why is he buttering me up now, Johnny wondered? "Thanks."

Changing the topic, Ritter asked, "Where are you headed today?"

"Des Moines, back to Booneville for a couple of days, maybe longer, not quite sure."

"Got time to meet over coffee sometime while you're back?"

"Maybe, what's up?"

"I need your help, but I don't want to talk about it over the phone. It's very important to me and my partners. We'd like to meet in person. Maybe an hour or two. What do you say?"

"I say you're holding back something. It feels like you're not saying what's really on your mind, and I'm not real anxious to continue on this path unless you come clean."

"You don't beat around the bush, do you?"

"I do not."

"I like that. Okay, well, here it is…in a nutshell."

Once Ritter revealed the nut in the nutshell, Johnny sat back in his chair with a thump, and the hubbub of SFO faded away. *Didn't see that coming!* Blindsided, completely out of left field.

SIXTY-FIVE

AFTER Johnny's presentation to the sales and marketing department where he replicated the vision robotics demonstration he'd done in Ryan Ritter's office, Norm Boswell asked him to do it again in front of the entire company. Johnny agreed, and the company meeting was hastily scheduled for the following day. They wouldn't be able to squeeze everyone into the conference room, so in late afternoon Johnny began putting together a simulation of the technology on the manufacturing floor. Most everyone had seen the technology work but not in such practical ways. Several workers would drop by and ask a few questions or say hello, shooting the breeze a bit but heading right back to work. Johnny noticed the vibe on the floor was different, and he suspected Boswell was behind the turnaround. There was a current of energy sparking through the staff like unseen electricity, available and ready, eager to come to life.

Johnny had experienced this type of work passion before when accomplished, skilled managers could rejuvenate a company simply by painting a picture of the future that included success and meaning for the company. He'd had a buddy that spent a decade with Apple, Jobs' first tenure, and he'd been an integral part of Jobs' engineering staff. His buddy would frequently tell the story of Jobs disrupting the workflow of a project with an unscheduled appearance. Jobs would just talk about the future and how he saw it (and he had a God-given ability to see the future). He talked about it like it was on the verge of happening, on the cusp, the precipice, and all he needed from his staff was the tenacity to drag the company along that well-defined path. *There it is, boys and girls, now just get us there!* He made it sound easy, like crossing a bridge or climbing a small mountain. Of course, the reality was much different; half the time the technology hadn't even been invented yet. For example, as a way to control the keyboard, the mouse was after all just an idea;

somebody had to figure out how to make the little sucker work. Steve Jobs was the genius idea guy, and his talent lay in not only his Nostradamus-like ability to see the future but to get others to buy into his vision and make it happen.

Norm Boswell was not Steve Jobs, and he wasn't a genius. Norm Boswell, as Johnny summed him up, was a talented and resourceful operations manager. People liked him, he spoke honestly and to the point, and everyone wanted to be around him. You felt better in his company. From everything Johnny had read, Steve Jobs was a butthead. And Johnny knew that most people—and especially people in Iowa— would rather work for Norm Boswell. Jobs' shtick wouldn't fly in Booneville.

As the late afternoon meeting the following day began, Boswell seemed a bit nervous, Johnny thought. His voice was not powerful and had a bit of a quiver in it. Probably hadn't spoken with a microphone to this many people in a while. But they had practiced at Johnny's insistence late the evening before, and Norm was remembering to hold the mic right against his chin like he was licking an ice cream cone. Boswell thanked the board for its confidence in him and introduced the board and others he had invited, including Johnny, Doc, and the local banker. He then jumped into a very short state-of-the-business in a hundred and twenty seconds. He had most of the first four minutes of his time at the mic almost memorized, and he started to relax. Johnny had suggested he tell a joke, but that was where Norm had drawn the line. I'm not Tom Boswell, Norm had said, I'm Norm Boswell. *That's puzzling,* Johnny had thought, *who is Tom Boswell?*

Next came Johnny's demonstration, and he elicited a few oohs and aahs from the crowd. He had primed the Sales department beforehand to start the oohing and aahing first, but others soon picked up the energy without much prodding from Sales. But Johnny's job was to showcase the technology only. He wanted Norm Boswell to paint the picture. And paint it, he did.

After Johnny sat down, the room went dim, and a video clip from the movie *Butch Cassidy and the Sundance Kid* came on. It was the scene where Butch is riding the bicycle around the cabin, trying to impress Katherine Ross.

At the point in the scene when Butch declares that the bicycle is the future, the lights came back on, and Norm Boswell declared, "Ladies and gentlemen, as the bicycle changed transportation from the horse, so does vision-guided robotics change the face of technology." It wasn't a perfect analogy, but the crowd loved it. He then described the three "inquiries" for new business around the VGR product, as he dubbed it, and how it looked like those might actually turn into real business for Johnson Controls.

As the crowd died down, Boswell broached an issue that he knew needed to be addressed. "I'm sure everyone knows by now that there is speculation that Ulysses will not be returning." A murmur went through the crowd like a stiff breeze from the ocean, bringing with it new scents, new possibilities.

"The authorities, including the FBI, are looking into his disappearance, but so far, no clues have been uncovered." A bigger murmur, almost a buzz—everyone loves a mystery. "And we will carry on, in his tradition, with a new purpose. A purpose to make what he started, better. To make what he and his father invented, new again. To make what he made successful, even more successful." A slow round of clapping, two or three people, then a more sustained round of polite yet respectful applause.

"We also suspect that Joe Dunham will not be returning to the plant in any capacity," Boswell diplomatically declared. Silence, then a lone voice from the back, audible enough to be heard but not attributed, said, "Buh-bye." Heads throughout nodded in unison, in solidarity.

"Now, I have a couple of announcements," Boswell said, beaming, his demeanor completely changed, buoyed. "The Bank of the Midwest, today represented by Vice President Aldridge Perko, has agreed to renegotiate the loan on the building."

The murmur had returned now with quizzical looks. Norm Boswell himself started the applause this time, and he got the crowd going. Mr. Perko stood up and took a bow.

"What that means is simply that we have more working capital on a monthly basis. We won't be saddled with such a high monthly payment on the building, and that'll be a real lifesaver for this company." And the applause started again, even more so.

"And one more announcement. You see on the easel over there, a schedule. Maybe you can't see it from the back of the room, but please stop by after the meeting and find your name on the schedule. These are times that I've set up for each of you to meet with Dorothy Bates in HR. You all know that we have an ESOP here, an employee stock option plan. The board has authorized us to take another look at that plan and make some adjustments. I don't want to go into all the details right now because I know there'll be tons of questions. Dorothy is going to talk with each of you. But the bottom line is that each of you, every single person in this company, is an owner.

"Basically, what we've done, with the bank and Mr. Perko's help, is to buy out Ulysses' shares. The bank gave us a loan, we bought his shares, or, technically, I guess we are buying his shares because we're paying off the loan, and eventually those shares will be available to you. We've drawn up a memo that explains it all. And Dorothy can answer your questions, but I believe it's a tremendous way to not only make this company viable again but make it viable for all of us."

Again from the crowd, "You da man, Norm!" And everyone broke out in laughter.

"Well, no hoorays just yet. We're still in debt, and we need to build and ship product. But I know you all can do that, arms tied behind your back. Give us a year or two, then we'll see where we are. I think we'll be fine and then we can celebrate!"

"C'mon, let's celebrate now!" somebody yelled. The laughter began again.

Norm Boswell wasn't a genius, but he was quick to see an opportunity, and he jumped on it with both feet. Johnny sensed a shift in the room, a heightening, like a tent revival with Boswell selling salvation.

"You're right, we should celebrate. You know why? Not because Ulysses is gone and not because Dunham is gone. We should celebrate because we survived. We came through it, the dark period. Listen! We don't know everything that was going on with those two. Something wasn't right. We all sensed that. But we're through that; we've come out the other side. We survived."

Johnny sensed a theme; he sensed one helluva speech coming on. Like the movie *Norma Rae*, rallying the crowd. He was ready to look around for a Sally Field showing, but Norm's now booming voice brought him back.

"I gotta say this. I am very humbled to be the acting president of this company. By golly, there are several of you in this room," Boswell said, pointing his finger directly at several people, "could do this job, not just me. But I'm also dang proud to lead this team. Some of the finest people I've known in my life are right here, right now. Hard workers! Dedicated employees! Good, God-fearing people who would do anything, and I mean anything, for this company. I've seen it a hundred times.

"Like the time Ed Purcell over there…Ed, raise your hand," he said, pointing to the back right corner of the room. "There he is. The time Ed had to cancel his anniversary trip to Florida with his wife to finish up that Bainbridge job. I imagine he paid dearly around the house for weeks, maybe months, with Jenny. But he stayed. We got the job done. We shipped it on time."

Boswell paused and walked closer to the front of the small platform they'd erected.

"And I remember the week before the ISO quality audit most of you worked late every night, without pay I might add, so we'd be ready. And the weekend before when all we did was live on pizza so we could work around the clock. And we passed! And we put that dang ISO logo everywhere, even on the building out front. Let me tell you this: I don't forget those sacrifices. It's almost like going to war with you folks. I'd trust you, no matter how hard it got, no matter how difficult the situation. You'd have my back, and I'd have yours. And we'd survive. We did survive! Not all companies come through a time like this, but we did. We all did. And we all did it together. As a team!" Boswell said as his right fist shot up into the air.

Johnny noticed the sweat running down the side of Norm Boswell's head. The crowd was beaming in unison. But he wasn't done yet.

"And one more thing, speaking of logos…I'm going to ask Johnny Roe there to design something new for us. A new us. A new name for us and a new logo. I know there are lots of legal reasons why that doesn't make sense, but I have a feeling the time is right. A new beginning. A phoenix rising out of the ashes. A new start. Will you do that, Johnny?"

"Guaran-dang-tee I will!" Johnny shouted back. He'd caught the fever, would somebody give me a big Amen out there!

A few final announcements followed, and then Norm dismissed the meeting. People mulled around the easel with the ESOP schedule, small groups convened to talk, and nobody wanted to leave the building. A few hugs were exchanged. Norm Boswell had grabbed a bottled water and was draining it dry. He'd earned it.

Johnny had already grabbed a pad and was scribbling down possible names for the new company.

Norm Boswell approached him and put his arm around Johnny's shoulder.

"I forgot to mention in the meeting, and maybe I wanted to do it personally, man to man, how much I appreciate what you did."

"Oh, the demonstration? No problem."

"No, not that. What I mean is how you contributed to me personally. How you had confidence in me, even though you didn't say it. Just looking at new opportunities with those venture guys really opened me up. Brought me out of the status quo. Made me look in new directions, broadened my horizons."

"Yeah, I got it, Norm. But I was wrong, dead wrong. My big idea didn't work. It never got off the ground. Died on the tarmac. I thought you could change it up, turn it around, re-invent it all. I was the big shot from the big city, coming to the small-town company as a savior. And it didn't work. I'm…I'm sorry."

"That's one way to look at it. But…searching for new ways to build the company was the only way we could've realized that we needed to stick to our business. To do what we are really good at. It gave us the vision to change things, improve things, make them better. We were struggling—I was struggling—and you brought me out of the abyss. Brought the whole company out. We may not have done that without your help. No, I know for a fact, we couldn't have. We would have been searching for a new destiny forever. Or till we died searching. And we would have died, Johnny. We were on life support. It was you, it really was. You save us, saved the whole plant, maybe the town. You, Johnny."

Johnny nodded his understanding.

"Thank you," Boswell said, shaking Johnny's hand and gripping it hard enough to convey his feelings.

"Welcome," Johnny replied. "But Norm?"

"Yeah?"

"You still da man."

Norm Boswell beamed a smile that reached ear to ear.

SIXTY-SIX

"**H**EY," was all Emmy said as Johnny appeared on the other side of her front door.

"Hi. Can I come in?" he asked.

"Sure. I'm glad you came." She smiled at him, but she didn't beam like she wanted.

"Been busy since I've been back," he explained as he grabbed a seat on the couch. No hugs, no kisses.

"You don't have to explain."

"I want to. You deserve it."

"How was your trip back west? I kind of lost track after the first few days."

"Hectic, whirlwind," he began. And he told her of the meetings at the office, a brief update on business, and his idea. Then he recalled in detail the trip to his home, recanting a few of the positive memories he was storing away. But he also told her how it didn't feel like he could live in that house anymore. That he was planning to sell it eventually, maybe rent a smaller apartment somewhere in the city, but he wasn't sure. After twenty minutes, he was done, drained.

"So…now what?" she asked in an uplifting tone. She didn't want to press him.

"Well, I've got some work to do for the plant, new name, new logo, and I want my people in San Francisco to do that. So I'm heading back tomorrow to get started. Not much else to do with the house, maybe just negotiate a contract to get it on the market. Those'll take a week or two. Then…" He didn't finish. His eyes met hers, but he couldn't hold the look long.

In the span of the next ten seconds or so, Emmy had a real come to Jesus talk with herself. Her lips tensed, her nostrils flared a bit, a look of determination spread across her face. As Johnny sat motionless on the couch, she rose and took a dozen paces toward the kitchen. She inhaled deeply and turned back to him.

"The last time we talked about this, you said you couldn't say you loved me, and I understood that. But I was a weenie. I let it end there," she began. "I told myself I wouldn't let that happen again. If I had the chance. Now I have the chance. No matter how hard it was for you to say, I wasn't going to let that interfere with my feelings for you."

"Just because you couldn't say you loved me," Emmy continued, straightening her back, standing taller, "that wouldn't prevent me from saying it to you. So here goes…I love you. Head over heels, butt over tin cup, nothing held back. Gaga. When you left for San Fran, I cried. Blubbered. Thought you'd never come back. My heart ached, horribly."

Johnny now held her stare, not looking away, not interrupting her. He nodded as if to say, *Go on.*

"I know I can never understand the pain you've been through. I actually hope I never experience that, even if it meant I could understand it. And I don't spend a lot of my time looking toward the future. I'm not much of a planner or a worrier. I'm beginning to realize that I should probably just leave that up to God. I just know how I feel right here, right now. I know it's love. Cause, well, I can tell…I know."

He still didn't speak, so she continued.

"My new girlfriends…you know, the ladies at the…at Doc's church…well, my girlfriends anyway, they've convinced me that if you…don't come back…that I'll be okay. I'm almost to the point where I believe that…and I want to believe it. Sometimes it just doesn't feel that way."

"Now…this is the part that I have to say…and you have to hear. I'm here, in Booneville. It's my home. But if you say 'Come with me to San Francisco,' I'd go with you. And if you said…I can't ask that or I'm not ready or even, Johnny Roe, if you said, I need to leave and figure out how I feel…I'm here, in Booneville, waiting for you. I have no idea how long I would wait. I'm thirty-one, and my clock has started to tick. And like I said, I'll be okay. Whatever happens, I'll be okay.

"So I'm not talking marriage or babies. I'm only talking loving you. Wholeheartedly, all in, with every ounce of my being, for however long I can."

She sat down and took a deep breath and smiled at him, tears running down her face.

Johnny stood up. "Okay, my turn. Emmy, I'm screwed up. My whole life was my business and my family. Now I have neither. I don't want to return to my business, and my home is…empty. It feels like my heart is, too. It feels like I've got no room in there. Sometimes it feels like I don't even know if I have a heart anymore.

"Booneville is wonderful, it's been such a surprise to me. Here I was, heading east, and boom, Booneville. Outta nowhere. And you…you were the first thing I saw when I woke up in the hospital. I've thought a lot about that day. It was like the beginning of a rebirth for me. Everything changed that day. I went from roaming around the country to…well, I don't know to what. But your eyes brought me back. From roaming. From the hell I was in. Those eyes…saved me somehow.

"Is that love? Probably. But I need…some time. I'm not healed yet. I have this place inside me. It feels dark, foreboding. It comes over me, and I can't keep it away. Like that time with the baseball bat and the Bettchers. I don't want it to overtake me, but it does. It's a darkness. And I don't want to expose you to it. I don't want you to see me like that, with that inside me. I know it's not fair to you, but I need to not be screwed up anymore before I come for you. And I will come for you. I will."

She rose, and they hugged for a long time. He leaned his head back but didn't step away.

He continued, "I need to go to San Francisco and tie up some loose ends. Then I'll fly back and pick up my car and my bike. Then…I'll probably head east again. I have a little bit more to shake out of me."

"I'm here," she repeated in a whisper, "in Booneville. Waiting."

"I need to find a little bit more of myself still."

"I know. It's okay."

"I don't want to leave…but I have to. I'm not ready yet…for…."

"I understand."

"I'm still grieving, I'm still hurting. I'm still searching."

Then Johnny thought of the words Doc had conveyed to him from the rocking chair before he left for San Francisco: *It's not hard to find God. What's really hard is to let Him find you.* Johnny wondered if that was part of his journey.

Now she just used her eyes to convey her love.

Johnny leaned back in and kissed Emmy. She reached up and put her hand behind his head, clutching him closer; she wouldn't let him pull away.

She didn't want him to think it was only sexual. But she wanted him. She wanted the two of them to feel like one. She wanted the intimacy that couldn't be found in words or hugs or kisses. At first, she was afraid that he might think she was using her body to hold him. Maybe she was, but she didn't care. She wasn't about to hold back now, not anything. If he never came back, she wanted to remember this moment. Memories could never be broken like promises.

Her breathing was suddenly sparked with need—hearty, lusty. Her kisses turned from caring to urgent. From loving to passionate, impatient.

He caught her fever.

"Are you sure?" he said, the words coming out in one single breath.

She hesitated. She looked into his eyes, hoping to see something she longed for.

Johnny pulled away to arm's length.

"Now it's me that's not sure," he finally said.

She wanted to turn, but his stare held her. She closed her eyes to try and break the hold.

He backed up another step but held her hands, their arms stretched taut. One more step and they'd lose touch completely.

"I'm coming back, Emmy. One way or the other, I'm coming back," he said looking into her eyes.

She wasn't sure what that meant but didn't dare to ask.

SIXTY-SEVEN

WHEN Johnny left, he made no promises. Only that he was coming back to pick up his car and his bike. Stationed in Doc's spare bedroom, his other belongings, including the bike, were silent sentinels reminding Emmy that he wouldn't just leave them without returning to get them. There was still a part of him in Booneville.

Managers at the plant made hard choices as they waited for a fresh identity in the new company name and logo. A few of the marginal workers were laid off with a decent severance package, even if they'd only been there a short time. Most everyone, including Norm Boswell, took unpaid time off to reduce payroll expenses. Some employees worked from home even though they weren't getting paid. The sales department doubled their efforts to win new business from their existing clients, amping up service when they had to, reducing prices when forced—all without seeming too needy. One salesperson handled the vision-guided robotics business and did his best to reduce the sales cycle and bring in new contracts. By the grace of God and a recession that finally lost its death grip on America, they survived.

Every day, either on her way to the hospital or on the drive home, Emmy went by Doc's house to see if Johnny's Grand Cherokee was still parked to the right of the house on the cement pad beside the garage.

As weeks passed, so did the holidays. Snow came in harsh blasts to Booneville, and temperatures fell into the teens and stayed there. Routine set in for folks and families living on the prairie borders during early winter.

Then one day in early January as Emmy drove by Doc's house, the car was gone. One day it had been there like he was coming back, and the next it wasn't, and Emmy thought he might be gone forever. She almost didn't notice it at first. She'd always seen it there, every day. This day, she stopped and looked a second time, even looking down the street to both her left and her right, hoping he'd just moved it. No, it was gone.

Emmy slowly slipped into despair. She worked but without her same exuberance. She socialized but only after coaxing. She spent her evenings painting to get her mind off of her gloom. She put away any romance novels and concentrated on reading non-fiction, the uplifting kind featuring a hero. She needed to stay in reality, not fiction. That mirrored her life. She couldn't let her mind slip into a fantasy world, a world where she pined and pained over life without Johnny Roe.

Johnny put the sun behind him, heading east. He frequently looked to the passenger seat, missing his copilot, Buster. He let SiriusXM radio lead the way, molding his mood, mostly with rock anthems of decades past. He stayed off interstate highways for the most part, keeping to the back roads, taking in the landscape, trees, sky, lakes. He let his mind wander into what-ifs and then-whats. His reality was like a movie in the background, playing with the sound muted, the definition fuzzy, and the dialogue almost non-existent.

Emmy wandered from day to day. She never looked past tomorrow and kept her sights aimed at her daily routine. Work was a landing spot for her, like a safe playground where she knew the terrain, a place where she never got lost. She found she had even more empathy for patients, spending extra time in their rooms listening to stories or holding hands. She volunteered for extra shifts and stayed late when needed and even when she wasn't. She purchased from a used bookstore the hardback trilogy on Theodore Roosevelt, each a million pages long, and tried to stay awake to learn as much as she could. She didn't venture out much after work, only occasionally accepting an invitation for dinner at Doc's home and reciprocating with a meal at hers. They often talked late into the night and often about God. Doc tried to teach Emmy to let go of Johnny and trust God, that faith in God would always work out, even if faith in Johnny didn't. Emmy took his advice to heart, and her faith in Johnny faded. But still, Emmy hung on.

Johnny wandered from town to town. Each day was completely different from the one before. A new hotel, a new restaurant, a new road to take him someplace different. He spent as little time indoors as possible, only sleeping in hotels but strolling after dinners through towns where sidewalks were rolled up early and town folk were pleasant if he found them, but mostly scarce. Pandora or Spotify paced his music mood when not in the car and rather than relying on tunes he knew, he plugged in new channels and learned new songs. Johnny hung out.

Emmy clung to Booneville, what she knew, home, safe ground. Johnny searched for identity, destiny, new territory, and new dreams.

Emmy stayed rooted to Booneville. Johnny drove east. Each further and further apart from one another as day passed to day, weeks turned to months.

SIXTY-EIGHT

AS June flipped to July in Booneville, summer hit its stride. Trees boasted full-blown green, grasses covered their designated spaces in lush carpets, and the cold, snow, and isolation of the harsh winter were long forgotten. Summer baseballs leagues kept kids, parents, and city parks busy most evenings and every weekend. Barbeques and picnics dotted the parks and sprang up repeatedly and unexpectedly like wildflowers. Preparations and anticipation were peaking for the Fourth of July parade, always a standing room only favorite, and the county fair in August.

Only Emmy Brownell was still in a winter's cocoon. Her skin still clung to its wintertime pallor. Inquiries and advances from the new young pediatric doctor at the hospital had been quickly rebuked. Fine lines around her eyes, not quite crow's feet but their precursor, had developed and were only made worse by dark circles. Her makeup was minimal, and she didn't notice the subtle changes nor did she have a woman friend to point them out. She'd lost fifteen pounds that tended to make her face drawn and a bit hollow, like she'd missed way too many meals, which she had. That also made her clothes loose and ill fitting, hiding her curvy figure, which was just fine with her. Life just plugged along, sputtering.

The past six months had a very similar effect on Johnny Roe. Even though his skin was deep brown and suntanned from his outdoor adventures, crow's feet were painted on each eye. Only an illusion—squinting in the sunshine left the marks, and when his eyes returned to their natural roundness, they appeared as white marks on his ruddy face. He'd purchased a new bike in Pennsylvania and crashed it in the White Mountains of New Hampshire, stranding him near Lake Winnipesaukee for a week with a broken collarbone. He'd lost his fifteen pounds in vigorous bicycle training. He had visited a barbershop in upstate New York, been butchered there, and hadn't had a trim for almost three months. He rarely shaved his whiskers and only occasionally remembered to trim the hair that had just begun to grow out of his ears when he hit thirty. Life for Johnny Roe had also simply plugged along, sputtering from town to town—until he returned to the outskirts of Booneville, Iowa, that first day of July.

He drove past Emmy's house early that Sunday morning and noticed her car in the driveway. He parked the Jeep down the street, out of view, and circled around the car to let out his traveling companion. They rang her doorbell, and Johnny stepped around the corner of the porch, again out of view.

Emmy answered the door and saw an eager and energetic Golden Retriever puppy straining at the leash that tied him to the porch post. An orange-and-black bandanna hung around his neck. At first, she thought she was seeing Buster but then noticed he was a lighter color and a bit smaller in stature. She rushed out, bent down to give him a hug, and he lathered her with doggie kisses. Her heart leapt.

"John Roe, if you are anywhere within the sound of my voice, this dog is getting all the lovin'," she shouted.

"Move over, pup. Let me have some of that," Johnny said, emerging from the side of the house and nudging the dog away with his leg.

They spent the entire morning catching up. Johnny did most of the talking because Emmy did most of the asking. She found out that Johnny had driven east and south, getting as far as Florida, where he spent most of the rest of the winter near Fort Lauderdale. When the spring breakers arrived, he left and snaked his way along the Eastern seaboard, ending up outside of Allentown, Pennsylvania. He traded his older bike for a new one and continued his journey north as the early spring blossomed. He'd met a few cyclists who were trekking through the White Mountains, and he rode with them for a week, leaving his car at the southern end of the mountains and staying in fleabag motels as they rode all day long. His bike slipped on wet pavement on a descent one morning, and an ambulance delivered him to a small, local hospital where they discovered the collarbone break.

The other bikers rode away, and Johnny spent a week convalescing in a small hotel. His car had been parked two hundred miles away, so he finally climbed back on the bike in heavy-duty pain and somehow made it back to the Jeep.

Emmy asked if the nurses in the hospital gave good customer service, and Johnny cracked up, noting that they paled in comparison to Booneville nurses.

She loved to hear him laugh and tell stories; he seemed rejuvenated and alive. He told her of new towns he'd seen, the sights and scenery of his journey, with a verve and charisma she'd only glimpsed the last time she'd seen him. But she avoided the big elephant questions in the room—What now? Are you staying? Where do you go from here? Where do *we* go from here?

Johnny asked about the plant, Doc, and her life over the past eight months, and she kept directing his questions away from her. The plant was hanging in there, Doc was back on the board of directors, and Norm Boswell had been nominated to run for town council. He'd declined, citing obligations at work.

Emmy kept petting the dog and rubbing his ears. She found out his name was Pablo, named after Pablo Sandoval, a favorite player of Johnny and his son. And the puppy tended to eat everything in sight, another attribute of Mr. Sandoval, Johnny said.

Around noon they headed to the kitchen, and she made them omelets filled with fresh vegetables. They settled on the porch to eat.

Emmy began, "I've been spending a lot of time with Doc lately. He's been teaching me about God. I never knew he was such a spiritual man."

"What have you been learning?"

"That it takes time to know God, know what he wants for you. You just have to trust, have faith, that he only wants good for you."

"It takes time for a lot of things, doesn't it?"

Johnny thought, *It's not hard to find God. What's really hard is to let Him find you.*

She nodded.

"I'd like to hear more about God," Johnny said. "Maybe we can learn about God together. Maybe that's one thing I've been missing."

That got Emmy's attention.

"I discovered somewhere around South Carolina that I needed to go back to work," Johnny said, setting his plate aside. "That I had too much creativity that didn't have an outlet to be expressed. I think that was part of my frustration. I'd been in contact with Walt back in SF, but that job, that city, that way of life didn't interest me any longer. So we struck a deal."

"What kind of deal?" Emmy asked.

"We hired a lawyer and put together a deal that Walt and the staff would buy me out."

"You're selling?"

"Sold it. Well, over time they'll buy me out. Lock, stock, and barrel."

"And how does that, pray tell, solve your creativity issue?"

"I never told you this because I really didn't know what to do with it myself. But during one of my trips back to San Francisco, I had a long talk with Ryan Ritter, you know, the venture guy down in Des Moines. Turns out he was the one who was feeding the plant here leads for their vision-guided robotics. He liked that technology so much that he spread the word, found a few companies that could benefit from it, and made the connection. He did most of the initial selling, so to speak, and by the time the firms contacted the plant in Booneville, the deal was halfway closed."

"Where do you come in?" Emmy asked.

"Yeah, sorry, got off track. He offered me a job with his venture firm. To join them, work my way up to being a partner. Find new technologies, match them with new clients, put deals together, the whole nine yards. I met them all on my last trip here, then took a few months to think about it."

"You took eight months."

"But who's counting?"

"I was."

"Right. So…anyway…I took the job. I start in a couple of weeks."

"In Des Moines?"

"Or wherever I happen to settle. I'm sort of footloose right now. See, I sold my house back…home."

"You have been a busy boy. Here, I thought you were just roaming around enjoying yourself."

"I was searching, Emmy."

"For what?"

"I didn't know. For a while. Then I figured it out. I wasn't really searching after all. I was escaping. I thought I was searching, but I could never find…what I was searching for. Then I realized I was simply escaping. Getting away from those memories. My past life."

"Sometimes escaping is what we need to do. We have to get away from the pain."

"It took me a while to figure that out. I thought I needed to face reality. To man up. Get right back into life. Keep moving, keep achieving."

"You needed to grieve, huh?"

"I did. I have. And I suppose I'll continue."

"You will; it'll take some time. Healing always takes time. Some kinds of healing take longer than others."

"And that darkness," Johnny said, "that feeling that I couldn't control, remember? It's gone, Emmy. Or at least it hasn't surfaced in five or six months. Maybe that was part of the healing, I don't know. I suspect it'll always be buried somewhere inside me, but I think, for the most part, it's controllable now. At least, I hope."

Johnny swallowed hard and took a few deep breaths. "And I think part of the reason for that darkness…I didn't want to admit I had something to do with what happened with my wife. Maybe she wanted to leave…because of me. And what I couldn't give her. Maybe I was too busy working and building a company and…just being too much of me. Not hearing her, including her. Maybe it all wasn't enough. Maybe I wasn't enough…for her. Only for me."

He blew out more air, "Hard to admit. But I'm done wandering. It's too lonely like that."

"Lonely is no fun," she said as she walked down the steps of the porch. "So, you're ready to start a new life, huh?"

"Almost," he answered, following her. "But I'm still missing something."

"Oh, yeah, what's that?"

He grabbed her and pulled her close, looking into her eyes. The eyes he finally knew he wanted to look into forever.

"You."

One big kiss, then one long hug, then many little kisses—all the time the dog trying to get between them as if that was going to happen. Not today, not on this first day of July in Booneville, Iowa.

EPILOGUE

MUCH to the chagrin and embarrassment of Eddie Walnuts, the body of Mr. U.S. Johnson was never found. It left a rather bitter taste in Eddie's mouth and cost him a handful of jobs over the next several years. But he did manage a level of job security with Joe Dunham.

The human resources manager perused the stack of resumes, and although he didn't dread the upcoming interviews, he never enjoyed finding replacements for card dealers at the casino. They tended to lie on their resumes, a generalization to be sure, but he'd had to fire several this year just for that fact alone. They also never stayed long on the job; there was always another casino needing to hire, and they were a wandering bunch.

And really, what questions could you ask that would indicate you were making a good hire? *Can you count? Do you cheat?* Really, how hard was it to deal cards? Most started out on the blackjack table and soon began to moan that they wanted to be in the poker or pai gow rooms. It was boring work for the most part, especially if the casino was slow, as some shifts always were.

The first interview after lunch was a middle-aged fellow from Iowa; at least that was his last permanent address. He seemed a bit over-qualified, but the HR manager never held that against a candidate. After all, card dealer wasn't exactly a career path; for most, it was a career diversion or necessity.

The candidate appeared well-dressed, clean-shaven, and his hair was well groomed, clean, and neat. He didn't have any noticeable tattoos on his face or neck—always a plus for this job.

The HR manager had hired a heavily tatted guy not too long ago who had convinced him that customers would spend too much time staring at his artwork instead of concentrating on their cards. He lasted six weeks.

The candidate's handshake was firm but not too firm. Good sign, thought the HR manager; you didn't want them to be too forceful. But something about the handshake felt off, incomplete. *Huh?*

He kept eye contact but not for too long; again, that was good. Can't be a dominant sort at the card table. During the interview, the candidate kept his hands mostly in his lap and every effort the HR manager did to get him to display his hands, like asking him to demonstrate his card skills, proved that the candidate was adept at keeping his hands if not completely out of sight, for the most part, at least barely viewable.

Finally, the HR manager said that in all card dealer interviews, he was required by the casino to take a good hard look at the hands of all possible new hires. It wasn't actually a requirement, more like a rule. But a good rule, from the HR manager's viewpoint. More than once, unkempt fingernail had cost a marginal choice the job.

The candidate hesitated, keeping his hands under the table so long that the HR guy was going to ask the question again. Reluctantly, he slowly placed his hands, palms down, in front of him on the desk.

The HR manager recoiled and did a poor job of hiding his revulsion, his eyes bulging. On each hand, the ring finger was missing below the second knuckle. It would certainly be a distraction to all card players, but the HR manager had learned his lesson from the tattooed guy. And the missing fingers were just too creepy. If he was shocked and a little repulsed by the hands, just think how his customers would react. The HR manager wasn't willing to take that risk, and besides, he still had half a stack of resumes to sift through.

"I'm sorry, Mr...." he checked the resume for the last name, "...Dunham, but you just don't match our ideal candidate. You may be better suited for Reno or Tahoe, but here in Vegas, we're pretty...eh, restricted...on the people we are able to hire in jobs that have a lot of customer interaction. I really appreciate you coming in, and if you'd like me to keep your resume on file for other jobs that come available outside of the casino, I'd be happy to do that."

Joe Dunham clenched his teeth and his fists, and HR thought he might get punched in the face. Then Dunham looked at his hideous hands, sighed heavily, and looked away from the man across the desk. He stuffed his four-fingered hands in his pockets and walked out without a word.

THE END

Thank you for reading *The Resurrection of Johnny Roe*. If you enjoyed this book, please consider sharing a review at your favorite online retailer, BookBub or Goodreads.

ABOUT THE AUTHOR

Bruce Kirkpatrick spent over thirty years in Silicon Valley as an executive and entrepreneur. Since his move to Southern California, he now divides his time between writing and serving on nonprofit boards of directors, including Christian Education Development Company and Extollo International. His nonprofit work includes helping to train Haitian men and women in employable skills so that they can find jobs, feed their families, and have hope for the future.

For more information, visit his website BKirkpatrick.com.